IP Book Reviewers!

In his latest novel, *Staged*, author Irwin L. Hinds returns to the Republic of Trinidad and Tobago where the criminal enterprise of kidnapping is explored. Hinds, author of *Betrayal and Deceit* and *Discourse*, fills the pages of his book with rich descriptions of the landscape and history of both islands.

Khleo Karch is a twenty-something elementary school teacher and the daughter of the owners of a successful lumber and hardware distribution company. Khleo is estranged, somewhat, from her parents because they do not accept her current boyfriend. Christopher is intelligent, polite, and kind, but all Khleo's parent's can see is his dark skin. What Khleo's parents want for their daughter is a man more like her old boyfriend, Eli: light-skinned and charming. The problem with that is Eli has a history of legal troubles. Hinds is open and transparent in his depiction of the internal racism among people of color and how the belief that light-skin is better than dark-skin can fracture relationships.

After a long absence from the islands, Eli returns home and Khleo is informed of his homecoming by her best friend Amanda. The return of Eli leads Khleo to damage her relationship with Christopher to focus on her first love. In an interesting turn, allowing Eli back into her life sets into motion a series of events that leads to a claim that Khleo has been kidnapped. But the story is not as cut and dry as it initially appears.

Staged is a well-layered story. The author combines interpersonal relationships with criminal activity while threading interesting facts about the origins of the two island country. The stories of Khleo, Christopher, and Eli are blended together allowing for seamlessness in the storytelling. This technique also encourages a moderate flow in the movement of the plot. However, there are scenes in the middle of the book that interrupt the pacing because information supplied earlier in the book is repeated.

Staged is a continuation of Hinds effort to present the beauty and history of Trinidad and Tobago. He succeeds in his mission while also presenting an intriguing work of fiction.

Melissa Levine
for
Independent Professional Book Reviewers
www.bookreviewers.org

STAGED

A NOVEL

IRWIN L. HINDS

Note for Librarians: A cataloguing record for this book is available from Library
and Archives Canada at www.collectionscanada.ca/amicus/index-e.html

Printed in the United States of America.

ISBN: 978-1-4269-1690-8 (sc)
ISBN: 978-1-4269-8380-1 (e)

Trafford rev. 03/14/2011

 www.trafford.com

North America & international
toll-free: 1 888 232 4444 (USA & Canada)
phone: 250 383 6864 ♦ fax: 812 355 4082

This book is dedicated to my wife and children.

ONE

THE PICNIC TO THE BANK of the Ortoire river was unplanned. Nevertheless, little Khleo Karch otherwise known as KK, was enjoying the company of Christopher Boyz. She was referred to as little KK during her childhood because she was the last of four children; two boys and two girls. As an adult the pseudonym stuck with her because of her diminutive size. At age 23 she was wearing a size four dress. That was comparatively smaller than other young women her own age in town.

Although they had arrived there two hours earlier, KK had just kicked off her shoes and leaned back against the trunk of an almond tree to admire the dense, green foliage, the large variety of colorful chirping birds, and the swirling currents as they rippled in the river on their seemingly endless flow toward the sea. Suddenly she was startled by a bolt of lightning which was quickly followed by a crack of thunder. The lightning was so intense as it traversed the atmosphere that it struck the mangrove with a rattling sound. Shortly thereafter the foliage on the opposite bank of the river was on fire. The danger of being in the area was imminent.

"The weather is beginning to change. We should leave now,"

said Christopher. "We wouldn't want to be caught here when those burst." He pointed to the dark clouds above.

"No," Khleo said.

"That's nice. For once you agree with me without any objections."

"Not at all. I am not agreeing with you," said Khleo. "I really do not want to leave right now."

"Even so, we would be safer in the car," said Christopher. "Let's make a dash for it."

Khleo did not resist. So they both scampered away to where Christopher had parked his SUV. It wasn't far from the Ortoire RC School and relatively close to the new housing development at the intersection of the Manzanilla/Mayaro Road and the St. Joseph Estate Road. As soon as they reached the vehicle and even before they had time to enter it, Khleo's cellular telephone started ringing. She scrambled to answer it. The call was from her friend and confidant Amanda Flagg.

"Girl! Where have you been?" asked Amanda. "I have been trying to reach you for the last two hours."

"I have been here all that time. My phone did not ring."

"Was it turned off?" Amanda asked.

"No. You were probably dialing the wrong number. You know that you make that mistake all the time."

"I know. So if that is what I did, I am sorry. Anyway, I heard Snake has been deported from the United States and the NPA (National Protection Agency) is on alert to arrest him as soon as the plane lands at Piarco International Airport."

"Why would they want to arrest him?" asked Khleo. "That embezzlement *thing* he went to the States to get away from was more that ten years ago. Don't they have other real criminals to arrest? Why can't they find all the unidentified murderers and drug dealers to incarcerate?" Khleo asked angrily.

Amanda sensed the anger in her friend's voice and asked, "You still have the hots for him, don't you?"

"You know what, let me call you back when I get home," Khleo said.

"Okay! But you still haven't told me where you are."

"I am at the Ortoire picnic grounds."

"Are you with Christopher?" asked Amanda. "You know your parents are going to freak out if they ever know that."

"I know that but I do not care," said Khleo. "They do not support me. I do not live under their roof so they cannot tell me who I can or cannot date."

"I can tell that you are becoming agitated so I will let you go and speak with you when you get home."

"Okay! I'll talk to you then."

Khleo was visibly upset when she folded her cell phone to end the conversation with Amanda. That caused Christopher to ask, "What was that all about?"

"What was what all about?"

"What was that conversation all about?"

"Didn't we agree not to be intrusive?"

"Yes."

"So why were you eavesdropping on my conversation?"

"I wasn't eavesdropping. You mentioned my name so I felt compelled to ask."

"Amanda was saying that Eli was on his way to Trinidad," Khleo said.

"Who is Eli?"

"Eli Ebbs. He is an old friend of mine."

"That doesn't tell me much. Eli Ebbs? Eli Ebbs?" Christopher repeated the name as if he had been trying to jog his memory. "The name just doesn't ring a bell," he said.

"Snake," said Khleo. "His real name is Eli Ebbs."

"Oh! The light skin guy who embezzled funds from the national bank and skipped the country," said Christopher. "So why didn't you say Snake in the first place? You know that is the name by which everyone knows him. If I am not mistaken, he is the chap your parents were crazy about."

"My parents have this obsession with color, shades of black I should say," said Khleo. "They are color prejudiced. Personally, I believe that they disinherited my older sister, Caroline after she married Karu."

"Karu Egtibe, the attorney?" asked Christopher. "He is a highly respected individual in this community if not in the nation at large."

"You and I know that. My parents, however, did not see it that way. In fact, my father refused to attend the wedding. Not only did he refuse, he was insisting that Mom did the same. For a while she seemed to agree with him. It was not until two weeks before the wedding that she decided she would attend with or without him or his permission."

"She defied him?"

"She certainly did. To my knowledge, it was the first time my mother had done anything against my father's wishes."

"Wow!" exclaimed Christopher. "What are my chances?" he repined.

"My parents will not like you. They will look at you and not take the time to know you. None of that matters though because I am in love with you. I would like to be close to my parents but I am living independently without them or their money."

"Are you happy?"

"I am happy with you."

"That does not quite answer my question."

"Happiness is a relative state of mind. You expect me to say that I am totally happy. I couldn't say that because I am not. I don't think that anyone is."

Christopher knew that the Karch family owned and operated the largest lumber and hardware distribution business in the South Eastern districts. It was a lucrative business operation and he often wondered why neither Khleo nor her sister Caroline worked in the family business. Both of their brothers, Melrose and Tyreik who were university graduates did. With the exception of Khleo, all the Karch children were graduates of the University of the West Indies. Khleo, because of her rebellious nature chose not to further her education beyond Teachers Training College. She found her parents to be controlling and feared that if they financed her education, she would never escape their dominance. She was a refulgent young woman who enjoyed her job as an elementary school teacher. Apart from the fact that she earned a salary that allowed her to live independently, although not luxuriously, she genuinely loved children.

The Boyz family was not an original Mayaro clan. That is, the family name only became known in town within the last ten years. Christopher's family arrived there as employees of the National Petroleum Prospecting Company (NPPC). As a teenager, he traveled to San Fernando every day to attend the prestigious J.T. Pennington High School where he was already enrolled when his parents relocated to Mayaro. He was thirteen then and knew very few people in his newly adopted hometown. It was seven years later that he was introduced to Khleo Karch on the first day of his appointment to the staff of the Mayaro Public Elementary School. The year was 2000 and the first day of classes was September 5th. It was also Khleo's first day as an elementary school teacher and from the moment Principal Tucker introduced them, she saw the sparkle in their eyes. They too immediately recognized their attraction to each other. That Tuesday they had lunch together. That soon became routine, a routine they looked forward to every day after that. So when Khleo became upset at the news from Amanda that Snake will be back home, Christopher couldn't help but ask, "Did he really mean that much to you?"

"Did who mean what to me?" Khleo asked.

"Did Eli mean a great deal to you?" Khleo did not answer, so Christopher asked, "Were you romantically involved with him?"

"We were close."

"That is not what I asked."

"I have never interrogated you about your past," said Khleo.

"What do you really want to know? Was he my man? Yes! Are you happy now?"

"I am sorry, KK. It wasn't my intention to upset you," Christopher said as he reached over to touch her.

"Please don't touch me. Whether or not you intended to upset me, you have done just that, and I am teed-off right now."

It was raining heavily, with constant flashes of lightning and rumbles of thunder. Returning to the picnic grounds was not an option. Christopher suggested that they leave the area.

"Let me take you home," he said.

"Why? asked Khleo. "Is it that you suddenly believe that I am unable to think for myself?"

"No! That never crossed my mind.."

TWO

THE BAD WEATHER SUBSIDED AND Christopher took Khleo home but not before she said that was what she wanted to do. The intense rainfall created some flash flooding in areas that were poorly drained and that made driving difficult for Christopher and other motorists. What should have been a five-minute trip from Ortoire to Khleo's home in *Plaisance* took fifteen minutes. By the time they arrived at her place the sun was shining again and a beautiful rainbow was visible over the ocean. It appeared to have risen up from the horizon.

Christopher parked the SUV and walked in with Khleo but he did not sit down. He told her goodbye and left graciously. She responded in kind and showed no regret at his early departure. Instead, she immediately dialed Amanda's telephone number.

"Hello!" Amanda answered.

"Amanda . It's Khleo."

"Don't you think I know that?"

"Don't you get smart with me, girl," said Khleo. "I couldn't talk freely with Christopher right there."

"Yeah, I understand."

"So what were you saying about Eli coming home?"

"That was a while ago," said Amanda. "Since I spoke with you he must have landed at Piarco International Airport."

"This is a nice time for him to be on vacation. School is closed so I do have some free time."

"You were not listening to me, Khleo. He is not here on vacation. He has been deported from the USA."

"You speak as if you are certain that he has already arrived here," said Khleo. "You are always so sure of yourself."

"Yes! When I spoke with you earlier today he had already left New York three hours prior."

"Altogether isn't that about five and a half hours?"

"I would say so," said Amanda. "He is probably clearing immigration or customs as we speak."

Khleo suddenly became silent. Her thoughts were projecting on what the future holds for her. *Would it be a quiet and progressive life with Christopher, or would it be an exciting and sometimes tumultuous life with Eli?* She wondered. "It is your call," said Amanda as if she knew what Khleo was thinking. "They are both educated young men. The only difference is that one is inclined to be a scamp."

"Are you reading my mind?"

"No. I am simply looking at your dilemma."

"My dilemma! Just what is my dilemma?" Khleo asked.

"As I see it, you are faced with a problem of choice."

"Why do you think that the ability to choose is a problem for me?"

"The ability to choose is not in or of itself a problem, making the right choice is," said Amanda. "You are not asking for my advice but I am giving it anyway. I cannot sit back and see my best friend go down the wrong path, one that can ultimately lead to the destruction of her social and personal life or God forbid, her early demise."

"Say what you want to say," Khleo said.

"Stay away from Snake," said Amanda. "He is nothing but trouble." She used the sobriquet *Snake* instead of his given name

Eli. To her the nickname described quite clearly the type of person she thought Eli was.

Khleo thought for a moment then said, "There are other differences between them."

"Like what?" Amanda asked.

"Their ages."

"How different are their ages?"

"Christopher is my age. Eli is ten years older."

"Chronologically, Eli might be older but Christopher is a lot more mature."

"How can you say that? We have not seen or heard from Eli in ten years."

"Do you mean Snake?" asked Amanda. "He is a creepy, crawly character."

"His name is Eli," said Khleo. "I am sure he is not like that anymore."

"Yeah! Right!"

"It's funny that you can be so judgmental. You are forgetting how upset you became when people referred to your friend Pastor Bertrand as *Wolf skin Preacher Man*, and you were not romantically involved with him."

"Why would you even go there?" Amanda questioned. "He was a friend. I tend to be loyal to my friends."

"A friend who wanted to take you there, even though he knew that you were engaged to Quin," Khleo said while laughing. Amanda was laughing too.

"In retrospect, I think he felt comfortable knowing that I was engaged to be married."

"Comfortable? How could that be?" Khleo questioned.

"Well, had I agreed to his proposition, I would have had to be discreet."

"You would have had to be discreet?"

"We both would have had to be discreet. He, however, would have had no obligation or responsibility."

"No one would have been any wiser. You spent so much time with him anyway."

"Yes! I know. We spent a lot of time talking. Sometimes we spoke for hours. We spoke about everything; scripture, education, politics, war and terror, relationships, family, you name it, we spoke about it."

"He reeled you in," said Khleo. "It seems to me he would have taken you across the valley had it not been for the rain."

"You are so bad," said Amanda. "At the time I was quite naïve, it never occurred to me that he could think......" Amanda did not complete her statement. She seemed speechless.

"Think of you as a woman, a beautiful, vivacious woman." Khleo completed what she thought Amanda intended to say.

"That's it," said Amanda. "To this day I am still puzzled."

"So what brought it all forward? You never did say."

"It fast-forwarded one July when I was supposed to meet Quin for a trip to Grand Tassé Bay."

"How?"

"Pastor Bertrand and I stood on the hill in front of the *House of Worship* for what had become a routine after service conversation. As usual the topics were varied, interesting, and intense. I completely lost track of time."

"So?"

"So after about two hours of waiting I guess Quin got tired and decided to meet me instead."

"Oh! Oh!"

"That was my reaction exactly when he drove up," said Amanda. "As soon as I entered the car, he went ballistic."

"Oh my world!"

"Girl, there was no reasoning with him. I tried to explain the nature of the conversation I was having with Pastor Bertrand but he was not buying it."

"What did he say?"

"He said a lot of things, none of which was pleasant but he kept repeating one thing in particular."

"What was that?"

"He kept saying the Pastor is just another man," said Amanda. "The more I tried to defend the integrity of Pastor Bertrand, the angrier Quin became. He described him as a wolf in a sheep's skin whose mission was to take me some place but it certainly was not to heaven."

"Did he say where Pastor Bertrand wanted to take you?"

"No. He didn't have to."

"Did you ask him?

"No! Girl, that man was so angry, I didn't dare ask him anything. I assumed what he was alluding to and it made me feel angry and worthless."

"How could you? You are always so confident."

"Strangely enough, Quin was right."

"Please say that you are kidding me."

"Not at all," said Amanda. It really came to light a month later."

"How?"

"Apparently he was being transferred to St. Kitts so he asked me to have lunch with him and I agreed."

"Even after Quin was so upset? Were you nuts?"

"Like I said before, I was naïve."

"So where did you have lunch?"

"At Elaine's, the little restaurant on the Old Road."

"That's a nice place."

"It was cozy, and as usual our conversation was most interesting until........"

"Until what?"

"Until he held my hand, told me he was leaving soon and that he wanted to spend some time with me."

"More time than you already spent together?"

"That was exactly what I asked him."

"So what did he say?"

"He said not necessarily more time but better quality time."

"What a creep!"

"That's not all," said Amanda. "When I said to him that I always considered the time we spent talking to be quality time. He said, 'I want to lie down with you.' That is when I realized that Quin was right. Everything he said about the man was true."

"I am willing to bet that he knew more that six months before that he was being transferred."

"He probably did. I can tell you though, wherever he wanted to take me, he had to either go alone or with someone else."

"You are a strong woman, Amanda. I feel sorry for the weaker ones of the flock."

"Congregation is a better word than flock," Amanda said.

"You know what I mean. Anyway, we have been on the phone for more than forty minutes now."

"You are right. I will speak with you later."

"Okay! Bye."

THREE

CHRISTOPHER BOYZ WAS AT HOME alone. He did not like the solitude, so very shortly after his arrival he decided to leave. That was somewhat out of character for him. Usually when he was at home and there was time to spare, he would read either from an e-book or from the large collection of fiction and non-fiction he owned. On that day he wanted to be with other people, so he decided to go to Pierreville. Although it was a relatively short time since Christopher and his family moved to Mayaro, he was very well known to all.

Liming (hanging out with friends) in town was comforting to most men of Christopher's age. It provided an opportunity for them to vent, laugh, and be one with the community. Christopher soon discovered that as a school teacher, he felt uncomfortable with it. Apart from their interest in cricket and soccer, he had very little in common with most of the *limers*. So when Mr. Cortez, the vice principal of the school where he worked, stopped in front of Chin Chin's Store and shouted his name, he had a strange feeling of relief.

"Where are you off to, sir?" he asked.

"We are heading to Balandra Bay."

"Balandra Bay?" Christopher questioned. He did not remember ever hearing about Balandra Bay and wondered, *Why would anyone leave beautiful Mayaro to go to Balandra?*

"Yes. It's a little Southeast of Sangre Grande." replied Mr. Cortez when he saw the look of wonder in Christopher's facial expression. "We are taking Carlton to meet some relatives there. Frank is tagging along for the ride." Mr. Cortez looked back at Franklyn Avila when he said that, and Frank nodded in agreement.

Carlton Stuyvesant was born in Curacao but came to Trinidad and Tobago with his parents when he was only six years old. The Stuyvesant family settled in Mayaro where Carlton Sr. worked as a chemical engineer in the petroleum industry. At age twenty-six, young Carlton Stuyvesant had become a model citizen. He too was a school teacher and a close friend of Mr. Alfredo J.R. Cortez.

Although Christopher wasn't overly enthused about a beach called *Balandra Bay*, he did not want to be at home alone. He was trying desperately to forget what kind of mood Khleo was in, or the circumstances that might have triggered it. He wasn't comfortable with the *limers* or the idea of *liming* at street corners. To him there could be no beach anywhere in the Caribbean that is worth leaving Mayaro to visit. Nevertheless, if only for the company, *Balandra* was beginning to sound like a great place to be. So when Mr. Cortez said, "Come with us. We shouldn't be long." He did not hesitate. He hopped into the back seat, sat next to Franklyn, waved goodbye to the group he was with, and they left.

Mr. Cortez crossed the Naparima/Mayaro Road, rushed up and over Peter Hill Road, turned left onto Manzanilla/Mayaro Road and sped off. From where he sat Christopher could see the odometer. It read 80 mph. "Aren't you driving too fast, JR?" he asked. Outside of the school setting they often called Mr. Cortez, *JR*. Before Mr. Cortez could respond, Franklyn said, "He is good . You are safe, man."

Mr. Cortez had always prided himself as the country's safest chauffeur. "In thirty-five years of driving every day, I have never had an accident. Not even a scratch," he said. By that time they were entering Ortoire Village. They quickly crossed the Ortoire River Bridge and entered Cocal. Although Christopher lived in the Mayaro area for at least sixteen years, that was only the second time that he had been in or through Cocal. His, and the family business had always taken them to *San Fernando*, the second largest city in T & T. There was never any justifiable reason for him or his parents to travel that route to *Port-of-Spain* the capital city. He was in awe of the canopy of coconut trees that lined the narrow but well maintained roadway for miles.

"Wow! This is awesome," he said, and was a little taken aback when no one else expressed the same level of interest.

As Mr. Cortez' car sped along, Christopher was fixated on the panoramic view of the blue waters of the Atlantic Ocean on one side of the road and the mangrove and other lush tropical vegetation on the other side just beyond the canopy of coconut trees. As the car sped up the road, suddenly a huge gap appeared in the mangrove. Although still green, the usually flat area looked savannah-like.

"What happened here, JR?" he asked with a sound of despair in his voice.

"Where?"

"At this clearing."

Mr. Cortez glanced to his left and said, "Oh, that is where the mangrove had been removed to grow rice and watermelons commercially."

"That was not a sound environmental decision."

"It was not. Unfortunately, mankind does this sort of thing everywhere," said Mr. Cortez. "The ability to earn a living is always placed ahead of environmental concerns."

"What about the species that lived there?"

"Eventually, they went the way of the mangrove that was

there," said Mr. Cortez. "One species was sacrificed for the survival of another."

"In this case JR, multiple species were destroyed for the survival of one species, mankind." Franklyn said.

"That is truly sad."

"It certainly is Christopher. It certainly is." Mr. Cortez said.

As they approached Manzanilla, he was forced to reduce his driving speed because of several areas of damaged pavement due to land slides. The slides heightened the danger of the undulating roadway that had so many hairpin-type curves. For two or more miles the roadway consisted of a single lane where vehicles teetered on the edge of the embankments. Only the superb skill of the local drivers, including Mr. Cortez kept those vehicles from going over the edge. Drivers were forced to be courteous by having to wait until others got past the mud slide before proceeding themselves. Some of course, were more courteous than others. There were always the bullies, the show-offs, the underachievers who pretended that they were driving aficionados and in the process endangered the lives of others.

About thirty minutes after Mr. Cortez and his friends left Mayaro, they were approaching Sangre Grande. The road surface had greatly improved and so too did the driving. JR was determined to get to Balandra and return to Mayaro before noon. It was 10:30 a.m. when they started the final leg of the journey. The weather had improved considerably from earlier that day when Christopher and Khleo's picnic was interrupted by torrential rain.

Forty-five minutes after leaving Mayaro they had arrived at Balandra Bay. It appeared to be a quiet, not secluded, but sheltered bay. There were several swimmers in the water but no life guards were seen on duty. A few individuals were trying to surf but none seemed to have achieved any noticeable success.

Carlton Stuyvesant did not see the relatives he went there to meet. He peered out over the breakers but could not recognize any of the swimmers as people he knew.

"Where could they be?" he asked without directing the question to anyone in particular.

"They could be further up the beach. Or perhaps they have not yet arrived," Mr. Cortez said.

"What time were you supposed to meet them?" Franklyn asked.

"At noon."

"So we are early. It is only 11:25 now." Franklyn said after looking at the time on his cell phone. He wasn't wearing a watch.

Soon after Franklyn's remark, a late model, German-made luxury car came to a stop a few feet away from where the group was standing. A female voice from the car shouted, "JR!"

Mr. Cortez turned around but did not immediately recognize the caller. She called again, "JR! JR. Is that you?" As she stepped out of the car, he recognized the lady as Patricia Ramdial and said, "Oh my God! Pat?"

They stepped forward, hugged each other and Patricia asked, "How long has it been?"

"It's been a while. Since Teachers Training College I believe."

"I see you two know each other," her male companion said.

"Yes, Peter. Meet an old friend of mine, JR Cortez."

"It's so nice to finally meet you. I have heard so much about you in the last two years," said Peter Stuyvesant before turning his attention to Carlton whom he was there to see in the first place. "You must be Carlton."

"I am, and I am so glad you made it."

Peter shook Carlton's hand. Then he reached out and shook Christopher's hand. The young men introduced themselves to Patricia before they sat down at a picnic table. It was an unusual meeting in that Peter had not seen his cousin, Carlton since he was ten . Mr. Cortez had not seen Patricia in as many years. It was a total surprise, a chance meeting that was very pleasing to Mr. Cortez. The last time he saw her she was leaving to further her studies in the USA. That is where she met and married Peter.

17

She, however, continued to use her maiden name. Her husband meanwhile, was fascinated at how much his younger cousin had grown.

"Carlton! You are all grown up." Peter Stuyvesant said suddenly.

"You have also, Peter," said Carlton. "I am so glad you came."

"Well, thank you for meeting us half way."

"The thanks really should go to Mr. Cortez," said Carlton. "I couldn't get here without his help."

Peter turned to Mr. Cortez who was engaged in conversation with Patricia, shook his hand and said, "Thank you. You are a kind man."

"You are welcome. I should tell you though, it's nothing more than I would do for any of these guys. They are all very nice chaps and they are my friends."

"Friendship! What a wonderful thing," said Peter. "Sometimes friends are more dependable than family."

"Yeah! You are so right." Franklyn said.

Everyone was talking and laughing except Christopher. He was extremely quiet and that did not go unnoticed by Mr. Cortez who knew him well and couldn't resist the urge to ask, "What is the matter, Christopher?"

"Nothing."

"You seem so pensive."

"I am okay," he said. By then all eyes were on him. Everyone was smiling and that brought a smile to his face also. Although he was a lot more comfortable with the company at Balandra Bay than he was with the *limers* in *Mayaro*, he still was not totally at ease. His thoughts were with Khleo who really wasn't thinking much about him. In fact, she was wondering why she didn't hear from Eli. She knew that his parents, two sisters and a brother were residing in the United States of America. She knew also that he had no other close relatives in T & T. He did have an aunt and uncle-in-law in Mayaro but they were never socially close. *Genetics alone will not bring people together,* she thought.

Mr. Cortez looked at the time. He realized that the proposed time for their return home had long gone. Yet, he was trying his utmost not to hasten Carlton away from his cousin. They seemed to have bonded so well. Nevertheless, he was becoming uncomfortable with the glances and winks he was getting from Patricia whom he dated briefly while in college.

Franklyn glanced at his cell phone. The time was 2:00 p.m. He then looked at Mr. Cortez, rolled his eyes as if to say, *JR, it is time for us to leave.* Mr. Cortez caught on and said quietly, "Say something." Franklyn read his lips and said, "Excuse me, JR. Don't forget we have a Lions meeting at three o'clock."

"Oh my goodness! You are so right," said JR. "Peter, Patricia, it has been a pleasure but as you heard, we have to be back home before 3:00 p.m."

"The pleasure was ours," Peter said.

"I am just so glad you came," Patricia said.

"We would do anything for Carlton. He is one of our model citizens," Mr. Cortez said.

"We agree," Christopher said as he gave Carlton a tap on the shoulder. At the same time, Franklyn nodded in agreement.

"Well, let us get you something to eat or drink," said Patricia. "You have a long drive ahead of you."

"Thanks Pat. But that is not really necessary," Mr. Cortez said.

"It is not necessary. We want to do it."

"We understand that you must leave but before you do, have something with us," Peter insisted. Mr. Cortez looked at Carlton, Christopher, and Franklyn and said , "Okay."

The trunk of the couple's car opened as Peter pressed the remote on the key chain in his pocket. Patricia walked to the car, removed a yellow tablecloth from the trunk and covered the top of the picnic table. Then her husband went to the car and fetched a basket of delicacies and placed it on the table. He returned to the vehicle and removed a red and white Styrofoam cooler which he placed on the picnic table. That cooler was filled to capacity with beer, sorrel, sweet drinks (soda), bottled water, and ice.

The group sat at both sides of the picnic table and Patricia served each person a neatly wrapped sandwich. Peter looked around and said, "Let's have a beer guys."

"Since I am driving, I will have a soda." Mr. Cortez said.

"I will have the same," said Patricia. "I have never done well with anything alcoholic." Everyone else had a locally brewed beer.

Why she wants to have the same thing I am having? Mr. Cortez wondered but asked, "What is your aversion to alcohol?"

"It gets me drunk." There was more laughter from the group.

"Doesn't it do the same thing to everyone?" Franklyn asked.

"Not with the first drink," Patricia said. They all laughed again. They ate, drank, shared jokes, and promised to stay in touch.

Mr. Cortez exchanged telephone numbers, e-mail and postal addresses with the Stuyvesant couple and invited them to visit *Mayaro* before he and his friends said goodbye and left.

FOUR

KHLEO WAS IN THE SHOWER but her cell phone was ringing. Like so many people in T & T, she had a landline but had stopped using it. On that day she rushed out of the shower, grabbed the phone, but the caller had already hung up. Her cell phone recorded, *one missed call 868 005-27615; name unknown.* Khleo did not recognize the number. She thought it might have been Christopher but hoped it was Eli, and if it were, he would call again.

Half an hour later, her phone rang again. She answered, "Hello!"

"Khleo. This is Amanda."

"Yes."

"What's the matter, girl? You sound as if you just lost your shadow." There was no answer from Khleo so Amanda asked, "Khleo, are you there?"

"Yes."

Amanda knew that something was very wrong when her usually glib friend had suddenly become monosyllabic "What are your plans for the rest of the evening?" she asked. Again there was no answer from Khleo so Amanda said, "Get dressed.

You need to get out of the solitude of that lonely room. I will pick you up in ten minutes."

"Okay," she said. She didn't know where Amanda intended to take her, and she didn't ask. She decided, therefore, that the t-shirt, jeans and sneakers she was wearing were suitable for any early evening adventure.

Amanda arrived within ten minutes as she suggested she would. She rang Khleo's door bell intending to wait for a response. Instead, the door opened before she could lift her finger off the bell. Khleo stood there smiling.

"It's good to see you can still smile."

"Of course I can smile. I am not dead," said Khleo. "Where are we going?"

"No place in particular. Did you have lunch?"

"Lunch? It is almost dinner time."

"That might be true but have you eaten since breakfast?"

"I have not."

"That means you have not eaten all day."

"I did have some coffee."

"Was that all?"

"That's all."

"Then we are going to Elaine's," Amanda said. Khleo did not respond to that so when they got into the car and fastened their seat belts, Amanda headed up the Old Road, drove into the restaurant's parking lot, stopped and said, "We are here."

Both women stepped out of the vehicle, entered the restaurant, and were quickly seated. The place was empty, void of patrons, but lunch was still being served. The waitress knew Amanda very well but Khleo was no stranger either. Although she was visiting the restaurant for the first time, the waitress knew her as Ramdeen's teacher. Ramdeen was the youngest of the waitress' three children. The waitress handed each of the women a menu and said, "I will be right back."

True to form, she returned within three minutes. She filled

two glasses with ice cold water from a pitcher. Then she asked Amanda and Khleo, "Would you have preferred bottled water?"

Both women answered, "Not really." The waitress then took their orders and left.

"Why would she ask if we would have preferred bottled water after she filled our glasses with this oily petroleum tasting tap water?" Khleo asked.

"I don't know. Perhaps it is restaurant policy."

"It seems more like a PR ploy," said Khleo. "Our glasses are filled with tap water, what are we to say?"

"They offered bottled water. We accepted tap water, so they saved a few pennies." Amanda said.

"That's clever."

"That is deceptive."

The waitress came back with the lunches. Khleo had ordered a Panini with avocado and shrimp salad on the side. Amanda had a roti (a type of flat bread) with curried shrimp and chick peas. They ate without interruption because both had turned their cell phones off when they entered the restaurant. It was not a requirement, nor was it even suggested. They did it so that they could eat and converse with each other.

"Have you heard from Eli yet?" Amanda asked in an effort to initiate conversation.

"No. The telephone rang when I was in the shower but the caller hung up before I could get to it."

"So you do not know who called?"

"I checked the call log but I did not recognize the number."

"Where is Christopher right now?"

"I have no idea," said Khleo. "Since he brought me home after our failed attempt at a picnic, he hasn't called."

"Huh!"

"Why the deep thought and look of disdain?" Khleo asked.

"I am wondering how you are going to resolve this?"

"Resolve what?"

"The problem of having two lovers in this little town. The

first with whom you never broke up, and whom your parents adore, and a second whom you adore but your parents dislike simply because of his skin tone."

"I do not see that as a problem."

"Don't you?"

"No. In the ten years that Eli had been away, I heard from him about ten times. That is once a year on average," said Khleo. "Secondly, I was young, very young when he left."

"You are not suggesting that at twenty-five you are now over the hill and he may no longer be interested. Are you?"

"No! I was innocent then. When he left abruptly he took that away."

"So? Are you expecting him to give it back?"

Khleo laughed but Amanda was very serious. She was thinking of the plight of other deportees from the USA and Canada, the sort of troubles they had gotten themselves into, and she was scared. To her Khleo was still innocent but she also felt the need to be cautious about giving advice that was not solicited.

"That's not what I meant." Khleo said.

"Just what did you mean?"

"I am not the innocent fifteen year old school girl he left here. I am older, wiser, and can make informed decisions."

At that point in the conversation the waitress came and asked, "Can I get you anything else, ladies?"

"No. The check would be fine now. Thank you," Amanda said.

"Together or separate?" asked the waitress.

"Together," said Amanda. "I will take care of it."

"No! You wouldn't," Khleo said.

"Why not? I invited you out."

"That doesn't matter. I will pay for it or we both pay for it."

Although she lived independently of her parents, she believed that her friends and others thought of her as the rich kid. While she wanted to dispel that notion, she also didn't want anyone thinking of her as the rich kid who sponged off others.

Eventually they settled on the compromise of paying for their lunches separately with Amanda tipping the waitress. They then turned their cell phones on. Soon after there was a half ring on Khleo's phone indicating she had a message or messages.

"He is tracking you down," Amanda said.

"I doubt it," said Khleo. "He is too stubborn and too proud for that."

"Check your messages, girl. You would never know otherwise."

Khleo stopped, took her cell phone from her pocketbook while Amanda proceeded toward the car.

"You have two new messages and six saved messages," Khleo heard when she listened to her voice mail. The first message was from Christopher. He said, "Khleo, we should be in Mayaro before three o'clock but remember I have that Lion's meeting at three. I will see you later. Love you."

"What the hell? Who are we?" Khleo wondered aloud. She immediately erased that message and listened to the second one.

"Khleo. This is Eli. I am home. Sorry I missed you but I will call again in about an hour from now." Khleo was so excited about that message she folded her cell phone and ran to Amanda's car.

"He is here! He is here!" She said.

"Who is here?" Amanda asked.

"Eli."

"Where is he?"

"I don't know. He didn't say"

"He didn't say where he was but you know that he is here."

"He said only that he was at home."

While they were talking, Khleo's phone rang again. She answered it, "Hello!"

"Khleo Karch? KK?"

"Speaking."

"This is Eli."

25

"My! My! Oh my! You are really here," Khleo said. Amanda couldn't believe what she was hearing.

"Yes, dearest. I am here and I need to see you."

"Where are you right now?"

"I am still in the arrival lounge at the airport."

"Are you coming to *Mayaro*?"

"That is what I would like to do but................"

Khleo did not ask what the *but* was about. She quickly figured it out and said to Eli, "Stay at the phone booth . I will call you back." She turned to Amanda and asked, "What are you doing for the rest of the evening?"

"Nothing in particular."

"So can I ask you for a ride?"

"You can ask. Whether or not I agree will depend on where you want to go."

"I want a ride to *Piarco*."

"The airport?"

"Yes, girl! What else is there?"

"The General Post Office."

"Are you trying to be funny?"

"Girl, I am not trying to be funny. I know that if I do not take you there, you will hire a taxi."

"So are you taking me?"

"Let's go."

Amanda knew that her kindness to Khleo in the matter concerning Eli, aka, *Snake* would not bide well with Christopher. However, she concluded that Khleo was her friend too and that the friendship was not conditional. Khleo was elated. She called Eli back and said, "Stay where you are, hon. We are coming to get you."

"Thanks Khleo. You are the best."

She was smiling broadly from ear to ear when Amanda asked sarcastically, "Stay where you are, hon?"

"Girl, you know........" Khleo attempted to say something but she was giggling too much.

"Let's get real, Khleo. You are going to run in to some serious trouble if you bring Snake to *Mayaro*."

"Well, he has no where else to go."

"Don't ever say I didn't warn you."

FIVE

CHRISTOPHER WAS HURTING EMOTIONALLY. He wanted very badly to vent and would have already done so had he been alone with Mr. Cortez. While he was friendly with Carlton and Franklyn, he wasn't at ease discussing his personal affairs with them or in their presence. They, however, recognized that something was bothering him and Carlton asked, "What's the matter, Christopher? You have been so quiet all day."

"Yeah! That is quite unusual for you, Christopher." Franklyn said.

"My egg nest is destroyed." Christopher said in his typical metaphoric fashion.

"That is what happens when your egg nest is exposed," Carlton said.

"Sorry, man. It looks as if a mongoose raided the coop."

"Cut it out guys. Christopher is our friend. If he is distressed and chooses to open up to us, we should not be joking around about it."

"You are right, JR," Carlton said.

"Sorry, man," said Franklyn. "Perhaps now you will understand why you shouldn't be too deeply devoted?"

"You couldn't just say *sorry* and leave it at that," said Mr. Cortez. "You had to be Franklyn and add your twist to it."

"I am Franklyn and I am truly sorry. Although, you haven't told us what the problem is."

"There you go again." Mr. Cortez said.

"It's Okay, JR," said Christopher. "Very soon the world will know anyway."

"Does that mean you are going to tell us first?"

"Franklyn?" Mr. Cortez questioned admonishingly.

"Yes, sir!"

"You just can't help yourself, can you?" Mr. Cortez asked.

"My problem really started this morning right after that heavy rainfall..........." Christopher detailed the events leading up to Amanda's phone call to Khleo informing her of her ex-boyfriend's arrival in T & T.

"............. She only didn't tell me to get lost but the message was clear," Christopher concluded.

"What the hell is wrong with her?" asked Carlton "That guy is such a loser."

"She doesn't know how lucky she is to have someone who is as caring as you," Franklyn said.

"This is really tough," Christopher said. His voice was cracking and he was holding back tears.

Christopher's emotional state of mind touched everyone in the car, each of whom tried to offer some words of consolation and encouragement. Mr. Cortez who was a mentor to so many ambitious young men in the district was himself an emotional wreck. Nevertheless, he felt compelled to offer some words of encouragement and comfort to Christopher.

"What you need to do right now Christopher, is step back. Give Khleo the space she thinks she needs. We know how much you love her. You know how much you love her, and she is aware of the love you have for her. If she chooses to throw it all away, there is not much you can do. You are young, healthy, bright and ambitious. There is no limit to what you can achieve, so at this point you should move on. You will be pleasantly surprised to know how many more deserving young women in the world would be willing to shower you with the kind of attention you deserve."

"JR is right Christopher. You do not deserve any of that. She is a nice girl but she is making a big mistake. That guy let her down once before. He is likely to let her down again. She is a smart girl and one would hope that she is smart enough to recognize that he is a creep, a *snake* as his nickname implies. If she does, hopefully she would stay away from him. He of course, would play on her sympathy and the stupidity of her parents with whom she longs for a good and close relationship," Carlton said.

"We all know that any close personal relationship Khleo may have with her parents would exclude you. So the disappointment you are feeling today just might be an unforeseen good, a blessing in disguise perhaps. Be strong, man. This might be the only safe port in an impending storm," Franklyn said.

"I could never have imagined it would come to this," said Christopher. He was calmer and more relaxed after listening to his friends. "I never thought of anyone else. Since we met on that first day of our employment as teachers at Mayaro Elementary, every little step I took in life was with her in mind. When I saved a dollar, I saved it for her. I realized that I may never be able to provide her with the life of luxury she had grown accustomed to with her parents but I was prepared to do my best."

"I know your faith is strong, Christopher. What you are experiencing today is minor compared to what life throws at others," Carlton said.

"Listen man, I have been dumped a couple of times. Every time it happened, someone better came along," said Franklyn. "At some point Khleo would look back at this with regret."

"We know that you do not want any hurt or harm to come to her but right now you must look out for you, Christopher. You are number one," Mr. Cortez said.

30

"Hey! JR is right. She is doing what she wants to do. You have to do what is good for you," Carlton said.

"Yeah! Move on," Franklyn said.

"That is easy for you to say Franklyn. You are not the one involved," Mr. Cortez said.

"Ultimately, that is what he would have to do," said Franklyn. "Khleo has already made her choice."

"All of that is true. However, had it been that easy for Christopher, we wouldn't be having this discussion."

"So what are you suggesting. He should continue to languish in despair."

"No, not at all. By opening up to us he has taken the first step toward overcoming that."

"The love trains are moving fast. Khleo is on the express so Christopher here must catch another train."

"One that can take him a lot further than she would get to," Carlton said.

"That train she is on with *Snake* is an express to nowhere," Franklyn said.

"Hopefully, Christopher would have more direction in reaching his life long goals with someone worthy," Mr. Cortez said.

"Treat this as a learning experience, one leg in the journey of life Christopher," said Carlton. "When it is over you will be stronger and better prepared for the next upheaval or let down."

Mr. Cortez was driving fast out of habit and because he and his friends were late for the Lions meeting. As he swung around the sharp curve where the so called *First and Last Store* is located, the driver of an oncoming vehicle honked her horn and waved to him. Unlike drivers in the capital and other busy cities in Trinidad, owners and or operators of private or commercial vehicles know one another and are generally friendly.

"That's Amanda's car," Carlton said.

31

"Who is driving?" asked Mr. Cortez, "I waved back but I didn't recognize the driver."

"She is driving," Carlton said.

"Is she alone?" Mr. Cortez asked.

"No," said Carlton. "There is someone with her."

"It's 2:45 p.m. They are probably going to 'Grande to shop," Franklyn suggested.

"I doubt that," Christopher said.

"Why?" asked Carlton.

"The passenger looks like Khleo to me," said Christopher. "As far as I know, she would not shop in *Sangre Grande*. She finds that it is always too congested there. "

The others in Mr. Cortez' car knew that Khleo was the passenger in the other car from the moment it approached. No one wanted to say so for fear that would have aggravated Christopher's already bad feelings. It was a welcome relief, therefore, when he made it known that he recognized her.

"Are you sure Christopher?" Carlton asked.

"Am I sure it's Khleo? Or, am I sure she wouldn't shop in *Sangre Grande*?"

"Both."

"The answer is yes to both questions. I realize that you are trying to soften the impact all of this could have on me and I am thankful. It is always so nice to know that one has friends who can be relied on in times like this. I am truly grateful. Thanks again," Christopher said.

"You are welcome," Mr. Cortez said.

About the same time Christopher and his friends arrived back in Mayaro for their Lions meeting, Khleo and Amanda arrived at the parking lot of Piarco International Airport. They parked as close to the International Arrival area as possible. They entered the building and walked right past Eli Ebbs without being recognized. Khleo was taller and 25 pounds lighter than when he saw her last. He did not know Amanda. She, like Christopher, was a newcomer to Mayaro.

Khleo was anxious and eager to meet Eli but Amanda was more concerned about getting a cup of coffee. She stopped at one of the many retail food distribution counters and ask whether she could have a cup of local coffee. She was assured that she could.

"We serve an internationally known brand of coffee but it is processed here from locally grown beans."

"That's fine," Amanda told the server.

"I should let you know though, that it is an instant coffee."

"That's okay."

"How would you like it?"

"With cream and sugar."

"We serve condensed milk so you may not need sugar," the server said.

"That would be fine."

Amanda took her coffee, paid for it and added the condensed milk to her taste. She then turned to Khleo and asked, "Are you sure you wouldn't like to have a cup?"

"I am sure," said Khleo. "That is a tiny cup of coffee you got for your five dollars."

"Well, this is the airport. One cannot expect more."

They started to walk away when Khleo spotted a young man she thought was Eli. "That's him," she said.

"Where?"

"Over there," she pointed to where Eli was sitting.

They walked over to the seats against the glass wall, Khleo stood in front of the young man and said, "Eli."

"Yes," he replied but with uncertainty in his voice.

"Khleo."

"Oh my God! You look so different."

"What! You didn't think I would grow up?"

"Not at all."

"Didn't you think I would grow up?"

"You know that's not what I mean."

"I do not know. Please explain."

"You are just so lovely. Too much for words to describe is what I mean. Come on give me a hug."

They hugged each other. Then Khleo said, "Please meet my friend, Amanda."

Eli stretched out his hand and shook Amanda's. "It is a pleasure to finally meet you," he said.

Amanda looked at Khleo as if to ask, *what did you tell him about me?* He was still holding her hand when she said, "The pleasure is really mine."

"Where is your luggage?" Khleo asked.

"Right here." Eli pointed to a navy blue backpack on the seat next to the one where he sat.

"Then, let's go," Amanda said while thinking, *Is he homeless?*

Eli picked up the backpack and he and Khleo followed Amanda into the parking lot. She popped the trunk open and he tossed the backpack in and closed the trunk. From where she was standing, Amanda released the door locks. Both Khleo and Eli attempted to climb into the back seat of the sedan, so Amanda shouted, "Oh no! I left my uniform and cap at home."

"What does she mean by that?" Eli asked Khleo in a whisper.

"I don't know."

Amanda heard the exchange and said, "I'll tell you. I am giving you guys a ride. I am not your damn chauffeur, so one of you better occupy this empty front seat now."

"Okay! Okay boss woman!" Khleo said as she rushed into the front seat.

Amanda headed to the exit. She stoped at the gate and handed the attendent her ticket. Khleo was offering to pay the parking fee which amounted to $5.00 but Amanda refused. She paid the fee herself and they headed out. Eli was in awe at the developments which had taken place along the Churchill-Roosevelt Highway in the ten years that he had been out of the country.

"This is impressive," he said.

"What is so impressive?" Amanda asked.

"All of this development."

"This is happening throughout the nation," Khleo said. There was no comment from Eli. He was still in a state of wonder. Amanda took that as an opportunity to ask him a few questions that bothered her since she saw him at the International Arrivals Terminal with a single piece of luggage, a backpack.

"Eli, how long would you be staying?" she asked.

"I am not sure. I guess I'll be here for a while."

"If you do stay a while, be sure to visit Tobago," said Amanda. "I think you would love the place."

"It is beautiful," Khleo said.

"Listen to her. She has never been there. I keep begging her to go but she always finds a reason not to," said Amanda. "Since you are going to be here for a while, she now has all the reasons she needs to go."

Khleo smiled, a delightfully charming kind of smile. Eli, however, was serious. He wasn't sure how much Amanda knew about his situation and he didn't want to reveal any more than he had to. Amanda was suspicious about Eli and determined to deduce from him what she wanted to know and what she thought Khleo should know.

"Where in the States (USA) do you live, Eli?" she asked.

"New York."

"What city?"

"New York City."

"That is a very crowded city. What borough are you in?"

"Brooklyn. It is *Kings* really."

"Khleo told me that all your family members and most of your relatives are there except your Aunt Mina."

"That is true," said Eli. "I do not know much about Aunt Mina. She is different."

"The outcast?"

"I wouldn't go that far. I do know that most of us find it difficult to get along with her."

"So, are you married?" Amanda asked . Khleo's jaw droped. *I can't believe she asked him that,* she thought.

"I was for a while."

"Are you divorced?"

Why is she interrogating the man? Khleo wondered.

"I am legally separated," said Eli. "My divorce is not yet finalized."

They were leaving Wallerfield and heading toward Valencia when Amanda's compact car sustained a flat tire. It was the right front tire so she was aware of it the moment it happened but she said nothing.

"What is that sound?" Khleo asked.

"Sounds as if you have a flat, Amanda," Eli said.

"I know but I am not stopping here."

It was only 5:30 p.m. but darkness had already set in, so Amanda continued driving until she reached the Valencia Police Station. She drove up onto the wide sidewalk and parked in front of the station. Everyone came out of the car and Amanda removed a spare tire and a jack from the trunk.

"Do you know how to do that?" asked Khleo with a bewildered look. Then she said, "I never saw a girl do that before."

"I am a woman! I can change a tire." Amanda snapped angrily as she attempted unsuccessfully to loosen the lug nuts. Two young men came from across the street to help but they too were unable to remove the lug nuts.

"This is the wrong tire iron," the younger looking of the two said.

"Damn!" Exclaimed Amanda. "That's what happens when you allow other people to use your car."

She stood there pondering what her next move should be when Eli asked, "Don't you have road side service?"

"No!" Said Amanda angrily. "This is not Brooklyn. You are in Valencia, Trinidad. It's country here."

"You don't have to be so mean to him," Khleo said.

"What! Are you blind? He hasn't lifted a finger to help since we got here." Having said that, Amanda walked away and entered the precinct. The sentry on duty was a corporal. Amanda realized that from the two stripes on his shoulder. *He is kind of young for his rank*, she thought. *He is very handsome too.*

She smiled and said, "Good evening, sir."

"Good evening," said the corporal while smiling back at her. "How can I help you this evening?"

"I have a flat tire and I am unable to get the lug nuts off."

"That is not in my job description but I think I can help."

The young, bi-racial, police corporal, picked up a tool kit from under his desk and walked out with her. When he saw the tire with several nails attached to a piece of board imbeded in it, he said, "Another one of these."

"What do you mean?" Amanda asked.

"You are the fifth person to come in with a flat today. All were sustained similarly."

"How could that be?" Khleo asked.

"Some person or persons might be tossing these contraptions onto the highway with the hope that people would stop when their tires are flattened," said the corporal. "It's a good thing you didn't."

"We would have been robbed, wouldn't we?"

"Robbed and or killed," the corporal said.

The officer tried several sockets on the nuts until one fitted perfectly. Then he proceeded to slacken the nuts before jacking up the vehicle. Meanwhile, Amanda kept looking at his profile. *He has features of both major racial groups of the nation*, she thought. *With such beautifully smooth, dark skin, a slightly receding hairline, and a perfectly fitted uniform, he is among the cream of the crop. Lord! I have sinned. Please forgive me.*

"You should get this flat tire fixed as soon as possible," said the officer after he changed the tire. "It is not safe to drive around without a spare."

They shook the officer's hand and said, "Thank you." Amanda walked with him back into his office. They stood in front of his desk and she said, "I know you cannot accept a tip. That essentially can be construed as a bribe. However, I want to say thanks again."

"You are very welcome."

"By the way, here is my business card." She handed him an embossed business card with her name, e-mail and postal addresses, and both of her telephone numbers on it. She had those cards made after Quin left to study in the USA. They were intended for situations just like the one she faced.

"If your wife wouldn't be offended, give me a call," she said.

"I am not married," he replied.

I knew that. she thought but she asked, "Does that mean you would call me?"

"I would."

"Okay. Anytime before mid-night on any given day of the week."

"What happens after mid-night?"

"You would like to find out, wouldn't you?" She smiled and said, "Bye."

"Bye," the officer said smiling.

Amanda walked out to the car. As soon as Khleo looked at her, she pumped her fist and said, "Yes!"

"Did you score?" Khleo asked.

"Ah sure did."

The women high-fived each other. Got into the car, buckled their seat belts, and Amanda drove off. Eli wasn't saying anything. He curled up in the back seat unsure of how he would handle any further questions that Amanda might throw at him.

SIX

THE DRIVE FROM VALENCIA TO Sangre Grande was uneventful. Traffic was sparse on that stretch of highway. The road surface was in fine condition, quite a difference from the last time Amanda traveled along that route. She took full advantage of the favorable weather and road condition to expedite that leg of the journey home by driving at or close to the speed limit. It was dark and although no one expressed concern, both Khleo and Amanda were becoming anxious about being away from home at night. Eli was asleep in the back seat, unaware of his surroundings or that Amanda had slowed her speed upon entering *Sangre Grande*.

The little town was not quite as bustling as it was earlier in the day. There were very few taxis around and absolutely none destined for *Mayaro*. As Amanda drove past the taxi stand she saw someone she recognized. "Isn't that Mr. Finch?" she asked Khleo.

"Where?"

"At the *Mayaro* taxi stand."

Khleo looked back but by then they had gone too far. She couldn't say definitely that the person standing at the taxi stand was Mr. Finch. Amanda drove around the block, returned to the stand, stopped close to the gentleman, rolled down her window and shouted above the sound of honking car horns, "Mr. Finch!"

He spun around and looked at her with uncertainty. She called out again, "Mr. Finch!"

He approached the car cautiously and asked, "*Mayaro?*"

"Is that where you are going?" Amanda asked with a broad smile.

"Yes," he said somewhat dazed.

"Then hop in," she said.

Mr. Finch got in the back seat and sat down. Eli merely stirred to make himself more comfortable.

"Why are you traveling so late?" Amanda asked.

"I didn't plan to. I was delayed in *Port of Spain.*"

"Do you realize that the *Mayaro* taxis are not coming back to *'Grande* tonight?"

"I know," said Mr. Finch. "I was praying that an angel like you would come along."

"So what would have happened if we didn't come around the block?"

"I was thinking of going to Arima. At least, there I would find a Bread and Breakfast for the night. God is good all the time," Mr. Finch said.

"You are a man of strong faith," Amanda said.

"Just like your Daddy, Mr. Flagg."

"You are amazing, Mr. Finch," said Amanda. "All this time I thought you did not recognize me."

"At first I didn't," said Mr. Finch. "When you smiled though, you are a younger version of your mother."

"Thank you, sir."

They had gotten past the landslides and were traveling a lonely strip of roadway that traversed a former cocoa estate in *Manzanilla.* The plantation was overgrown with bush. Although, a few banana trees and an occasional cocoa plant could still be seen among the tall weeds. Amanda suddenly slowed her speed and Khleo asked, "What the hell is that?"

"I don't know but I am taking no chances." She stopped the car and backed up about thirty to forty feet.

"It is either a dead body, a drunk, or someone is hurt." Khleo said.

"Dead or alive, he or she better get out of the way now." Amanda reved up the motor, put the car in drive and raced off directly toward the figure lying in the road. The person playing drunk or dead quickly realized that the driver of that oncoming vehicle wasn't playing anything. He or she scrambled out of the way. Amanda stopped about thirty yards away and looked back. Mr. Finch was praying but what Amanda saw scared her. A minute before there was one person lying on the roadway. Suddenly there were three standing. She drove off as three flashlights shone on the back of her car. "That was *staged*," she said to Khleo.

Amanda was nervous but pleased in the thought that once again , as she had done an hour earlier, she made a decision that probably saved her and the passengers in her car from being robbed, injured, or killed. No one in the car spoke for at least ten minutes. Then Mr. Finch said, "Never underestimate the power of prayer."

"Never!" Amanda said. She knew that her father always prayed for his family and that he and Mr. Finch attended the same church - The United Christian Ministries.

"Obviously those people had bad intentions," Khleo said to break her silence.

"That might be a new scheme," said Amanda. "It is late in the evening. Someone appears to be hurt, and an unsuspecting motorist stops to help and is attacked."

"Girl! It's a good thing you were driving this evening," said Khleo. "I would not have known what to do."

"You will learn, Khleo. You had been sheltered too long but if you continue to hang with us, you will gain some street smarts."

".....hang with us? Who are us?" she asked.

Amanda looked in her rearview mirror to see if Eli was still sleeping. He was. She heard him snoring softly, so she said, "Christopher and me."

They came down the hill at the cemetery slowly because of the rough terrain caused by constant mud-slides. As they turned right around the corner, a full moon was seen shining through the canopy of coconut palms that lined the Manzanilla/Mayaro Road.

"What a beautiful moon," Khleo remarked.

"It surely is a bright spot considering the kind of day we have had," Amanda said.

They were on another nice roadway. It was narrow but the surface was superb and Amanda took full advantage of it. She was certainly eager to get home after a harrowing evening. What to do with or about Eli, she considered to be none of her concern. That was a matter strictly for Khleo to deal with. She felt she had interfered enough, although that was never her intent.

They approached the Nariva Bridge feeling somewhat at ease. As they reached the next bridge, a smaller structure that spanned a lagoon less than a mile away, they observed three parked cars on the side of the road. Among the mangrove and coconut trees, as many as twelve people were tramping around with flash lights in their hands and chattering loudly. Khleo and Amanda were afraid. In the back seat, Eli was asleep but Mr. Finch didn't seem bothered. Amanda drove a little closer and stopped to observe the activity.

"There is no chicanery here," she said. "They are just crabbing (catching crabs)."

"Are you sure?" Khleo asked.

Amanda drove forward and Khleo observed and said, "They are all males."

"Males?" Amanda questioned.

"Yes. There! There is a crab, and another, and another one there," Khleo pointed to crabs at the roadside.

Amanda started laughing. "Male crabs do not ...."

"The crabbers (crab catchers) are all males, not the crabs," Khleo said.

"Oh! So you do understand the phenomenon?"

"What phenomenon?"

"The spawning phenomenon."

"What is that?"

"It's a bit of a long story."

"Don't we have time for it?"

"I guess we do."

"Then tell your story."

"As you probably know, the blue crab which is essentially a land crab, is a *crustacean*. It belongs to the family *Portanidae*. The female crabs migrate to salty, shallow waters with a tidal stream to spawn. That is, to release the *zoea larvae* or *embryos* which may survive and develop into adult blue crabs. The male crabs do not participate in the migration. Only the ovigerous crabs (females with eggs) migrate."

"So these people who are catching the crabs are acting as predators," Khleo suggested.

"They are not acting, Khleo. They are predators."

"By catching and eventually killing and eating these crabs, these individuals are threatening the actual survival of the species."

"Here in Trinidad that is true. Hopefully, the same thing is not happening in other Caribbean countries."

"More likely than not, it is happening."

"To add insult to injury, humans are not the only predators of the blue crabs. Alligators, large fish, and snakes also eat them."

"Certainly not in the quantities that we do."

"That is the travesty, Khleo."

Amanda had introduced Khleo to the world of biology. She alerted her to the fact that because of our appetite for crab and dumplings, callaloo with crab, crab cakes, and curried crabs, the crustaceans we call blue crabs are teetering on the brink of extinction in Trinidad and Tobago.

43

"Don't forget me!" Mr. Finch shouted.

Amanda pulled up at the curb a short distance away from Mr. Finch's home.

"Thank you ," he said as he eased his tired body out of the car.

"You are welcome, Mr. Finch. Have a good night," Amanda said.

Eli woke up. He stretched, looked around, unsure of where he was, and unaware that another passenger shared the back seat with him for at least forty-five minutes.

"Where are we?" he asked.

"In your old hometown," said Khleo. "You slept for almost the entire trip."

Eli still seemed confused. He gave no indication that he knew what old home town Khleo was speaking about so Amanda said, "Wake up Eli. You are in *Mayaro*."

"Already? We got here quickly," he said.

By then, Amanda reached Khleo's place. She pulled aside, popped the trunk and said, "We are here Khleo. Eli get your backpack."

SEVEN

ELI AND KHLEO WALKED INTO her one bedroom apartment and sat down. It was an awkward situation for both of them but more so for Khleo. She was thinking of Christopher. How was she going to explain Eli's visit and the fact that he was spending the night at her place. At first she thought, *This is my home. I live here. I pay the rent and no one could tell me who can or cannot spent the night with me.* Little did she know that Eli would be there for many nights. He had no where else to go. *How will I explain this to Christopher?* Again she wondered. Then she looked at Eli and said, "You can sleep in the bedroom. I'll spend the night on the couch."

"No! I cannot inconvenience you like that."

"Okay! Then you stay on the couch. I am going to bed and we will talk in the morning."

"Thanks."

"Good night."

"Good night."

Khleo got up, walked into her bedroom and locked the door behind her. She had never before looked her bedroom door. She threw herself on the bed and thought about Christopher, just like she thought about Eli ten years earlier when she was only fifteen. Back then it was Eli's goof. He made the mistake when he left Trinidad on a student's visa to join his parents in the United States but never went to school. His visa lapsed and he remained there as an undocumented alien until he got married to an American citizen.

That night Khleo was worried that she might be the buffoon that time around. She was about to give up what could have been a promising future with Christopher. She had no conversations with Eli. So she knew nothing of his plans, his desires, his ambitions, or his direction. She was confused, bewildered, and disgusted about everything she had done so far. "Amanda should never have called to let me know that Eli was being deported from the USA and was on a flight to Trinidad and Tobago," she muttered to herself.

Khleo laid in her bed wondering what can be done. She had never really had much adult responsibility apart from her own personal care. Someone came in once a week to wash and clean for her. She had most of her meals at *Joe's* or one of the other restaurants in town. She went to bed at a time of her own choosing and got up whenever she felt like it. Very often when on vacation, she would not answer her telephone when it rang but would check her messages periodically and return the calls she considered important. The life of luxury she enjoyed at her parents' was replaced with a life of leisure she was becoming accustomed to from living by herself. *I am independent and happy. All that could end if I allow Eli to stay here,* she thought before dozing off to sleep. She slept soundly until 8:00 a.m. the next morning. Nevertheless, she did not get out of bed until ten o'clock.

Once she was up, she looked in the mirror, brushed her hair back, put on a robe, and unlocked her bedroom door. To her surprise, when she walked out into the living room, Eli was not on the couch. She looked out onto the veranda and the street below. He wasn't there. Khleo looked around and saw that his backpack was on the floor under the end table. She proceeded to take a shower before getting dressed. She was especially careful in choosing what to wear that morning. She wanted to look attractive but not salacious. She selected a pair of navy blue slacks and a loosely fitted yellow knit top. She creamed her skin, got dressed, and brewed some coffee which was the only breakfast drink she had at home.

Eli walked in with several ripe Julie mangoes in his hand. "Look at what I have got," he said.

"Where did you get those?" she asked with skepticism.

"About a block down the street."

Khleo knew right away that the mangoes came from the Burket's yard. "You can go to prison for that," she said.

"For five Julie mangoes?"

"Yes."

"Since when do people get locked up for picking fruits in Mayaro?"

"Picking fruits that are not your own or picking them without the owners permission can get you jail time.

"In *Mayaro?*"

"Not only in *Mayaro*. Anywhere in the country. It is called praedial larceny."

"Yeah! I know. Those laws were on the books since I was a kid but they were never enforced."

"They are now. If one is found guilty of such a crime, the penalty could be three years in prison."

"Isn't that harsh?"

"It is but it's the law. You have to be careful."

That last statement from Khleo caused Eli some concern. He had gotten in trouble with the law before, both in Trinidad and in the USA. He didn't want a repeat of those experiences any time soon. Khleo noticed the concerned look on his face and said, "Why don't we have some coffee."

"That would be nice," said Eli. "Do you have coffee here?"

"Of course. Don't you smell it?"

"Now that you mention it, I do."

"How do you take your coffee?"

"With cream and sugar."

She poured two cups of coffee and added cream and sugar. She placed the cups in saucers on a tray and took the tray to the living room. At any other time she would have had her coffee at the dining table. That morning, however, she felt it would be more relaxing to sit in the living room and have coffee with Eli while they conversed.

"How is life in the USA?" she asked abruptly.

"Was! I am not returning," Eli said.

"Okay! How was life in the USA?" she rephrased the question.

"It was not what I expected."

"What did you expect that wasn't available?"

"In the first place, the money I had was woefully insufficient to pay for college. Secondly, I couldn't find a decent job. The next thing I know my mother and stepfather asked me to leave their house."

"Why did they do that."

"My mother was fine with me there . It was my step-dad who instigated it."

"Why?"

"He claimed that I wasn't pulling my weight."

"Were you?"

"I was doing the best I could," said Eli. "I didn't have a job"

"So what eventually happened?"

"I moved in with a friend."

"Without a job?"

"She was working."

"She was working but you still didn't find a job?"

"She was okay with that."

"And you didn't mind sponging off her?" Khleo asked. She was thinking of the situation she could be in.

"I wasn't a sponge. We had an agreement."

You weren't a sponge. You were a leach, she thought but said, "So you had a place to stay. What did you do about food, clothing, transportation, recreation, and spending money?"

"She was very generous."

"What does that mean?"

"She provided everything I needed."

"That doesn't sound like you, Eli. Certainly not the person I knew and loved ten years ago."

"Ten years is a long time, Khleo. People go through changes in their lives; some good, some not so good."

"So what was the point of leaving Trinidad in the first place? You could have stayed here and done a lot better."

"I probably would not have done any worse."

"You would have done better," said Khleo. "You may recall that my father offered you a job after you left the bank. That is the same level at which my brother Melrose, you remember him, got started. Today he is the general manager of Karch Lumber and Hardware Company. His salary exceeds $12,000.00 per month."

"You are forgetting a few things Khleo. First, I did not leave the bank. I was fired. Secondly, I was young, proud, and extremely sensitive. Getting fired was the most embarrassing and humiliating thing that could have happened to me."

"So what happened to all that pride and sensitivity?" Khleo asked in a reprimanding manner.

Eli shrugged his shoulders. He couldn't answer her question. Instead, he clammed up. He wasn't angry, he was just sad. Khleo sensed his despair and said, "It is a pity you didn't make the best of a great opportunity."

"It is not my fault that I couldn't find a decent job."

"Eli, people from all over the world go to America and find work. You could have too if you tried hard enough."

"Yes! People find jobs. What line of work? What do they do?" Eli sounded annoyed but Khleo persisted.

49

"They work in restaurants. They work as landscapers, taxi drivers, housekeepers. They harvest crops."

"You really expected me to do those things?"

"Yes. None of those constitute a crime," said Khleo. "What type of work was your girlfriend doing?"

"She was a waitress. She wasn't my girlfriend."

"She wasn't your girlfriend but she worked hard to support you? How long did you live at her place?"

"I lived there for about a year."

"A year in which you didn't work. You didn't pay rent or make any monetary contributions, and you were not romantically involved with her," said Khleo. "Is that the reason you said she was very generous?"

"Yes. She was."

"Either she was a fool, or you think that I am a damn fool," said Khleo. "Suppose I accept it that you were entirely truthful with me. Although, I do not believe it for one minute. You were receiving free lodging. Any type of job would have allowed you to save enough money for your graduate studies."

"You really have no concept of the cost of attaining an education in the USA. Do you?"

"I know that it is costly but I also know of numerous individuals who endured hardship, sacrificed, and were ultimately successful. Why couldn't you persevere? It is no disgrace to work. That pride and sensitivity of yours prevented you from seeking or accepting a job that you considered menial. Somehow it didn't prevent you from being a dead beat who sat back and depended on your mother or some other female to take care of you, a grown man."

Eli couldn't believe that he was being rebuked by Khleo Karch, who as a fifteen year old was stupidly in love with him. Although their love affair was short lived, her parents condoned and encouraged it, in spite of the difference in their ages. There was no doubt in Eli's mind that the relationship would have blossomed had he not left Trinidad in a hurry. In the ten years that he had been away, Khleo has had one serious relationship. From her perspective, the worthy young men were all attached, with the exception of Christopher whom her parents despised. Others in the community were either too poor or not educated enough. As for Christopher, her color conscious parents felt he was too dark-skinned. That was the same issue they had with Karu, her sister's husband. *Could Eli turn his life around?* she wondered. She longed for a close relationship with her parents again, and felt that with Eli's return, things could be back to normal soon. For a moment at least, she seemed to have forgotten about Christopher.

The conversation Khleo wanted to have with Eli had taken a completely different turn from what she intended. She was feeling badly but didn't quite regret her line of questioning. It yielded some valuable information that hopefully would not be obliterated or overruled by her emotions. However, she realized that if she listened more and spoke less he might have volunteered even more information.

Eli was sullen. He looked depressed and Khleo was looking for a way to lighten things up a bit. "Would you like to go out and get some breakfast?" she asked.

"I would like that," said Eli. "I must first have a shower though."

Khleo looked at her watch. It was 10:45 a.m. She got up, walked to a linen closet, took out a towel, soap and tooth brush and handed them to him. "If we hurry we can have breakfast at Elaine's. They serve breakfast up to 11:30 a.m.

Eli took the toiletries and towel from Khleo, said "Thank you," and headed to the bathroom. He was out and dressed within ten minutes.

"Shall we go?" he asked.

"Not before I get a hug," said Khleo. "I am so glad you are here." They hugged each other tightly before leaving.

EIGHT

CHRISTOPHER'S CELL PHONE RANG. He reached for it reluctantly, thinking perhaps it might be Khleo. Although he wasn't longing to see her, he was eager to speak with her.

"Hello!" He answered.

"Christopher. This is Franklyn."

"What's new, man?"

"Are you sitting down?"

"No. But these soccer legs of mine are strong."

"I had breakfast at Elaine's this morning and you wouldn't guess who I saw when I was leaving."

"I wouldn't try because I cannot guess."

"I saw your home girl, Khleo, with *Snake*. It looks as if they were going to lunch."

Christopher did not respond so Franklyn asked, "Are you there, Bro?"

"Yes! Sorry. I was thinking, I heard the name *Snake* yesterday. Isn't he the same guy whose real name is Eli?"

"Yeah, man! Eli Ebbs is his real name," said Franklyn. "I was surprised to see him. I thought he was in the States."

"Okay, Franklyn. Now that you have told me, what am I supposed to do?"

"I don't know, man. At least you know what you are dealing with."

"Thanks anyway," Christopher said and they hung up.

Christopher knew that in that small community where most people are known to the rest of the population very few things can be kept secret. Khleo's rekindled flame was no exception. He was only surprised that she chose to flaunt it after telling him the day before how much she loved him. He decided that the best way to handle the situation was to lay low for a few days. He packed a small travel bag with clothing, four new novels, and other necessities. Then he got dressed and called a taxi to take him to the airport. Fifteen minutes after he made the call, the taxi arrived. Christopher came out, placed his bag in the car trunk, then sat in the front seat next to the driver. That was not at all unusual in Mayaro where every taxi driver was well known to everyone else. Generally, a passenger would sit in the back only if the front seat was already occupied.

"Where are you heading, Teach?" the taxi driver asked Christopher whom he knew was a school teacher.

"To the airport."

"You are going on a little vacation I see."

"Yeah, man. I need to get away for a while."

"Without your lady?"

"There is no lady."

"Don't tell me you broke up. You were so good together."

Christopher sighed, *Somebody else is getting into my business,* he thought but said, "All good things must come to an end some time."

"Don't you worry , Teach. When one door closes another one opens."

"A wider one I hope."

"Usually it's wider and better."

"I hope you are right."

"I am right. I have experienced it myself."

Christopher sighed again as he thought, *This is the second time in two days that I have heard that proverb.* Before he could say anything, the taxi driver said, "You sigh a lot. This thing is really bothering you, Teach?"

"Not really. I have reconciled myself to my lot."

The cabby did not quite understand Christopher's last statement but he could see that there was no real sadness in his mood or appearance. He decided , therefore, to engage Christopher in a less personal dialogue.

"Did you read about the latest kidnapping?" he asked. Before Christopher could answer, someone was flagging down the cabby. He slowed, then asked Christopher, "Do you mind if I pick up those two people?"

"Not at all," Christopher said.

The driver pulled the car up to the curb and a young man and woman entered. The driver did not ask the new passengers where they were going. He knew them well. They traveled with him regularly to the same destination. As the passengers settled into the back seat , they greeted Christopher and the cabby. The young man was carrying a local daily paper and comented on the latest kidnapping which was headline news.

Christopher had hoped to hire the cab all to himself so he could have some peace and quiet as he enjoyed the scenic view which he admired so much the day before. That was not to be. People knew one another in Mayaro and they loved to talk. They spoke even when they didn't know someone or were not familiar with the circumstances surrounding a given event. They spoke, seemingly with authority about things they knew nothing about.

"Before you stopped, I was about to ask whether the kidnapping you were referring to was the case of the US army veteran?"

"No. It's the one in today's paper."

"It's here in the Daily," said the female passenger. "It's another vicarious act."

"What exactly do you mean by that Miss Mercy?" Christopher asked. Her name was Merciless Tudor but for some unknown reason everyone called her Miss Mercy.

"It is all politics," Miss Mercy said.

"I still don't get it," the cab driver said.

"These kidnappings are *staged* by party supporters to benefit the opposition."

"Are you suggesting that these heinous acts are orchestrated by the opposition party?"

"I do not know whether the party officials were involved or whether supporters just took it upon themselves," said Miss Mercy. "I do believe that the kidnappings are *staged*."

"Really?" the taxi driver asked.

"How could that be when the Police Department is actively investigating the cases?" Christopher asked.

"The Police Department does not know yet but it will soon find out." Miss Mercy said.

"Excuse me ," said Christopher. "I must give Ma a call."

He took out his cell phone, unfolded it and dialed his parents' home telephone number. It rang and his mother answered. "Hello! Boyz' residence."

"Good afternoon , Ma."

"Oh Chris! What is the matter , son?" asked Mrs. Boyz. "We haven't heard from you all day."

"I am fine. I intended to call you earlier but............"

"But what, son? That is not like you at all. Something must be terribly wrong."

"No, Ma. There is nothing wrong. In fact, I am on my way to the airport right now."

"Airport? What are you running away from?" You never travel without consulting us."

"I am not running from anything , Ma. I am going to Tobago for a few days before school reopens."

"You are going to Tobago and you think it is okay to tell us when you are already in a taxi on your way to the airport?"

"I apologize for that, Ma."

"Okay. I hope Khleo is with you. Give her my love."

"I will give her your love, Ma. Tell Dad that I will call him tomorrow."

"Have a safe trip, son."

"Thanks, Ma. I love you."

"I love you too. Bye."

Christopher folded his cell phone to end the conversation with his mother. He did not tell her that Khleo was not with him or that he was going to Tobago alone.

"A mother's intuition! She knows, doesn't she?" the canny asked.

"She thinks something is wrong but she doesn't know what it is."

"Is something wrong , Teacher Christopher?" the female passenger in the back seat asked.

"Just a little personal matter. Nothing to write home about," Christopher said.

"You are a handsome, well educated, progressive young man; a model citizen. Do not allow your first serious relationship to ruin your promising life," the male passenger said.

What do they know? Why can't they keep it to themselves? Christopher wondered but said, "I will be fine."

"I am sorry , Teach," said the cabby.

"It is okay! I am okay," Christopher said.

Christopher wasn't sure whether the cabby was apologizing for the intrusiveness of the passengers he picked up after Christopher hired the taxi, or whether he was sorry for Christopher's ordeal, or both. Whatever the reason for the apology, Christopher didn't care much. He accepted it.

The male passenger in the back seat handed the driver the fare. "It is for two," said the man. "You can drop us off just before the Hi Lo Supermarket."

"Are we in *'Grande* already?" Christopher asked. It was not a route with which he was very familiar.

"Yes," said the cabby. "When there is interesting conversation, we tend not to pay attention to the drive."

"True," Christopher said. *Especially when it's other people's business*, he thought.

"Have you been to Tobago before?" the taxi driver asked.

"No," said Christopher.

"You are going to love it. It is like *Mayaro* in many ways: The people are gracious, the food is excellent, and you don't have to worry about crime."

"I also heard the beaches are great."

"The water is great. The beaches themselves don't quite compare to *Mayaro Beach*."

"What about accommodation?"

"Oh! There are plenty places to stay," said the cabby. "There is something for every pocket."

"That's good to hear."

"I take it that you did not make a reservation."

"I did not."

"Then don't worry. When you get there, go to the Tourist Information Counter and ask for Lynette. She would be able to recommend a decent place with reasonable rates."

The taxi driver turned on the car radio for the first time since he picked up Christopher on Alexis Street in *Mayaro*. That was somewhat unusual. Most taxi drivers in *Trinidad* keep their radios blaring on an all music station. On that evening, the driver taking Christopher to the airport chose to tune in to an all news station. The recent kidnapping was at the top of the news.

"We are experiencing a break down in social behavior," Christopher remarked on hearing the news.

"It all started when a so-called brilliant young defense attorney was winning so many cases because witnesses for the prosecution were disappearing."

"I think it started long before that," said Christoper. "The prelude to this anarchy we are experiencing came when teachers were forbidden from disciplining children in schools. Shortly after that the government literally took away parental authority by prosecuting the strictest disciplinarians amongst us."

"I understand your point," said the cabby. "Those indisciplined children are now grown up criminals."

"That's not the whole story though," said Christopher. "Those youngsters also seem fearless. Their lack of respect for authority is translated into a lack of respect for themselves and for everyone else."

"My ! Oh my! How or when did it come to this?"

"That is what happens when governments of developing nations like ours adopt failed policies of the so-called advanced nations like the USA."

"You in education are probably seeing a mirror image of the tried and failed education policies that are adopted here."

"Yes. We no longer teach for the sake of educating our students. We teach for the test; the Common Entrance Examination, the CXC Examination. We teach for examinations and engage students in rote learning. We have abandoned essay-type or constructed response-type examination formats in favor of true or false and multiple choice approaches in evaluating our students. They are not expected to be able to recall anything as long as they can recognize a fact if or when they see it. Our expectations of them are low. Therefore, they in turn, have low expectations of themselves."

"That's too bad, Teach," said the taxi driver. "The system that made you and me successful is now abandoned."

The taxi driver, himself a retired school teacher, clearly understood Christopher's concerns. For Christopher, the discussion was an avenue for expression on a subject that was troubling to him for quite some time. It also provided an opportunity, if only momentarily, to take his mind off Khleo. By then they had arrived at Piarco International Airport. The cab driver popped the car trunk, stepped out of the vehicle, took

Christopher's small piece of luggage from the trunk and placed it on the sidewalk at the entrance of the *Tobago* terminal.

"It is not crowded , Teach. You should have no trouble getting a seat."

"Thanks," Christopher said. He paid the fare and said, "Thanks again."

"You are welcome, Teach. Enjoy your vacation. Don't forget to ask for Lynette."

"What is her last name?"

"Oh! I am sorry. I should have told you. Her name is Lynette Tripp."

"Okay! Thanks. Be safe." They shook hands and the taxi driver left.

Christopher had no difficulty in purchasing an airline ticket and procuring a seat on the evening flight to *Tobago*. After clearing security, he purchased a newspaper and sat in the lounge awaiting his flight. He became engrossed in reading an article about the kidnapping that was discussed in the taxi on the way up to the airport earlier that day. He was paying such rapt attention to the detail as it unfolded, he did not realize that someone sat in the seat next to him.

Because Christopher sat with the paper parallel to his face or at right angle to his field of vision, the lady who sat next to him was unaware that he was someone she knew. It was not until the announcement was made that boarding was in progress, they recognized each other.

"Christopher Boyz?" inquired the female passenger with a sound of surprise in her voice.

"That's me. How are you, Ebita?"

"Oh my God! I am so glad to see you," said Ebita Leah Scott. "I have not heard from, or about you since we left UWI (University of the West Indies)."

"Well its nice to see that you are still in T & T," said Christopher. "If I remember correctly, you intended to do graduate studies abroad."

"That was my plan but I had a little setback."

"I am sorry to hear that."

"Don't feel sorry for me , Christopher. I am blessed with good health. My setback was financial and, therefore, temporary."

NINE

It was quite a while that Khleo and Eli returned home from breakfast at Elaine's. In fact, they skipped lunch because breakfast was so late and so large. It was approaching evening and although they had been conversing amicably, she was tense and fidgety, a clear sign that all was not right between them. She could not recall ever feeling that way with or around Christopher. She knew him well. She was familiar with his likes and his dislikes, and was certain that whatever he did, he did with her best interest in mind. Eli on the contrary, was self-doting, narcissistic, rude and crude.

Khleo found that Eli had an obsession with money. Although at the time he didn't have any. He was overly concerned about material things, or as she thought, immaterial things. There were earrings in both of his earlobes. He wore designer sneakers, gold caps on his teeth, a gold necklace and a Rolex watch but he had an empty wallet and no savings. He had been unemployed in the USA for years and arrived in *Trinidad* broke and empty-handed. Had it not been for Khleo, he would also be homeless.

Amanda had not called Khleo since she gave her and Eli a ride from the airport. Previously, a day would not elapse without them speaking on the telephone at least twice. Khleo looked at Eli and wondered, *Could he be the cause?*

"What was that about?" Eli asked.

"What?"

"That look."

Khleo smiled and said, "I was wondering what it is my parents liked about you."

"The same thing you liked," said Eli. "That is my guess."

"That is so wrong."

"So you do know what it is?"

"No."

"So how can you say it is wrong?"

"I was speaking for myself."

"What is that supposed to mean?"

"Just forget it," said Khleo. "Forget I said it."

"Then come over here and give me a hug."

Khleo moved from where she sat on the couch and inched her way closer to Eli at the other end. He put his arm around her and she responded in kind. It was the first time they hugged each other since before breakfast. Khleo inhaled deeply and exhaled the same way. Eli held her tightly and her deep breathing continued. He ran his fingers through her hair as their faces came together. They were both breathing hard when, without asking he kissed her. She reciprocated and they leaned back in the couch. They appeared relaxed for the first time since their reunion. Khleo kissed Eli again as if to ascertain that it was real.

Then she asked, "Would you like to go to the beach?"

"Not right now."

"Maybe later?"

"Maybe tomorrow."

"Okay! Then we can have lunch."

"Are you going to cook?"

"You are joking, aren't you?" I have never cooked," Khleo said.

"I am not joking. If you do not cook, where or what do you eat every day?"

"I only eat breakfast and dinner. That's two meals per day."

"Do you eat out twice a day, every day?"

"Essentially, yes."

That started Eli thinking, *All that money she is spending on daily meals she could spend on me.* He immediately decided that in order to get Khleo to do that, he must have a plan; one she will not see as conniving.

"Today is already Thursday. If you do not mind, I would relax with you for the weekend and Monday I will start my search for a job."

"Do you have an updated résumé ?" Khleo asked.

"No."

"Well, we should work on that this weekend."

"That is a good idea," said Eli. "However ......"

"However nothing! The situation that you found yourself in before you left *Trinidad* may come up in your job search. Anyway, it is more than ten years now so you can no longer be prosecuted for it."

Eli's countenance changed. The mere fact that Khleo mentioned the situation with the bank checks made him cringe. Although it was reassuring for him to know that he would face no further legal action. He still flirted with trouble but was terrified of the idea of going to jail.

"I do not have much to add to my résumé," he said.

"Even so, it will still be impressive," said Khleo. "At an interview you may be asked to account for the years of unemployment."

"That could be difficult."

"Why?"

"My student visa lapsed, so I had been an undocumented alien for quite some time before I got married."

"What does that mean?"

Eli was skeptical. *She really doesn't know what that means?* he wondered but answered, "It means that I couldn't find a decent job."

"You could have done any type of work," said Khleo. Without waiting for a response from Eli she continued, "No! UWI honors graduate, former accounts executive with a major Caribbean bank, you couldn't take just any job."

"You knew the answer. So why did you ask?"

"I wanted to hear it from you but you were evasive."

"That shouldn't matter if you knew what the reason was."

"In T & T we call that false pride. I think you know that." Eli did not respond so Khleo continued, "Sometimes you have to set aside your foolish pride and do what is good for you, even when it is not what you want. I know, and I am sure you do too, that there are foreign trained physicians, dentists, and other professionals who accept unskilled jobs until such time that they can get exactly what they want or are qualified to do."

"So?"

"You could have done the same, Eli."

"Why are you dwelling on the past? I am here now. Let's look to the future."

"You are right," said Khleo. "Sometimes though, we have to look carefully at the past and adjust accordingly, so we do not repeat the same mistakes."

"I can look at my past. In fact, everyone does. That does not mean that I have to wallow in past sorrow."

"If that means you are willing to make a new and different start, I am with you," Khleo said.

"Thanks," said Eli. "Your phone is ringing." He felt relieved.

"Hello!" She answered.

"Khleo, it's Amanda."

"What happened to you, girl? You just dumped us here and forgot about us."

"Hey! I dropped you home. Your old man is back. I figured you needed some time together alone."

"Still, you could have called."

"Yeah! I know. For that I apologize."

"You are apologizing? Is that some kind of omen?"

"I hope not. Anyway, can you talk?"

"I will try."

"I read you. Where is Christopher?"

"I don't know. I tried calling him but got no answer and no one returned my call."

"He must be quite upset."

"If that is the case and I am told, I will be able to explain." Khleo was being especially careful about what she said to Amanda on the phone while Eli was present.

"What are you doing later?" Amanda asked.

"Nothing in particular."

"Do you want to go to the Seawall later?"

"What time?"

"Around five o'clock."

"Yeah! Why not?"

"Are you sure that is okay with Eli?"

"I spoke for myself. If anyone else is interested it's fine. If no one else is interested, it is also fine."

"Okay! I will see you at five," Amanda said.

When Khleo ended the conversation with Amanda, she turned to Eli and asked him whether he would like to attend the Guaya Fest.

"What is the Guaya Fest?" he asked.

"It is short for the *Guayaguayare festival*. It is held at the *seawall* every year at this time."

"What else is there to do?"

"Nothing I can think of."

"Then let's go."

"Good! Amanda will pick us up at five o'clock."

"Does Amanda take you everywhere you want to go?"

"Why? Do you have a problem with that?"

"No."

"So why did you ask?"

"I was just curious."

"Now that your curiosity has been satisfied, let me make something quite clear; I think and act independently. Since I left home, I pride myself in my independence. I am not about to give that up for any reason whatsoever."

"That's cool. I am okay with that."

"You do not have a choice," Khleo said. Eli did not respond but he thought, *Let's see how long that will last.*

When Eli left Trinidad and Tobago Khleo was too young to know much about him. She thought she was in love. He however, thought it was just infatuation. Her parents encouraged the relationship even though she was a minor. On one occasion she asked to accompany Eli to Las Cuevas Beach and they consented. Not only did they give their consent, they gave Eli a ridiculously large sum of money (TT$4000.00) to ensure that while they were gone all of their needs were met for that weekend.

The Karch family was very successful and philanthropic. Unfortunately, that is not what they were best known for. Their notoriety was as a result of their prejudice. By all social norms, they were people of African descent. Both Mancilia and Dejongh Karch were of fair complexion, an indication that they may have inherited slightly more genes for skin color and hair texture from their European and/or Asian ancestors than they did from their African ancestors. As a result, they were slightly fairer in complexion than many other people in the region. That became the basis of their well known prejudice. They were overly concerned about shades of skin color. That stupidity came to the fore when, over their objections, their older daughter Caroline became engaged to Karu Egtibe, a first generation Trinidadian whose parents migrated from Nigeria to work as physicians at the Port of Spain General Hospital. Karu himself was renowned, a successful attorney in the South Eastern districts. Yet, Mr. and Mrs. Karch found that he was not a good enough suitor for their daughter. They much preferred her former boyfriend,

Kendall Blunt, a fair-skinned lumberjack who did business with the Karch Lumber and Hardware Distributing Company. His level of education as an elementary school dropout, was of little concern to them. They made their wishes known to Caroline but she rejected them. That infuriated Mr. and Mrs. Karch so much that they rewrote their will and excluded Caroline as a beneficiary.

TEN

LIKE CHRISTOPHER, EBITA LEAH SCOTT was traveling to Tobago alone. She too chose Tobago as a place to find respite. Although traveling alone, Ebita didn't particularly want to be alone. She wanted to enjoy some tranquility after a tumultuous relationship in which she found herself ended abruptly. She knew that Tobago was the best place on earth to find what she was looking for. She had been there several times before and had acquired a time-share condominium overlooking the ocean in Plymouth.

The regional airline flight on which they were booked was on time. There were no seat assignments so Christopher and Ebita were able to sit together. They both knew that the flight would be short, no more than 15 to 20 minutes. Christopher was content to just sit back and enjoy the ride, and perhaps shut Khleo out of his thoughts in the process. Ebita on the contrary, was so excited about meeting Christopher, she was trying to tell him in 15 minutes all the things she wanted to say during their three years at UWI but never did.

Ten minutes into the flight she realized that there was not enough time for her to say to Christopher all that she wanted to. Fearing that if they land at Scarborough, Tobago's Crown Point

International Airport, and went their separate ways, she might experience a recurrence of what happened when they graduated from the university. That is, they will drift apart and not see each other again. She decided, therefore, to make a bold move.

"Christopher! How long do you plan to stay in Tobago?" she asked.

"No more than three or four days."

"Where in Tobago would you be staying?"

"I don't know yet."

Ebita smiled and asked, "Didn't you reserve accommodation before making this trip?"

"No. A friend suggested that when I arrive I should go to the Tourist Information Counter at the airport and ask for Lynette. He said that she can assist me in finding a decent place at a reasonable rate."

"Is that Lynette Tripp?"

"Yes. I think he said her last name is Tripp."

"I know Lynette. She can be very helpful but she cannot guarantee anything.

"Oh!" Christopher sounded surprised and concerned.

"Don't be overly concerned. This late in the season there are always vacancies," said Ebita. "Alternatively, I have a condo with an extra room. If you don't mind, you can stay with me."

"I wouldn't mind at all," Christopher said. He was cognizant of the fact that lodging facilities were lucrative forms of investments in that world famous resort island, often referred to as Crusoe's Island, the second T in T & T. He, therefore, assumed that Ebita's offer was an offer to let or sublet. He was wrong.

After the aircraft landed at Crown Point, Ebita suggested that they rent a car for however long they decided to stay. Christopher agreed, so they collected their small pieces of luggage and walked over to the auto rental place. As they walked in and said good evening, the sales associate looked at Ebita but spoke to Christopher.

"Welcome to Tobago. What can I do for you this evening, sir?" he asked.

Ebita looked at Christopher. Then she looked at the sales associate as if to ask, *What's up with that? Do you only speak to men?* However, she allowed Christopher the opportunity to respond.

"We want to rent a car for the weekend," he said.

"Would you like a stick shift or an automatic?"

"It doesn't matter."

"Would you like an all terrain vehicle or a sedan, sir?" the sales associate asked as he continued to look at Ebita while he directed his questions to Christopher.

Christopher looked at her and asked, "What do you think?"

"It's up to you."

"Okay! Then we will have the sedan."

"Good choice. I have a brand new vehicle for you. It has only seventy kilometers," said the sales associate as he turned around and unhooked some keys from a rack. "Come with me. I like to show my clients their vehicle before we do the paperwork."

"I will wait right here. You go with him" Ebita said.

Amanda was punctual in picking up Khleo and Eli and taking them to the Guaya fest at the Seawall. They arrived there at 5:15 p.m. and Khleo decided to call Christopher. She walked a short distance away from her friends and dialed his telephone number. As soon as Christopher and the sales associate walked out of the door, Christopher's cell phone rang. He took it out of the case attached to his belt, and answered, "Hello!"

"Hey, Christopher! This is Franklyn." His call reached Christopher before Khleo's could get through.

"What's up, Franklyn?"

"That's what I want to know," said Franklyn. Then he asked, "Why is Khleo here at the Guaya Fest with Snake?"

"Maybe she likes reptiles. I don't know," said Christopher." Don't you forget Franklyn, that she is an adult and we live in a democracy where one has the freedom to choose."

"When did you become so damn liberal, Christopher?" Franklyn asked.

"My guess is that I have always been like that. It is just that there was never a time or an occasion for me to express it. You get my drift?"

"I get it my friend. Good luck. I will check in with you tomorrow."

"Enjoy the festival."

"Thanks. Bye."

Christopher turned to the sales associate and said, "I am sorry about that."

"That's okay. The reason we have cell phones is that people can reach us anywhere at anytime," said the sales associate as they reached the car. "Here is the car. I am sure you would like it"

"It is fine. We are just looking for convenient, reliable transportation."

"Okay! Then I am sure your wife would like it too. So let's complete the paperwork."

I didn't say I like it. And who said Ebita is my wife? You are fishing. Christopher thought but said, "Okay."

As they turned to return to the office, Christopher's cell phone rang again. "Excuse me." he said. The sales associates continued walking back to the office as Christopher answered the phone, "Hello!"

"Christopher! It's Khleo."

"Don't you think I know that?"

"Where are you?" she asked.

"Why is that important to you when you are enjoying yourself at the *Guayaguayare festival?*"

Khleo was in shock at Christopher's response and for a few seconds she didn't quite know what to say. Christopher did not overlook the silence. He asked, "Are you there?"

"Yes." She paused, then said, "Christopher we need to talk."

"Talk about what? The fact that your ex-boyfriend, the embezzler, *Snake*, spent the night at your place, you had breakfast and lunch out together and now you are taking in the festival at Guayaguayare?"

"My God, No!"

"Then what?"

"I was being compassionate in trying to rescue him."

"Yeah! What is he, a stray cat or an injured snake?"

"You are being unreasonable right now. I will speak with you a little later."

"Okay! Bye," Christopher said and hung up.

He took a deep breath in an effort to compose himself before walking into the auto rental office. When he eventually did, the sales associate was trying to converse with Ebita but she was not receptive. She was obviously angry at what she thought was his male chauvinism when doing business. She was so annoyed that she refused to sign the agreement the associate had prepared for the car rental. She looked at Christopher and said, "Please sign that thing and let's get out of here."

Christopher did as she requested. The associate handed the keys to him and said, "There are two sets of keys. You have tonight free but there is full comprehensive insurance from now until you return the car anytime on Monday. If you wish to keep it for another day or two just give me a call. I have enclosed my business card in that envelope. He pointed to the envelope which he had given Christopher earlier but he was looking at Ebita as if to say, *You can call me too if you feel up to it.*

Christopher said, "Thank you." He shook the associate's hand. Then he placed the two pieces of luggage in the car trunk. When they entered the vehicle and buckled themselves in, Ebita said, "The easiest way to get to the condo is via the Claude Noel Highway."

Christopher turned the key in the ignition to start the car. He moved off tentatively and Ebita said, "Turn right here." She pointed to where she wanted Christopher to turn. He made a sharp right from the Auto Rental parking lot and within a distance of 100 to 150 yards away they were on the Claude Noel Highway heading North.

"In about seven minutes or so you would reach the junction at Plymouth Road. There you would turn left onto Plymouth Road. When we get to Great Cortland Bay, you would bear left. That would take us to Stone Heaven Bay. The condo overlooks the bay."

"Do you really expect me to remember all of that?"

"No. I will remind you as we go."

ELEVEN

KHLEO REUNITED WITH HER FRIEND after a very disturbing conversation with Christopher. Her disappointment was obvious to Amanda who asked, "Did he hang up on you?"

"No. But it would not have been worse if he did," said Khleo. "He just wasn't himself."

"Do you mean his kind, gentle, accommodating, indulging you self?"

"He just wasn't nice to me."

"Well, what did you expect?"

"I had no expectation really," said Khleo. "I was surprised that he knew everything I did in the last twenty-four hours."

"Why does that surprise you? This is Mayaro, a small town where everybody knows everybody else's business."

"Amanda! It is as if he had someone tailing me."

"I doubt that. He is well liked, so people who think that he is being hurt will volunteer information to him."

"What good does that do for them?"

"That usually is not their concern. They like him and do not want to see him hurt."

"Isn't that exactly what they are doing by telling him that they saw me with Eli?"

"That may be so. In their minds, however, they are somehow averting any further distress to him if he takes heed."

"That is nuts."

"No! You are nuts." Amanda was blunt because intuition told her that Eli was nothing but a scoundrel.

Khleo wasn't thrilled by the remark but she offered no objection. She knew from her conversations with Eli that he was of questionable character. She was also aware of the fact that ten years earlier her parents adored him. She had no reasons to think that they would react much differently. For one thing, their values had not changed. She knew without asking that her parents would prefer her to be with Eli rather than Christopher. She also knew that the only reason for their preference would be the skin colors of the two individuals. Quite frankly, both young men were of similar intellect. Both graduated from UWI with honors. The paths they took in life were markedly different though. *Would her parents be mindful of that?* She didn't think so.

Over the years Khleo Karch had tried desperately to think and act differently from her parents. In some instances she did succeed. However, having grown up with those values herself, they were engrained in her subconscious mind. It became very difficult at times for her to detach herself from them completely. There were times when she tried but her love for her parents got in the way. She wanted to be close to them again and was fully aware that her involvement with Christopher prevented that. Also, the experience of her sister, Caroline, did not escape her.

In an effort to put the negatives to rest even if only temporarily, Khleo told Amanda, "Let's see what there is to eat around here."

"Girl, you know me. I do not care to eat anything from those open stalls with so many people moving around, coughing and sneezing."

"I know, but could you really come to the Guaya Fest and not eat something?"

"I sure can," said Amanda. "I will walk with you anyway."

"Thanks," said Khleo. "Where is Eli?"

"I don't know. He walked off with one of his home boys when you were on the telephone."

"Who are his home Boys? He got back only yesterday after ten years abroad."

"Two of the Aranguez brothers greeted him and they went to get something to drink. Maybe they always stayed in touch. I don't know."

"Amanda, those brothers are nothing but trouble."

"I know that. You know that, and Eli would soon find that out."

"They are not even in his age group. They were just kids when he left T & T."

"So were you."

"What is it with you?" asked Khleo. "You are always so matter of fact."

"That's just me Khleo. You can never say that I did not tell it to you just like it is."

They did not like what they saw at the first stall they visited, so they decided to walk around the food court. After about five minutes, they finally arrived at a stall that piqued their interest.

"Everything looks so good," said Khleo. "Have you noticed how the foodstuff is protected by the glass case ?"

"Yes. It is innovative. Definitely better than anything we have seen so far and probably better than anything we will see all evening."

Khleo was moving her hips in rhythm to the soca music that was blaring from the loud speakers around the periphery of the festival grounds.

"Are you trying to prove that those hips don't lie?" asked Amanda. "No one except your little pupils there will care." She pointed to three children who were admiring shapely Khleo

Karch shake her booty. As soon as the children realized that they were being observed, they started giggling and ran off.

Not only were Khleo's hips moving, her salivary glands were exuding amylase at the sight of the corn meal coo coo, corn bread, corn dumplings, payme (*a corn pastry that is steamed in banana leaves*), and Chili bee-bee (*parched, dried, corn kernel ground with brown sugar*). In addition to the corn meal preparations, there were curried cascadura and curried tators (*also known as mama tators*). They are river fish that are relatives to the cascadura, and indigenous to Trinidad and Tobago.

At the same stall with the finest of corn meal preparations, were the best selections of cassava (*yucca or manioc*) delights. They included farina, cassava bread, crab and cassava dumplings, and cassava pone. There were also breadfruit pies, breadfruit oil-down, callaloo, and stewed ox tail.

"So, are you going to have something to eat?" Khleo asked.

"I think I will try the breadfruit oil-down," Amanda said.

"I cannot wait to taste that cassava dumpling and stewed ox-tail," Khleo said as they both placed their orders.

TWELVE

EBITA DID NOT HAVE TO remind Christopher where to make the turns. He drove as if he was guided by a GPS navigating system or he had driven that route a dozen times before. He was decelerating as if he knew exactly where he was supposed to stop. In fact, he was so impressed with the area, he was slowing the speed to admire the view.

"It's that building right there," said Ebita. "The green and white one to your left."

Christopher pulled up and parked the car at the side of the building. "It is quite nice here," he said.

"I am glad you like it," said Ebita. "There is only one drawback."

"What could that be?"

"The apartment is on the third floor and there is no elevator."

"Oh! That is not a problem."

Christopher popped the car trunk, took out both travel bags and said to Ebita, "You lead the way."

"Let me help you with one of those bags," she said.

"It's okay. I can manage if you just lead the way."

She started walking and Christopher followed her up the stairs. When they reached the third floor, she stopped at the door and said, "This is it." She opened the door and they entered. "There are two bedrooms here. Only one overlooks the ocean though. They are both the same size, so take your pick," she said.

"It doesn't matter," Christopher said.

"Then I will take the back room."

"Okay," Christopher said. He was unaware that Ebita's choice was because she sleeps better in the back room. He may never ever know that.

It was six o'clock when Christopher emerged from the bedroom. Ebita was sitting on the veranda and he joined her there.

"This is awesome," he said.

"The best thing about it is the tranquility and the beautiful array of flowers," Ebita said.

"The water appears to be so calm and the sand is so compact."

"It is always like that on this side of the island."

"No wonder there are so many people on the beach this late in the evening."

"Yes. It is relatively safe here too."

"Do you have a caretaker?" Christopher asked.

"The place seems to be immaculate, doesn't it?"

"It certainly does."

"It is a time share so management takes care of everything," said Ebita. "Whenever one tenant leaves, they make sure it is ready before the next one arrives."

"I am impressed but also concerned ."

"What are you concerned about?" Ebita asked.

"How much all of this luxury would cost me for the weekend."

"You already paid for the car," said Ebita. "Whether or not

you came, I would have incurred the same expense. So we are even."

"I don't know what to say."

Say I always loved you, Ebita thought of saying but she said, "Thank you would be fine."

Christopher got up, walked over to where she sat, put his arms around her and said, "Thank you so much."

She leaned her head back and said, "You are welcome...." She was hoping he would kiss her.

Christopher was hungry. He had not eaten anything since breakfast. Nevertheless, he was reluctant to make that known to Ebita. So it was a relief to him when she said, "I don't know about you but I am hungry."

"Is there some place around here to eat?" he asked.

"There are a couple of restaurants here but they close around seven-thirty."

Christopher looked at his watch. It was 6:35 p.m. "We should hurry. There is very little time left," he said.

"We will get there when we get there. I am not rushing. I came here to relax so if we miss dinner, we would have to make do with the snacks that are in the refrigerator, or we can drive over to Scarborough. The restaurants there stay open later."

"That's okay with me," Christopher said.

"What is okay with you?" asked Ebita. "Is it the snacks in the fridge, or is it the drive to Scarborough?"

Christopher laughed and said, "Whatever, dear."

That brought a broad smile to Ebita's face and she said, "Let's try to catch the restaurant down the street while it is still open."

They left the condo immediately and arrived at the eatery before 7:00 p.m. They were warmly greeted and served as soon as they placed their orders. Ebita turned off her cell phone and said to Christopher, "I do not want anyone calling me while I am having dinner with you."

Christopher did not comment. He simply took his phone from the case attached to his belt and turned it off. Ebita smiled and said, "We have so much to talk about, Christopher . I don't know that one weekend is enough."

"Well, it's a good time to start," said Christopher. "You can begin by telling me how it is you are still in T &T. You were supposed to return home to Barbados then go on to graduate school in the United States."

"That's just where the story gets long and unwieldy," said Ebita. "I did go home but shortly after I arrived, my father died. He had been ill for quite some time. I was distraught to say the least. In addition, my stepmother and I weren't getting along very well. I had no job, I had no money. My father was my sole support but after his death, she took control of the finances and virtually excluded me."

"Where was your mother in all of this?"

"Mamie died when I was twelve years old. I will be twenty-four next month and would you believe, that woman is the third adult female who has directed and controlled my life until I was nineteen and left St. Michaels to study here?"

"You actually had three stepmothers in seven years?"

"Virtually, is more like it. Daddy was never married to either of the other two women."

"I see," Christopher said. *So my problem pales when compared to yours,* he thought but didn't say it.

"The funny thing is, both of them were nicer to me than she ever was."

"Huh!"

"Yeah! That is what I meant when I said it was a long story."

"Now I understand why you never went home during all those years at the university," said Christopher. "I wish I knew then. My parents would have loved to have you with us when classes were out."

"As close as we were Christopher, I couldn't burden you or anyone else with my problems."

"You are amazing, Ebita! That's very courageous indeed. With all that was going on in your life you still managed to study and graduate with honors. Your father must have been very proud of you."

"I think so. However, that is one of the things my stepmother used against me."

"How could that be?"

"I don't suppose you know Bajans."

"I know you. One could not wish for a nicer person or a better friend."

"Thanks for the compliment," said Ebita. "Anyhow, she told everyone who listened that I was such an ungrateful little B...., that all I ever did was take, take, take from my father and I never came to see how they were doing. What she never did say, was that when I was at home she treated me like shit and did everything she could have done to prevent me from achieving my goals."

Christopher sensed that Ebita was becoming upset, so he said, "She may not admit it openly but deep down inside she is proud of you. Everyone in your district I am sure is proud of you. I am proud of the smart, beautiful person you are."

The waitress came to ask whether there was anything else they would like to have. She noticed the tracks of tears flowing down Ebita's cheeks and asked instead, "Is everything okay?"

Ebita placed a napkin to her nose and nodded to indicate yes. At the same time Christopher looked up at the waitress and noticed that her eyes too were welled with tears, so he said, "It is okay. We will take the check now."

The waitress took the check from her apron pocket, handed it to Christopher and said, "Have a good night." She then pulled up her apron and wiped her eyes.

Christopher himself came close to tears. *I have never experienced anything like this,* he thought. *In a strange sought of way, it is beautiful.* He certainly didn't mean that it was beautiful to see Ebita cry. What he didn't realize was that Ebita Leah Scott went to Tobago often and frequented that restaurant. While most of the other patrons were transients, she was a regular there. She was known and well liked by all the employees. In general, the people of Tobago are caring and loving. They are helpful and accommodating to strangers. Ebita, however, had become one of their own, so when the waitress saw her crying after observing how good she and Christopher were together minutes earlier, she simply assumed the worse. Ebita was hurt, so she too was hurt. That's just the nature of Tobagonians. They share the love and they share in the sorrow.

"Let's go back to the hotel," Christopher said.

"Condo," Ebita corrected him. They both smiled, held each other's hand and walked toward the door. The waitress was standing there.

"Good night. Please come again," she said.

"Good night." Christopher and Etiba said in unison as they walked through the door. The waitress smiled as they walked away hand in hand.

THIRTEEN

THE ARANGUEZ BROTHERS, PETER AND Paul, together with Eli, came around to where Khleo and Amanda sat to enjoy their local gastronomical delights. Peter Aranguez, the older of the two brothers, seemed to have consumed a considerable amount of alcohol. His speech was already slurred. The younger brother, an ex-police officer was still sober and so too was Eli.

"How are you lovely ladies?" Paul Aranguez asked.

"We are fine," Amanda said.

"Lovely ladies?" Peter repeated sarcastically in his state of drunkeness.

"They are the loveliest on the planet," Paul said.

"You never had any sense," Peter said to his younger brother.

"You never thought of me as sensible but look at you."

"What is wrong with me?"

"You are drunk and acting like an ass."

"I will pretend that I didn't hear that," said Peter. "We will talk about it later."

In an effort to divert attention from what could have become an embarrassing situation, Amanda asked Eli, "Have you had anything to eat?"

"No," he said.

"Who cares about food when we have liquor," Peter said.

Khleo ignored the silly statement. She reached into the pocket of her jeans, took out a blue note (TT$100.00) and handed it to Eli. "Get yourselves something to eat fellas (men)," she said.

Eli took the money without saying thanks. His newly found buddies did not have the presence of mind nor the manners to say thank you either.

They walked a short distance away. When neither Khleo nor Amanda could hear them above the sound of the music, Peter said to Eli, "You found a golden goose there, man."

"It is not the goose that is golden," said Paul. "It is the eggs the goose lays."

Eli smiled although he wasn't sure what the brothers meant by their comments. All three young men walked to one of the food stalls where they ordered three roti (a type of flat bread), each with a different filling. Peter had curried chicken in his, Paul had curried chip chip (a mollusk harvested from Mayaro beach), and Eli chose curried beef. They sat together at a table for three instead of rejoining Khleo and Amanda.

"When did you come down from the States?" Peter asked Eli.

"Yesterday."

"Are you driving a rented car?"

"I am not driving at all."

"Then, how did you get here?"

"Amanda drove us in."

"Oh boy! That is not good," said Peter. "You need to have your own ride (transport)."

"Why is that necessary?"

"It puts you in control," said Peter. "You would be able to decide where you go, when you go, and how."

"Right now I cannot afford a vehicle," Eli said.

"We can hook you up. Or you can start using some of those golden goose eggs."

"What the hell are you talking about?" Eli asked.

"You just arrived. The sky is a little cloudy right now. Give it a week. and you will see it clear up."

Peter Aranguez was considering how he and his brother Paul could use Eli Ebbs and his girlfriend Khleo to extort money from the Karch family. The Aranguez brothers like everyone else in Mayaro, were very well aware of the Karch family lumber and hardware distributing business. They viewed it as a highly successful venture. That being the case, one might think they would consider seeking employment there. Not at all. On the contrary, those vagabonds had no intention of working with the Karch family business or any other business for that matter. They were living easy, parasitic lives, and living well, judging from the huge dwellings they owned and the luxury vehicles they drove. Strangely enough, the law had not yet caught up with them.

As the men consumed their roti and beer, two other waif-like guys whom Eli did not know joined them. They pulled up chairs from an adjoining table, greeted the brothers, and introduced themselves to Eli. They were relatively newcomers to the Mayaro/Guayaguayare area, so Eli did not recognize their family names. He sat with the group for a little while longer then said, "Excuse me gentlemen. I must check on the ladies."

"Okay, man! Remember what I said about the sky," Peter Aranguez said laughing. Peter liked speaking in parables, his own parables. Unfortunately, or fortunately, depending on how one looks at it, Eli did not understand him.

When Eli got back to the table where Khleo and Amanda sat, he pulled up a chair from the next table and sat down. He was smiling broadly when he said, "Those are some really great guys."

"You are not talking about Peter and Paul, are you?" Amanda asked. "

"Yes," Eli said.

"Those guys are not gracious at all, let alone great."

"They are scam artists," said Khleo. Then she asked, "Do you know why Paul was kicked off the Police Force?"

"No. I didn't know that he was ever in the force."

"That is very typical of them," said Khleo. "They always try to conceal any damaging truth."

"Yeah! They kicked him out of the force for demanding and accepting bribes. Then he claimed that he was set up. What gall!" Amanda said with anger in her voice.

"From whom did he demand bribes?" Eli asked with disbelief.

"From everybody; store keepers, taxi drivers, hoteliers, caterers, contractors and fishermen," said Amanda. "I am willing to bet that he and his brother are here scheming and planning to deprive some innocent individual of his or her possessions."

"Yeah! They prey mostly on the weak; women, children and the aged, but they are opportunists, so no one is entirely safe with them around," Khleo said.

"Without their presence, a festival like this will be a truly grand affair," said Amanda. "It has grown so much since it's inception."

"It is now an annual affair," said Khleo. "People from all over the country come here for this festival."

"The Minister of Culture is here. There, also is the MP (member of Parliament) for Mayaro," Amanda said as she pointed to a portly Afro-Trini man who was casually dressed and wearing a white baseball cap which had no logo on it.

"Who are the organizers of this festival?" Eli asked. It was the first time he had spoken for at least ten minutes.

"I believe there is an organizing committee that works year round on the planning and preparation," said Khleo. "All of the major companies in the Mayaro/Guayaguayare area contribute to make the event the resounding success it is."

"Do you mean that they contribute financially?" Eli asked.

"Yes! Of course," Khleo said.

"It will soon rival carnival," Amanda suggested.

"Don't push it now , Amanda," said Khleo. "This is a very localized festival and the participants do not wear costumes. Carnival on the other hand, is a national affair. The costumes are richly colored."

"Okay, Khleo! You win this one. You will agree though, that Guaya Fest rivals all other celebrations in Trinidad and Tobago," Amanda said.

"Listening to you, one is inclined to believe that you live, work, and play in Guayaguayare," Eli said.

"I did not intend to give that impression and I doubt whether that was Khleo's intention," Amanda said.

"When does this thing normally end? Eli asked.

"In the past, it went on to 11:00 p.m. or to mid-night. These days, however, it is wrapped up around 9.00 p.m.

FOURTEEN

CHRISTOPHER AND EBITA SAT TOGETHER on the couch. The door to the veranda was open and there was a constant flow of cool, refreshing sea breeze. There were no divisions between the living room, dining room, and kitchen so the entire condominium was constantly being permeated with fresh air. It was for that very reason Ebita always kept the bedroom doors open. She enjoyed that benefit in the back bedroom without having to contend with the noise from the surf. Christopher, however, found that noise to be negligible when compared to the sound of breaking waves at Mayaro Bay. He felt that he would be quite comfortable in the bedroom overlooking the bay. Ebita, however, had other things in mind.

The beds in both bedrooms were unmade. Management did not supply linens so Ebita brought her own. However, when she decided to spend a few days at beautiful Stone Heaven Bay, she never expected to have a guest. She had taken only one set of bed sheets and pillow cases with her for a three-day stay. She was concerned that the leather couch in the living room would not be a particularly comfortable place for either she or Christopher to sleep but decided the night was young, they had a lot to talk about, so the issue of where, or how they would sleep could wait a while.

Ebita had always been very direct in her approach to getting information she wanted, not necessarily what she needed or what was most beneficial. On that night she was true to form. She wasted no time on trite or trifles and asked Christopher exactly what she wanted to know. "Are you currently involved with anyone , Christopher?" she asked without flinching.

"Until yesterday, I was."

"I am not kidding, Christopher.

"Neither am I."

"Then, would you please explain, because I am lost, totally confused."

"It is not all that confusing when you hear it," said Christopher as he went on to describe the circumstances that led to his visiting Tobago to get some relief from the stress of a broken relationship with Khleo Karch. One that resulted from Khleo's reunion with her ex-boyfriend who was recently deported from the USA.

"Oh Christopher! I am so very sorry," said Ebita. "You seemed so composed. There is no way I or anyone else could have known."

"Looks can be very deceiving, my dear."

"Our experiences are very similar."

"Maybe not," said Christopher, "Based on what you told me earlier, I would think mine is not as dreadful."

"Dreadful! Isn't that kind of extreme?"

"Under the circumstances, no," said Christopher. "I do believe that together we can comfort and complement each other.

Christopher's last statement was exactly what Ebita wanted to hear. As far as she was concerned, the problem they faced of having two beds and only one set of bed linens, would easily be solved. Christopher was unaware of the problem so Ebita decided to make him so comfortable, that he would never know that one ever existed. She got up and searched through the collection of CD's in the condo until she found one that she thought was appropriate for the occasion. She said to Christopher, "Excuse me," as she turned off the television and placed the disc in the CD player. She turned off the light switch so that the only light in the room came from a full moon that shone through the open door and windows. She then moved back to the couch where Christopher sat at one end facing the entertainment center. She rested her head in his lap and pulled both of her legs up onto the couch. The music was soft, delightful, and romantic. Ebita took a deep breath and said, "Oh! This is so relaxing."

"It certainly is. I could be lulled to sleep right here."

"It is quite relaxing but not a comfortable enough place to spend the night."

"It is a leather couch. I don't think it was meant for sleeping in all night."

Ebita smiled and said, "I have to tell you something."

"What?"

"You have to sleep with me."

"You can't be serious."

"I didn't mean it that way," said Ebita. "What I meant was that we would have to sleep in the same bed."

"Why?"

"I brought only one set of bed linens."

"That's not a problem. I can sleep right here on the couch."

"Didn't you just say that a leather couch wasn't meant for sleeping in all night?"

"That doesn't mean that I couldn't, or wouldn't sleep in it."

"Why would you want to? Is it that you find me to be so repulsive?"

"Not at all, sweetheart. I am very sorry if I came across that way. You are truly adorable"

"You know, if it would make you more comfortable, I can place a divider in the middle of the bed."

"That wouldn't be necessary , dear," Christopher said as he stroked her hair back gently with the palm of his hand.

Ebita closed her eyes, smiled, and turned her face toward

him. He continued stroking her hair and she started breathing rapidly. That continued as one soft, romantic tune after another was being played. When the oldie *'Let's stay together'* started playing, Ebita became emotional and teary-eyed. She then wiped the tears from her eyes and said, "Let's go to bed."

She did not wait for Christopher's response. She got up and proceeded to the shower. She wasn't there very long, and as soon as she came out, Christopher entered. He showered, got dressed for bed, and returned to the couch. He laid down intending to make himself comfortable. He was unable to and realized that he was wrong when he said earlier, *That doesn't mean that I couldn't, or wouldn't sleep in it.*

Two hours elapsed and neither Ebita nor Christopher fell asleep. She was becoming restless and he, more uncomfortable by the minute. Eventually, she got up, walked back to the living room where Christopher lay awake. She touched his shoulder and asked, "Christopher, are you awake?"

"I have not been able to sleep."

"You see! I told you so."

"What did you tell me again?"

"That you have to sleep with me."

"You can be really funny at times. Do you know that?"

"Yes! I can be sometimes but that is not my intention right now."

"What do you have planned?"

"My intention is to see that you get a comfortable night's sleep."

Christopher sat up. Ebita held his hand. They both got up and walked to the bedroom and laid down. It wasn't long before they were fast asleep.

Back in Trinidad, the larger of the twin-island nation, the music at the Guaya Fest stopped at 9:30 p.m. and the vendors packed up what was left of their goodies. Visitors began leaving the seawall, a clear indication that the annual festivities had come to an end. Amanda drove Khleo and Eli back to Mayaro. When they arrived at Khleo's place she suggested that they meet for breakfast at Elaine's the next day.

"That would be nice," said Khleo. "Would you like to join us for coffee now?"

Amanda looked at the clock on her dash board. The time was 9:47 p.m. *It is still early,* she thought and said, "Certainly! Why not?"

Together they entered Khleo's second floor apartment. Amanda and Eli sat on the couch while Khleo went to the kitchen to get the coffee percolator started. Amanda knew Khleo's place very well, so when she sat down she wondered, *Which one of them sleeps on this uncomfortable couch?* She quickly dismissed the thought and asked Eli, "Do you plan on returning to the USA?"

"No," he answered tersely. He was uneasy with the questions Amanda tended to ask.

"My boyfriend is up there. I intended to join him but I am having a change of heart."

"Why? Is someone else's picture in the frame?"

"Not really."

"Not really? Either there is someone else or there is not."

"My mother wants me to go to Canada instead."

"Why?"

"She knows people there."

"Are those people closer to you than Quin is?"

"Did Khleo tell you about Quin?"

"No. I went to high school with him."

"While that might be true, how do you know that he was my boyfriend?"

"This is Mayaro. Everybody knows that. Anyway, why are you speaking of him in the past tense? Apart from the fact that your mother prefers that you study in Canada, there is someone else in the picture. Isn't there?"

Eli had gone on the attack in order to deflect any further negative questions from Amanda.

"Well, her good friend who is there wants me to meet her son."

"What is it with Mayaro women? Do you always do your mother's bidding even when you are grown?"

"I heard that," Khleo shouted from the kitchen.

"Not always," Amanda said.

"So why are you doing so now?"

"In this instance, my mother's friend, Unesta, offered me a place to stay. She is also making arrangements for employment that will eventually get me landed immigrant status in Canada. If I ignore Mom and go to the USA, I would be there as an international student. She is concerned that she does not have the financial resources to cover all of my expenses."

"I can relate to that. However, I have to ask, does the son of your mother's friend live in the same house as his parents?"

"I don't think so. I do know, however, that his father is not there."

"How old is this young man?"

"He is thirty."

"Does he have a girlfriend?"

"I don't think so."

"He is a healthy thirty year old Trini man living in Canada and does not have a girlfriend. Is something wrong with him?"

Just then Khleo came into the living room with the coffee and answered for Amanda, "Maybe he hasn't met the right woman yet. You are thirty-five and you do not have a girlfriend."

"That is kind of open-ended," Eli said.

"What is that supposed to mean?" Khleo asked. Eli did not answer. Amanda rolled her eyes and sipped her coffee so Khleo continued, "As far as I can see, there is nothing wrong with you. So why do you think something has to be wrong with that young man in Canada?"

"Khleo! This started as my fight. Remember?"

"Sorry. Sometimes I get carried away."

The fact that Eli gave Khleo no indication that he had any interest in her as a girlfriend, heightened Amanda's suspicion of him as a creepy, crawly character, a *snake* who would use Khleo or anyone else to satisfy his own selfish needs. *I hope after all this, you are not still thinking of Christopher as your boyfriend,* Amanda thought but said to Khleo, "You are in for a few fights of your own, girlfriend."

"I can handle myself," said Khleo. "Some people seem to think that I am fragile but I am not."

Amanda finished her coffee. She thanked Khleo, then said, "It's getting late, girl. I have to go now."

"We had a lovely evening Amanda," said Eli. "Thank you."

"You are most welcome," said Amanda. "Have a good night."

Amanda left and Khleo decided to call her parents. She spoke with them every day although she rarely visited. It was unusual for her to call them that late at night but she felt it was better to call late than not call at all. She dialed her parents' number and her mother, Mrs. Mancelia Karch answered, "Hello!"

"Ma, it's Khleo."

"All day I was wondering about you. I tried calling you but got no answer."

"I am sorry, Ma. I was out most of the day."

"Are you okay?"

"I am fine."

"I am always so glad to hear that," said Mrs. Karch. "Anyway, your father just retired to bed, so I will call you back early tomorrow morning."

"Okay, Ma. Have a good night."

"You too. Good night." They both hung up.

Khleo looked at Eli and smiled. He did not smile back. Instead he asked, "What?"

"That was Ma," said Khleo. "I was going to tell her that you are here but she had to go."

"Where was she going?"

"To bed I guess." That got Eli laughing, and Khleo said, "I think I am going to do the same. Good night." She was angry at Eli for his indifference.

Once again Khleo entered her bedroom and locked the door behind her. Eli sat on the couch alone. He had enjoyed the day but the evening wasn't going as well as he had hoped. Amanda probably would never know that he would be the one sleeping on that uncomfortable couch. He, however, resigned himself to the fact that the couch in Khleo's living room was a lot more comfortable than a sheet of cardboard on the sidewalk at a store front, or in the park. He sat and mused about his situation for a while but eventually, he laid down and fell asleep.

FIFTEEN

THE NEXT MORNING CHRISTOPHER WOKE up early. He sat on the veranda overlooking the turquoise waters of the Caribbean Sea. The sounds of chirping birds were everywhere. A soft gentle breeze blew over the veranda and into the condo as his thoughts drifted momentarily to Khleo. *It is so peaceful here, we could have ....,* he started thinking of all the wonderful things they had done together and could have been doing still, had it not been for Eli's return. He quickly interrupted that thought and said to himself loudly, "I should wake up Ebita. It is a nice morning to walk down to the beach and take advantage of the low tide."

Christopher sat deliberating whether or not to awaken Ebita but she came out and said, "Good morning, my dear!"

"Good morning! You seem to have slept well."

"Thanks to you," said Ebita. "I had a great night's sleep."

"I am happy to have contributed."

"You didn't just contribute, honey. You made it happen."

"It's not as if you were a spectator. You were an active participant. I mean active, baby!"

"Is that the reason you rushed out of bed so early?" They

both laughed before Christopher said, "No. I wake up early every morning. I have done that all of my life."

"You seem eager to get out onto that beach."

"How can you tell?"

"Let's just call it a woman's intuition," said Ebita. "I will get into my swim suit."

She left the veranda to get dressed for the beach and Christopher did the same. It wasn't long before both were running down the stairs on their way to the surf. There were very few people on the beach that early in the morning, so they decided to stroll along the white compact sandy beach. It was not a long expanse of coastline but it was lovely.

After thirty minutes or so of walking and playing in the sand, they waded into the warm sea water of Stone Heaven Bay. Neither could swim very well, so they ventured no further than waist deep into the water. The tide was low and the water was calm. There were virtually no waves and absolutely no riptides but they were taking no chances. They dove, they laughed, they hugged, they kissed. They seemed to have found happiness in the activities and in each other.

Khleo was not experiencing the same kind of joy with Eli. She woke up early but he was not there. As she looked out the window to see whether he was on the street below, her telephone rang.

"Hello!" she answered.

"Khleo! This is Peter.

"Yes?"

"Is Snake there?"

"First of all, his name is Eli. Secondly, where did you get my number?" Khleo did not like the nickname *Snake* by which Eli was known in Mayaro and she had forgotten that her telephone number was public knowledge.

"Your number is listed, honey." Peter reminded her.

"Don't you honey me."

"Okay! Let's cut to the chase. Where is he?"

"I don't know. He wasn't here when I woke up this morning."

"Thanks. Bye."

As soon as Peter hung up the telephone he spotted Eli walking past the Anglican church at Two Beach. He stopped his car and shouted, "Snake!" Eli turned around and approached the car.

"Where are you heading?" he asked.

"I was coming to meet you. I called Khleo before I left home but she didn't seem to appreciate that."

"She probably thought I went against her wishes and gave out the phone number without her permission."

"Don't worry about that. I reminded her that the number is listed."

"Thanks for that. I didn't know that it was."

"What are your plans for tomorrow?" Peter asked.

"I have none."

"What are you doing this afternoon?"

"I don't know. I have to see what Khleo's plans are."

"You do that, and I would check in with you later."

"Just what did you have in mind? Give me some idea so I can plan accordingly."

"We wanted to go hiking tomorrow but we were hoping to check out the area this afternoon."

"Sounds good. I will get back to you in a couple of hours."

"Great! You take care." Peter drove off and Eli continued walking toward Khleo's place.

When he arrived there and said good morning to Khleo, she responded cordially but nonchalantly. As soon as he sat down she asked, "Did you have breakfast?"

"No," he said in a resounding sort of way. His response conveyed his thinking, *You know that I have no money for breakfast.*

"You know that I do not cook," Khleo said.

"Yes. You did tell me that."

"Then are you willing to go to Elaine's for breakfast?"

"Sure!"

"Okay! Let's go."

"How are we getting there?"

"We are going to walk," said Khleo. "How else did you expect to get up there?"

"I thought Amanda was going to take us."

"Where is she?" asked Khleo sarcastically. "Didn't she tell you once that she is not your damn chauffeur?"

"Okay! Okay! I got it loud and clear."

"Then stop the argument. Let's go"

They left the apartment, walked to the Guayaguayare Road, and headed toward the outdoor market. Neither spoke. Khleo was obviously very angry but she wasn't sure why herself. Eli was extremely bewildered. There was no one else he could look to for assistance out of the situation in which he found himself, yet he seemed to have been falling out of favor with Khleo. *Was it because of the friendship I struck up with the Aranguez brothers? Or was she reconsidering her decision to let me stay with her?* he wondered.

They arrived at Elaine's and were quickly ushered to a table for two. Khleo ordered breakfast and offered to pay for it in advance.

"Do you want to take it out?" the waiter asked.

"No. We are staying," responded Khleo.

"Then you can pay when you are finished."

"I usually do. Today, however, I want to pay in advance." Khleo handed the waiter her credit card. He took it and left without any further questions.

"Are you angry at me?" Eli asked in an effort to break the silence that was beginning to make him feel uncomfortable.

"No."

"Then why wouldn't you speak to me?"

"Why do I have to be the one speaking?" she asked. "Is something wrong with your tongue?"

"It really takes two to converse."

"Then start talking." That statement from Khleo made Eli laugh. He was still laughing when the waiter came back with their breakfast. That was a bit awkward for Khleo. She was not laughing. Her thoughts were on Christopher who, of course was not thinking of her.

"Would you like to have anything else, Ms. Karch?" the waiter asked.

"No. That will be all. Thank you."

Neither Eli nor Khleo enjoyed the breakfast. As delectable as it seemed, both individuals appeared to have lost their appetites. The lack of desire for food was no less pronounced than the hostility and resentment they felt toward each other. They were both perplexed, Eli because of poor choices he had made throughout his adult life and Khleo, because of her recent decision to give preference to him over Christopher.

As they got up to leave the restaurant, Khleo's cell phone rang. Without checking the caller ID she answered, "Hello."

"Khleo, dearest. This is Peter."

"What did I tell you about that earlier this morning?"

"Oh! Yes. I remember you said that I should not call you honey."

"So why are you calling me dearest?"

"Dearest is not honey."

"My name is Khleo and it does not require any description or qualification from you."

"I am sorry , Miss," said Peter. "Can I speak with Snake?"

"Eli!" Khleo said.

"Yeah! Whoever. Can I speak with him?"

Khleo did not respond to Peter's last comment. She handed the cellular telephone to Eli who was snickering at the part of the conversation he overheard. He wasn't sure who the caller was but assumed the person knew him. That was part of the problem Khleo was experiencing. She expected to receive from Eli the same sort of attention she got from Christopher and it was not forthcoming. Eli seemed inclined to spend more time with his male friends. He was trying desperately to make re-acquaintances with old friends and close associations with new ones like Peter and his brother, Paul. Peter was still talking when Eli put the cell phone to his ears. The words "You are going to come down a peg girl, caught his attention but he said only, "Hello."

"Snake! It's Peter."

"Hey! What's up, Peter?"

"We are going back to Guaya this afternoon. Would you like to come along?"

"Certainly. What time are you going?"

"Some time between 1:30 and 2:00 p.m."

"Then pick me up around that time."

"You've got it."

"Okay," Eli said. He was smiling again. Khleo was not.

She remembered Peter Aranguez' sarcastic remark when his brother, Paul referred to her and Amanda as *lovely ladies* and wondered, why was he trying to kiss up to her lately? She knew for certain that she would not be interested in him and was confident that if he didn't realize that yet, he would soon get the message. She looked at Eli and thought, *I have been unnecessarily mean to him. I really have no good reason for that.* Eli caught her glances and asked, "What is the matter?"

"Nothing. I was just thinking."

"What were you thinking about?"

"The fact that you have no money and you accepted Peter's invitation to go out."

"We are not going far," said Eli. "Would you like to come along?"

"Where are you going that is not far?'

"We are going to Guayaguayare."

"I don't think so."

"Don't you think we are going to Guayaguayare, or is it that you just do not want to come along?"

"I prefer to stay at home. Thank you."

Khleo was smiling again. Suddenly the thought of being out

with Eli as pleasing, though not quite as exciting as when they met at Piarco International Airport three days earlier. She started thinking that she might have been too hard on him and decided that she would give him a chance. She wanted to see whether they could rekindle the flame that once burned so brightly but was extinguished too early in their youthful relationship. *This is the right time to bring everyone up to date. At least those who matter,'* she thought but said, "When I speak with Ma later today I am going to let her know that you are here."

"Don't you think she already knows that?"

"She might but she still needs to hear it from me."

"Fair enough."

That seemed to be just what Khleo needed to hear. She held Eli's hand as they started to walk down the Old Road. Just then her cell phone rang. She released her grip on his fingers and scrambled to get the phone out of her purse before the caller hung up. She managed to accomplish that and answered quickly.

"Khleo! It's Amanda," the caller said.

"I thought by now you would know that I can recognize your voice."

"I know that. It is just protocol. Or is it telephone etiquette?"

"What's the difference?"

"Is there really a difference?"

"Whatever!"

"Whatever! What are you doing this afternoon ?"

"Nothing. Nothing at all. The man is going to Guayaguayare so I'll be at home alone."

"The man?" Eli questioned softly. Amanda didn't hear the question he asked, and Khleo ignored it.

"I would come and pick you up," Amanda said. Khleo never question what Amanda's plan was, or if there was a plan at all. She simply said, "Okay."

"What is a good time?" Amanda asked.

"Any time after 2:00 p.m.

SIXTEEN

CHRISTOPHER AND EBITA RETURNED TO the condo, showered and changed, and walked down to the restaurant where they had dinner the night before. They conversed amicably as they enjoyed their meal. After breakfast, they decided to drive to Scarborough, the main city in Tobago. Christopher asked Ebita to do the driving so he could enjoy the view as they traveled. Knowing that it was his first visit to the island, she obliged.

They left Stone Heaven Bay and drove across the island along Plymouth Road. Ebita knew the area well so she turned onto Windward Road, then up Bacolet Street and into Main Street. From Main Street, she made a left turn into Castries Street and bore right to Carrington Road. There she told Christopher, "We are going to visit the Scarborough Regional Library, then check out the Mall where I hope to find some postcards. If I do, we will make a stop at the Post Office. After that, we will pick up some fresh fruits at the market."

By then they had reached Gardensite Street. Ebita parked the car and told Christopher, "We can walk to all the places I told you we need to visit."

"That's quite an itinerary. Did you have it written down?"

"No. It is just something I do all the time."

"How often do you come to Tobago?"

"As often as I can. That is, as often as the condo is available."

"I imagine that is not very often, given the demand for facilities here."

"Well, it is more difficult during the North American and European winters. Also, during the months of July and August here when all teachers and many civil servants are on vacation."

"Is it readily available during Easter weekend?"

"No! Easter, Independence, Indian Arrival Day, and Emancipation are difficult. All times in between are okay."

Ebita retrieved three books she had placed on the back seat and walked into the library with them. The books were long overdue but the librarian waived the fees. She knew that Ebita lived in St. Augustine in Trinidad and came to Tobago at every opportunity she got. As they left the library, Christopher asked, "Are you the Mayor of Scarborough?"

Ebita laughed and said, "You are truly funny. No. I am not. I just happen to know a few people here. I like to talk, Tobagonians are friendly, so the match is easy and perfect."

Christopher saw nothing he personally needed or wanted at the Mall but Ebita found some postcards and a few personal items she felt she could use. While she was selecting those items Christopher excused himself, walked over to the florist and purchased a bouquet of roses for her. He sneaked out of the Mall and placed the bouquet of yellow roses on the driver's seat of the rented car before Ebita paid for the items she selected. By the time he got back she was ready. She looked at her watch and said to him, "I can write out these cards in the Post Office and drop them in the mail right away."

"Then what?" he asked.

"Don't be so impatient, honey. We will stop at the market and get some fresh fruits."

Christopher turned his thoughts to Khleo temporarily. He was feeling badly that for several years he had focused his attention on her, invested so much time in trying to nurture their relationship only to be hurt when some guy named Snake suddenly re-entered her life. *What a let down,* he thought. He regretted not staying in touch with Ebita whom he always knew to be an extremely nice person. Although it was through no fault of his that they drifted apart, he was saddened at the difficulties she experienced since they left the university. *If only I can turn back the hands of time,* he thought. Knowing that to be impossible, he vowed never again to be out of touch with her. In fact, he was determined to reassure her about how much he cared for her and still does.

After she purchased a variety of local fruits from the market, she suggested that they visit the Botanical Garden which was a short distance away. Christopher didn't know that so he asked, "How far away is it?"

"It is within walking distance. Even if it hadn't been close, we have a car and we have the time. I know you always had a love for nature. If that has changed and you don't want to visit the garden, I will understand."

"No! No. I am okay with it."

"Just okay with it?" she asked.

"I know that didn't sound enthusiastic sweetheart but I really would like to go."

She smiled, a delightfully gracious smile. It was as if Christopher had written a sonnet just for her. "You are so sweet," said Ebita. "I promise that we wouldn't stay very long."

As they entered the Botanic Garden, Ebita pointed to a cluster of beautiful flowers in long strands of magnificent vermillion and said to Christopher, "There is your national flower." He appeared puzzled by her statement as he stared at the flowering plant without saying a word.

"Don't tell me you are not familiar with it," said Ebita. "That is the Chaconia, the pride of Trinidad and Tobago. The plant blooms around this time. Remember that T & T became independent on August 31, 1962."

"It is very interesting," said Christopher. "Perhaps you have forgotten that I was born in Aruba. I am still not a citizen of Trinidad and Tobago."

"Oh! Oh! I really messed up. I am sorry."

"There is no need to be sorry. You had no way of knowing if I did not tell you. I came to Trinidad when I was very young so the only accent you are hearing is that of a Trinidadian who, in reality, I am not."

"You are an imposter," she said while laughing hysterically.

"It's strange that you find that to be funny," said Christopher. "I never made a conscious effort to change my speech."

"I believe you. It seems funny to me because for some reason we *Bajans* just never lose our accent."

"Good for you."

"Anyway, the Chaconia, and Chacon Street in Port of Spain were named after Don Jose Maria Chacon (1749-1833). He was the last Spanish Governor of Trinidad.

"Why did you say Trinidad and not Trinidad and Tobago?"

"The islands were not always united. *Bella Forma*, as Columbus called Tobago when he thought he discovered it, changed hands some 33 times among the Spanish, Dutch, British, and French colonial powers."

"Wow! So when did they become united?"

"Had you asked that question while we were in the library it would have been easy for me to use the computer there and look it up but I'll do the best I can from memory."

"Are you serious?"

"As I recall, In 1763 Britain gained control of Tobago from the French. The French, however, recaptured the island in 1781. It was not until 1793 that British forces regained control of the colony from the French. Four years later in 1797, British forces captured Trinidad from the Spaniards and claimed it for the British Crown. In 1802 Trinidad was declared a British colony. Eighty-four years later in 1886, a decree from the British government united Trinidad and Tobago as a single colony for purposes of finance and administration. They have remained politically united ever since."

"I get it. They progressed from British Crown Colony to self-government, to independence. Now they are a self-governing Republic within the British Commonwealth."

"You certainly got it. That has been their status since they gained independence from Britain. Today we speak of them as T & T; one nation, with a national flower, one national bird, one flag, and one coat of arms."

"Although you are from Barbados, you have taken quite an interest in this nation."

"I live here. It is now my home."

"I live here too. There is little or no chance that I would ever return to Aruba to live, so I have to brush up on my history of the nation."

"It is not that difficult because all of the Caribbean countries have similar histories. For example, Christopher Columbus re-discovered them all. In 1838 the British abolished slavery in all of them. Sugar and sugarcane plantation owners played a major role in the trading of slaves from Africa and later, after the abolition of slavery, the introduction of indentured laborers from India."

Ebita held Christopher's arm as they strolled through the Botanic Garden. "There is your Chaconia again," she said as she pointed to another of the Wild Poinsettias nationally known as the Chaconia.

They trekked all over the garden and viewed the many different types of flowers including the anthuriums, ginger lilies, orchids, bromeliads and heliconias. They took the time also to observe the large trees that were native of the region. Trees such as the cedar, purple heart, silk cotton, immortelle, poui, and sand box were particularly impressive. Christopher expressed regret that he did not bring along a camera. He left home so haphazardly, and simply did not think of taking a camera with him. One thing was certain, he was no longer rued by the thought he had lost Khleo, the love of his life, to the rascal Eli who had been her former boyfriend.

Ebita seemed very much in control of the situation and Christopher was comfortable enough to accept that. When they were leaving the Botanic Garden she suggested that they take a ride to Charlotte Ville.

"Charlotte Ville! Where is that?" he asked.

"It is at the Northeast coast of the island."

"What else do we have to do?"

"On a weekend like this, we do not have to do anything. What matters is what we want to do. So do you want to go or not?"

"Ebita, right now I am willing to go anywhere you want to take me."

"Okay! Then we must fill up with gasoline here in Scarborough."

Christopher looked at the gas gauge on the dashboard and said, "We have a half tank. That should be sufficient. The island is not that large."

"It is true that the island is small but the roads are narrow, bumpy, and undulating. In addition, there is a thirty miles per hour speed limit that is enforced throughout the island . Also, there are not too many gas stations. In fact, there are none in the countryside and those that are available in the more populated areas are more often than not, closed on the weekend."

They filled up the tank at the nearest gas station and Ebita paid for it over Christopher's objection. "You will pay for lunch," she said. "It's called sharing expenses."

"Gas might cost a great deal more than lunch."

"Things like that matter very little when two people are as comfortable with each other as we are."

"I am afraid," Christopher said.

"Afraid of what?"

"I might be falling in love."

"I thought you already had."

"I did once or twice before but this is different."

"This, meaning the situation with both of us?" she asked as she pulled the car up to the curb and parked.

"Yes my dear. You are now the chosen one."

"Oh Christopher! For years I longed to hear you say that. Even when we were out of touch after we graduated I hoped that a day like this will come. I love you, Chris."

She called him Chris for the first time. No one ever called him that so he never had reasons to object. He was not about to object then. He felt he was having the best weekend of his life and was determined not to allow anyone or anything to spoil the fun.

From where they were on Gardensite Street, they came down to Main Street via Carrington and Castries Streets. From Main Street they turned right onto Bacolot Street and left off Bacolot toward Roxborough by way of Windward Road. They were leaving the city on their way to rural Tobago. The roadway was meandering and undulating along the Atlantic coast. As they were passing Barbados Bay, Ebita pointed out that the first British capital of Tobago, Georgetown, was once located there. "A fish market is now in operation at the site," she noted. About five hundred yards away she said to Christopher, "This area is called Fort Granby. As you can see, it is now a picnic area. That tiny island just beyond the shore-line is Smith's Island."

At that point she was driving at 10 miles per hour, and Christopher finally understood why it was necessary to fill up the gas tank in Scarborough. Although he never questioned Ebita's decision, he had his doubts. As they drove through the quiet village of Belle Garden, she mentioned that there is another island, Richmond Island off the coast there but it could not be seen from the roadway. "Are you in the mood for walking?" she asked.

"I do not mind."

"Then we can visit the waterfall."

"Is there a waterfall here?"

"There are several waterfalls in Tobago. This one, Argyle Waterfall is the highest. At its base is a pool that is good for swimming," said Ebita. "There is only one catch."

"What could that be?"

"Visitors must use a guide."

"That is not such a big deal."

"The catch is that there is a fee."

"How much?"

"The last time I visited it was forty dollars. It might be a little more now," said Ebita. "Do you still want to go?"

"Of course."

As they parked and stepped out of the vehicle, they were approached by a tall handsome young man who asked, "Would you be interested in a guide to the Fall?"

"Yes," said Ebita.

"I will be happy to take you," said the young man

"How much will it be?" Christopher asked.

"We suggest forty dollars, TT that is, but it is really up to you."

Christopher interpreted that to mean, $TT40.00 is the minimum that will be accepted but one can give more, so he said, "Okay."

"It is a 15 to 20 minutes walk," the guide said.

"That's Okay," Ebita said.

"Then lets go," the guide said.

The guide was very knowledgeable and answered all the questions Christopher had. Ebita, having been there several times before, had nothing to ask. She was making the trip solely for Christopher's benefit.

"Magnificent!" said Christopher when he saw the Fall. "Girl, I am so glad I met you at the Airport yesterday. I cannot begin to tell you how much."

"I am very happy that I can do this, not just for you but with you."

"We are together again. Let's stay that way."

"That is my greatest wish," Ebita said.

"Togetherness! That's a great thing," the guide said.

SEVENTEEN

AT THE SAME TIME AMANDA arrived to pick up Khleo, Peter Aranguez came to take Eli to seek out a prospective picnic area in Guayaguayare. The fact that Khleo was going out did not escape Peter but his presence made her suspicious and uncomfortable. Eli on the contrary, was oblivious to Peter's planned chicanery. He assumed that the Aranguez brothers' interest in him was due to his happy, fun loving ways. He was wrong. He did not let Khleo know where he was going but that was not out of disrespect for her. As it turned out, he didn't know exactly where himself.

Minutes before he walked out the door, Khleo said to Eli, "I am not sure how long I will be out. If you should return before I do, there is a key to the front door under the potted palm at the top of the stairs."

She kept that key there so that no one would see her hiding a key on her way out of her apartment. Her mother knew that it was there. Amanda knew it was there but until then, no one else knew. Eli said, "Thanks, Khleo," and rushed down the stairs to Peter's car. Peter had already picked up Paul from his home in Beau Sejour. He was sitting in the back seat. As soon as Eli sat down and before he had time to buckle his seat belt, Peter sped off in the direction of Guayaguayare. He drove fast and foolishly and that made Eli uneasy.

Paul observed Eli's discomfort and asked, "Are you okay, Snake?"

"I will be," said Eli. "I have to readjust to the speed at which you guys drive on these narrow roads."

"Alright Peter, take it easy," said Paul. "Snake here is scared to death."

The sound of the word death really heightened Eli's fear as Peter swerved his SUV between two eighteen- wheelers to avoid an oncoming truck that was approaching at 80 mph. Eli, sitting on the left in the front passenger seat of the right-hand driven car, was stepping on imaginary brakes and holding on to anything he could grasp.

"Peter! Slow down," Paul pleaded.

"Do you want to drive?"

"No, but Snake is uncomfortable."

"If you don't want to drive, then shut up little brother," said Peter. "Under no circumstances would I let you drive me anywhere. So just sit down and be quiet" Peter Aranguez had always used the terms ....*little brother* and ....*senseless kid* to convey to Paul that he, Peter, as the older brother, was somehow superior.

Five minutes after Eli's departure, Khleo carefully and casually walked down the stairs to Amanda's car. She entered the vehicle and buckled herself in. "Where are we going?" she asked.

"We could start with Tropical Fruits, the exotic fruit juice bar in Plaisance."

"That sounds good," said Khleo. "The last time I was there the Kharmina sting was their signature drink."

"It still might be," said Amanda. "Let's go in and find out for ourselves."

They entered the elegant seaside lounge and sat near a window overlooking the ocean. A waiter approached them and said, "Good afternoon ladies. How can I help you today?"

"Please get me a cold Kharmina sting," Amanda said. The waiter then looked at Khleo and she said to him, "Make that two Kharmina stings. Thank you."

"Coming up! One Kharmina sting for you and two Kharmina Stings for you," the waiter said.

"No!" said Amanda. "Just two Kharmina stings."

"I knew that," he said as he laughed and walked away.

"Is he trying to be funny?" Khleo asked.

"He was the only one laughing."

Peter Aranguez was still speeding along the Mayaro/ Guayaguayare Road. He drove past his luxurious Lagon Palmiste home without even looking in. His brother was still questioning the wisdom of speeding to no place in particular but Peter continued to ignore him. With speeds of up to 70 mph, they quickly reached New Lands. Other drivers and pedestrians alike were giving way to Peter. Within minutes they had reached Guayaguayare Village. Only then did Peter reduce his speed. He did so either because he knew that speeds were monitored by radar in the area or he realized that he was relatively close to his destination.

When they reached the oilfield gate, a guard approached the car cautiously. "Where are you heading?" he asked.

"I thought *Oxtail* would be on duty today," said Peter. He did not answer the guard's question. He couldn't because he did not know where they were going. There was no plan.

"Oxtail? Do you mean Frank DePass?"

"Yes."

"He is working the late shift."

"Oh man!" Peter sighed.

The guard assumed that Peter knew his colleague very well so he offered to help in any way he could. Peter, however, didn't know exactly where he wanted to go or what he wanted to do. All he really knew was that beyond the oilfield the area was forested. Paul came to his brother's rescue when, from where he sat in the back seat, he told the guard, "We are trying to get to the Wildlife Sanctuary and Reserve."

"Oh! That's up in the Trinity Hills," said the guard. "You need permission from Petrotrin to visit. You can call the office but they are closed today. The office is open Monday to Friday from 9:00 a.m. to 4:00 p.m."

"Oh man! Oxtail could have told me that," Peter said.

"Don't make it a problem," said the guard. "About a mile and a half from here you would get to the Rio Claro/Guayaguayare Road. That would take you to the sanctuary. The road is very bad though. You might be better off hiking in."

That was exactly what Peter wanted to hear but he wasn't elated . He showed no emotion but said, "Thank you. We may try that tomorrow. Would you be on duty?"

"No. DePass will be though."

"Great! Thanks," Peter said.

The guard opened the gate and Peter said, "We are going to make a quick spin."

"Stay to your left."

Peter was driving at about 20 mph. That was a welcome change for Eli who, nevertheless, was astonished by the wilderness he saw after only ten minutes of driving. When they reached the Rio Claro/Guayaguayare Road, Peter said, "This is good. Let's head back."

Amanda sipped her drink and said to Khleo, "I see Eli is still hanging out with those brothers. You need to caution him about that. Those guys are nothing but trouble."

"What can I tell him?"

"Tell him what you know," said Amanda. "They are scoundrels."

"I can't do that."

"Why not?"

"That may seem controlling."

"Listen, Khleo! That man waltzed back into your life from

nowhere and with a lot of baggage. If you do not take control, he could ruin you."

"You know that he came back from the States with only one bag. So why are you being so harsh?"

"Please! Stop being so naïve, girl," said Amanda. "I did not mean that literally."

"I am so stressed out," said Khleo. "Just what can I do?"

"You can start by having more conversations, and deduce from him by skillful questioning what you want to know. You do that with your students in the classroom all the time."

"Yeah! However, he is not a child. Moreover, he does not listen to me."

"I can tell how frustrated you are. The stresses are beginning to show on your face."

"Perhaps what I should do is get away for a few days."

"That's a good idea," said Amanda. "You may want to consider going to some other beach resort."

"Las Cuevas would be nice."

"It would be a nice change from Mayaro."

"I have been there before."

"I know that you were there with Eli when you were only fifteen," said Amanda. "What you need now is quiet seclusion, so you can reflect on your life and what you can do moving forward."

"Are you implying that I go without Eli?"

"I am not only suggesting that you go without him, I am indicating that you do not tell him where you are going."

"I don't think he would like that."

"Then he may understand how it feels when he goes out without telling you where he is going."

"You may be right."

"I am right."

"It is already Saturday. When can I go?"

"Go tomorrow." Amanda said. Khleo did not respond, so Amanda continued, "I can accompany you if you wish."

"That's great. Then let's plan to leave early."

"As early as six o'clock?"

"Why not?"

"Then six o'clock it is."

Eli and the Aranguez brothers returned from the fields (oil fields). They located the Rio Claro/Guayaguayare Road, a road that few of the younger people in the Mayaro/Guayaguayare area knew existed. Hardly anyone under the age of thirty had ever heard of this Road. Although history teaches us that Guayaguayare, affectionately known as Guaya, the southernmost area in T &T, was the first land mass sighted by Christopher Columbus on his third voyage to the West Indies, very few visitors to the area ventured beyond the seawall.

Historically, Guayaguayare has played a prominent role in the petroleum industry. The first oil well was drilled there as early as 1902. The area still remains in the forefront of petroleum and natural gas production in Trinidad and Tobago while the wildlife sanctuary and the largest mud volcano in the nation, *Lagoon Bouffe*, remain virtually unknown.

Among the reasons tourists, school officials, and local residents are not too familiar with this great natural resource are the facts that the area is remote and restricted, the wild life in the area includes venomous snakes, and the terrain is rugged.

Peter Aranguez himself was not familiar with the protected reserve but his brother Paul, experienced the beauty of this relatively large forested area during his years as a police officer. He belonged to a team of elite officers whose mission it was to track kidnappers and rescue their victims. He became impressed not only with the forest, but also with the wildlife within. The pristine waterfalls, though small, were to him the most beautiful to behold. *Lagoon Bouffe* had also impressed him but when he was dishonorably discharged from the police service, his interest in the area waned considerably.

Until late that Saturday evening, neither Eli nor Paul knew what drew Peter to the area. In fact, the Wildlife Sanctuary and Reserve was not in itself of particular interest to Peter. He was looking for some remote place where he could perpetrate his hoax, a *staged* kidnapping, or if forced, execute an actual kidnapping. First, he considered Vespry Road but after a visit there, the thought of using the area as a venue was abandoned because a few people lived there. Peter felt that although there were only a few residents in the area, even one witness to his planned activity would be too many. He knew his intended victim but had not yet revealed his evil intention nor the possible victim to either his brother or to Eli.

Peter was driving slowly on the return trip from Guaya. When he reached New Lands, without indication he stopped and turned right into the parking lot of the Roadside Inn. He parked the SUV, took the keys from the ignition and stepped out leaving the windows rolled down. The others followed him without asking any questions. They entered the Inn and the bartender asked, "What will it be gentlemen?"

Peter looked at his brother and at Eli, a quizzing sort of look that they both understood and said, "Cold beer."

"The usual," Peter said to the bartender.

"Three?"

"Yeah."

The bartender took three local beers from the freezer, opened them and placed them on the counter in front of Peter. He in turn gave one to Eli and one to Paul. They sipped their beer while they enjoyed a game of football (soccer) that was being televised. A few minutes later Peter said to the bartender, "Let's have another round, Smiley."

The bartender again gave them three cold local beers. Peter paid for them, left a tip on the counter, and they proceeded to the parking lot.

"Are you going to drink that beer while driving?" Eli asked.

"What else will I do with it?"

"That is a violation," Eli said.

"A violation of what?" asked Peter. "Maybe in the States it is against the law. Here it is the law."

"That can't be," Eli said.

"It is not written but everybody knows that on a hot day like this, you have a cold beer, whether or not you are driving."

The trio drove without much conversation until they reached Indian Bay, formerly known to the locals as the glassy beach. Just before reaching the bridge, Peter made a sudden right turn and parked the SUV on a sand bank. He had found a quiet place where he could put forward his proposal to Eli and Paul without anyone else hearing the discussions. Their presence under the palm (coconut) trees on the beach appeared to be nothing more than a beach lime (the act of hang out) among friends.

Peter wasted no time before saying to Eli, "Snake, I see that you still have no transport of your own, and as I understand it, you have no spending money either. That's not how a nice fella (man or guy) like you should have to live."

"This situation is only temporary," said Eli. "Keep in mind that it is only three days now that I have been here."

"Three days! That's a long time to be without your own transport if you are over the age of eighteen," Paul said.

"Having no liquidity, no spending money makes it even worse."

"On Monday I will be sending out my résumé to several corporations. I am confident that very soon I will be offered a job."

"Yeah! How soon is very soon?" Peter questioned skeptically. "That could be a week, a month, a year. Who knows?"

"Like I said, I am confident that I would find something soon, within a week perhaps," said Eli. "If I am unable to find something on my own, Khleo promised that she would ask her parents whether they have an opening that I may be able to fill."

"You have a golden goose for a girlfriend. Why do you want to work for her parents?" Peter asked.

"It is the egg the goose lays that is golden," Paul told his brother for the second time since the Guaya Fest."

"Shut up little brother," said Peter. "Snake here needs money and he needs it fast."

"I am okay," said Eli. "Really! I am fine."

"No! You are not. You can't be," said Peter. "Take this." Peter pulled out an envelope from above the visor and handed it to Eli who opened it and said, "I am sorry. I cannot accept this." The envelope contained $600.00.

"Why can't you accept it? Are you afraid of money?"

"No. It just wouldn't be right for me to take that much money from you."

"Did Khleo tell you that?"

"No! She has no idea that I am out here."

"Where is she right now?"

"I don't know. She is wherever Amanda took her I imagine."

"Are you saying she didn't tell you where she was going?"

"She didn't but I saw nothing wrong with that. Perhaps she didn't know herself."

"Now, I would take that to mean she didn't care a damn."

"I was cool with it."

"You are just too laid back, Snake. Anyway, hold on to the cash. If you prefer to think of it as a loan, do so."

"If I were you Snake, I wouldn't borrow money from my brother," said Paul. "He is known in Mayaro as Shylock."

"Shut up Paul!" Peter shouted. "For the rest of the evening you should speak only when I speak to you."

Eli was becoming a bit leery about Peter's bullying of his younger brother but elected to say nothing about it. He folded the envelope Peter gave him and stuck it in the left front pocket of his jeans. Then Peter asked, "Did Khleo take her cellular phone with her?"

"I suppose so," said Eli. "She seems to always carry it whenever she goes out. You are not thinking of calling her, are you?"

"No! Not at all," said Peter. "I was wondering what kind of cell phone she has."

What that has to do with anything? Eli wondered but said, "I really don't know."

"You wouldn't happen to know how much she paid for her cell phone?"

"No."

"I suppose she carries it in her purse all the time."

"I really don't know," Eli said.

"Snake, you know very little about your girl friend. Don't you ?" Paul asked.

"What did I tell you, Paul?" Peter asked but his brother did not answer.

Peter wasn't able to deduce from Eli what he wanted to know about Khleo. His line of questioning was either ineffective, or Eli was determined to reveal very little of what he knew about her or her family to the Aranguez brothers. Peter, therefore, began to question the trustworthiness of his newly adopted friend and the wisdom of his own plan to reveal to him and Paul his intention to *stage* a kidnapping of Khleo Karch in order to extort money from her wealthy parents, or rather, perceived wealthy parents. He was unwilling to abandon the plan altogether and made a spur of the moment decision to have one of the Gardeners, the bad boys in town, snatch her purse that Saturday evening. He knew from an earlier discussion with Eli that Khleo was out with Amanda. However, he had no idea where they were or how long they intended to be out. Because it was Saturday and Eli was also out, he conjectured that neither Khleo nor Amanda had any reason to rush home. He was right. They left the Tropical Fruits Bar in Plaisance that afternoon and drove to Ortoire where they hired a boat to take them to the site of the offshore volcano.

Peter's stubborn and tenacious nature would not allow him to abandon an idea once he had given it considerable thought, though not necessarily careful thought. He took out his cell phone and called someone nicknamed Imp and told him, "I want one of the gardeners to run an errand for me."

"That would not be a problem," said Imp. "What time?"

"I would let you know when I come up to Pierreville."

"What time will that be?"

"In about twenty minutes."

"No problem," Imp said.

"How much will that cost?"

"That will depend on the nature of the errand and what it's worth to you."

"Okay! I will see you in twenty minutes. We will talk about it then."

"No problem," Imp said and hung up.

EIGHTEEN

CHRISTOPHER AND EBITA ARRIVED AT Charlotte Ville after having a late but delectable lunch . They had traveled the entire length of the Windward Road through hills and valleys making somewhat of a brief stop at the Argyle Waterfall and a more extended visit to Little Tobago also called Bird of Paradise Island. There again, Christopher was impressed the moment he stepped off the little boat that took them to the island. Birds were everywhere. The number of different species were numerous, just too many for Christopher to count. Once again he expressed regrets for not having a camera. Although there were no longer any Birds of Paradise on Little Tobago, Christopher wasn't any less delighted . In fact, he would not have known had it not been for Ebita's keen acumen. She gave him a brief history of the little island as she noted its early use as a cotton plantation, and the introduction of sugarcane there when cotton was no longer profitable as an industry. She also noted the introduction of the Birds of Paradise to the island by Sir Ingram who brought them from New Guinea where they were threatened by extinction. Sadly, she also noted the disappearance of those birds from Little Tobago after its devastation by a hurricane in 1963. Finally,

Ebita informed Christopher that the island was donated to the government of Trinidad and Tobago on the condition that it was to be used only as a bird sanctuary which it continues to be today. Christopher couldn't be more impressed with Ebita's knowledge. *She is a walking encyclopedia,* he thought but told her simply, "I am impressed."

Life in Charlotte Ville was mundane to say the least. However, the scenery of this little village that fringed Man-o-war Bay on the Northeastern end of the island was simply exquisite. Ebita was delighted that Christopher was with her. She probably would never have made that trip by herself. Once they were there, she began to view it as an eco-vacation, and Christopher was just as enthusiastic. He needed no prodding when asked to walk with her on the jetty. They walked hand in hand to the very end, turned around and looked back at the beautiful quiet village nestled at the foothills of Tobago's forested central mountain range.

"Oh Ebita," said Christopher. "It is so peaceful and picturesque here."

"I am happy to hear that you like it, and happier still that you came," Ebita said.

She hugged him tightly before they started walking back to the shore. She then went on to explain that the forested central mountain range is a protected nature reserve, perhaps the oldest in the hemisphere.

"When we visited Little Tobago, I somehow understood that it was also a reserve," Christopher said.

"Little Tobago is a bird sanctuary. Remember?" asked Ebita. Before Christopher could answer, she said, "Here everything in the forest is protected."

"There are so many protected areas on this little island. I got the impression that was also true for the area of the Argyle Falls."

"The Falls are in the same central mountain range. In fact, there are several falls here but the Argyle is the largest."

"I am so impressed with your knowledge of the natural world."

"I love the natural environment and there is such a variety of flora and fauna here, it is part of the reason I bought the time share. Being a woman though, I sometimes hesitate to visit places like this alone. Now that we have reconnected, I am hoping that we could spend more time like this together doing the things we love." As soon as she said that she corrected herself and said, "Doing the things that I love and enjoy and hoping that you too would grow to love and enjoy them."

Christopher and Ebita looked up and noticed that the sun was going down over the hills. "That must be a scene of the most beautiful sunset," Christopher said.

"Would you like to stay and see the sunset?" Ebita asked.

"Where will we stay?"

"There are several guesthouses here and a few hotels also I believe. If I remember well, there may be two four star hotels somewhere in the area."

"For just one night, a guesthouse should be fine."

"Then let's reserve a room, get something to eat, and come back out to view the sunset."

"Beautiful," Christopher said.

In Mayaro, Peter Aranguez, his brother Paul, and Eli arrived at Pierreville and went directly to *The Junction*, a well known watering hole (lounge or bar) where Peter met Imp. He ordered drinks for everyone at the counter. Then he and Imp walked outside with their drinks.

"I have just the right chap for you," said Imp. "He is here from Salybia but he is leaving tonight."

"How old is he?"

"I don't know," said Imp. "Eighteen or nineteen maybe."

"Can he run fast?"

"Now, how the hell will I know that?" Imp asked with frustration in his voice.

"The reason I ask is that I want him to snatch someone's purse and run like hell with it. She used to be the best female high school athlete in town so she probably will chase after him."

"Oh man! That must be worth a lot to you."

"Actually, I am not interested in her purse per se. I only want the cell phone that she carries in it."

"Is a damn cell phone worth the risk you are asking me to take?"

"To me it does."

"Then that is going to cost you."

"How much?"

"Ten blue ones ($1,000.00)."

It was as if Peter anticipated the cost of the operation. He took ten crisp, blue, one hundred dollar bills from his wallet and handed them to Imp.

"It is always so nice to do business with you," said Imp. Then he asked, "Who is the intended victim?"

"Khleo."

Imp did not feel the need to ask for the intended victim's surname. Her first name was so unusual that there was no one else with that name in the telephone directory. Instead, he said, "I will take it from here. You go back in there and enjoy your drink."

"Oh! I am sorry. That is not all."

"What else now?"

"I want her land line disabled too."

"That would be additional."

"How much?"

"Two hundred."

Peter did not question the charges. He took out another two hundred dollars and handed them to Imp who said, "Business is good today. This thing must be worth a lot to you."

"It could be," Peter said.

"Okay! I will handle this part of the task myself."

Without hesitation, Imp walked over to Ling Chin Bar and beckoned a young man he called Tart who responded right away.

Imp handed Tart two hundred dollars, the two hundred he last received from Peter. He then said to Tart, "I have a job for you."

"Okay!" Tart said.

"Come with me," said Imp. "You can wait in the car while I run an errand." He drove over to the two-family house where Khleo lived on the second floor. He parked the car about two hundred yards from her home, took a pair of pliers from the glove compartment of the vehicle and placed them in the right rear pocket of his jeans. Then he walked over to the building where Khleo lived, calmly walked up the stairs, climbed up onto the banister as if he had been a telephone company worker, and cut the telephone wire leading to her apartment. He then taped the cut ends together so that they didn't appear as hanging wires. Just as calmly as he entered, he left and left Khleo's land line disabled, or so he thought. She had stopped using that telephone months before but never had it officially disconnected.

Upon his return to his vehicle, he sat down and explained to Tart what he wanted him to do. Then he said, "I will park at the Two-Beach Bridge and wait for you. When you get there with the thing (purse), I will drive you to St. Anns Road, drop you off on the beach and return. You can walk up the beach to Plaisance and catch a taxi or a bus to Sangre Grande on your way back to Salybia."

"That seems okay Boss, except that I don't know who ah dealing with."

"She lives here," said Imp as he pointed to the house where, minutes earlier he had cut the telephone wire.

"However, she is not at home now."

"How will I know who she is, Boss?"

"I will point her out to you," said Imp. "It is Saturday evening close to month's end, I am certain that she and her friend, Amanda will stop at *The Junction* this evening. They always do on Saturdays. Today should be no exception. Let's go to *The Junction*, have a drink or two and wait."

127

Imp and Tart didn't have to wait long. Ten minutes after they entered *The junction*, Khleo and Amanda arrived and satin the lounging area where a waitress quickly took their orders. As they sat back and waited, Imp said to Tart, "There she is. The one in the red blouse with the black purse."

"Piece ah cake," said Tart.

"Not so fast! She used to be an athlete in high school, a very good sprinter"

"So? She is a has been. I am the athlete now."

"Okay Buddy. I will wait for you at the bridge. I can tell you, more likely than not, she will walk home from here. The rest is up to you."

Imp was right. Tart didn't have to wait long. Khleo and Amanda finished their drinks, agreed that they will meet again later that evening, and left *The Junction.* As expected Khleo Khleo started walking the five hundred yards or so from The Junction to her home. She wasn't concerned about the type of petty crime to which she was to become a victim because it had never before happened in that town. Tart started following Khleo the moment she left *The Junction.* She was totally unaware of his presence or that she was being followed. Approximately 25 yards from the entrance to the building in which she lived, she heard rapid footsteps behind her. Before she could turn around , the little vagabond snatched her purse from her right shoulder and sprinted off to the Two Beach River Bridge. Khleo was stunned. She never anticipated anything like that. Neither she nor anyone she knew had ever experienced such a horror. Consequently, she was unable to respond rapidly. In fact, she did not respond at all. Tart jumped into Imp's car and they sped off to St. Ann's Road as planned.

A bystander who witnessed the event, took out his cell phone and called the police. They assured him that they would take action but they never did. They either did not believe the caller, or they were convinced that such a thing would never have happened in Pierreville, Mayaro.

In a confused state of mind, Khleo walked back to *The Junction*. Amanda was still standing in front of the establishment having a conversation with another patron. As Khleo approached, Amanda was just as surprised to see her looking so shocked.

"What is the matter, girl?" she asked.

"Some son of ah b….. just stole my purse."

Amanda had never before heard Khleo swear. What she heard that day made her realize that the situation was dire.

"Let's go to the police right away," said Amanda. "That should not happen in this town."

They walked over to the station and reported the incident to Officer Sookram who was on desk duty that evening.

"I am so sorry to hear that, Madam," said Officer Sookram. "However, at this time, we do not have an available squad car. What I will do though, is communicate with the officers on foot patrol and ask them to investigate."

"Thank you , sir," said Amanda. "Let us get out of here," she said to Khleo. She was very dissatisfied with what the police officer had to say and was determined to investigate the matter herself. They walked out of the police station and over to Peter Hill Road where Amanda's car was parked. When they entered the vehicle she asked, "What does this creep look like?"

"He was wearing a hooded sweatshirt."

"In this tropical heat?"

"Yes! He was dressed in a light grey sweat shirt and blue jeans."

"Was he African or Indian?"

"I couldn't really tell. I only saw him from the back. He appeared to be about five feet eight inches tall and perhaps weighed 170 to 180 pounds."

"Well, let's go and see if we can find him."

Amanda made a broken u-turn on narrow Peter Hill Road and drove down Guayaguayare Road in search of the culprit. She drove slowly, to the annoyance of other, more aggressive drivers. It did not bother her that people were honking their car horns and cursing at her. All she wanted was for Khleo to cast her eyes around in an effort to spot an identify the thief. They reached as far as Ste. Marguerite's Village without seeing anyone who fitted Khleo's description of the culprit. Meanwhile, Tart , the thief was in a taxi and well on his way to Sangre Grande. Imp lifted Khleo's cell phone from her purse but did not remove her wallet, ID, or other personal papers. Cunningly or stupidly, depending on how one looks at it, he returned to Khleo's place, drove up the driveway, tossed the purse onto the veranda and quickly backed out."

When they realized the futility of their effort in trying to find the thief, Amanda said to Khleo, "Let me take you home, girl." Khleo did not object so Amanda headed back. When they arrived at Khleo's place, they walked up the stairs and Khleo opened the door timorously. Before they could enter, Amanda glanced around the veranda and shouted, "What the hell!"

That heightened Khleo's trepidation. She stood at the door frozen with fear when Amanda asked, "Isn't that your purse there?" She pointed to a black leather purse with a broken strap on the floor up against the wall. Without waiting for a response from Khleo, she picked up the purse and handed it to her friend. Khleo took the purse and opened it. She removed her wallet and checked its contents. All of the cash she had that evening, $310.73 was intact. She was relieved and said to Amanda, "It's all there."

"Thank God for that," Amanda said.

Khleo never realized that her cell phone was missing. Once she saw that the cash was in the wallet, a feeling of relief and contentment came over her. She tossed the purse on her bed and sat down in the livingroom with Amanda.

"That puzzles me," Amanda said.

"What?" Khleo asked.

"The fact that someone would steal your purse and then return it with everything in place."

"His Christian teaching probably got to him."

"That I believe is what we call his conscience."

"Whatever!" Khleo said. "I am just glad to have my stuff back."

"Now we have to be more vigilant," said Amanda. "We probably should wear our purses like the women of New York City."

"I know," said Khleo. "I have seen them on TV with their purses hanging in front of them."

"No one can ever doubt the security in that."

"Certainly, no one can." Khleo said. At that moment though, she wasn't feeling quite secure and Amanda sensed it.

"You know what, Khleo?"

"What?"

"I think I would stay with you tonight. In the morning I would go home and get dressed. Then I will come back and pick you up."

"I will greatly appreciate that."

"What are friends for?"

"Thanks, Amanda."

"You are most welcome."

Imp called Peter to say he had accomplished the mission and that the merchandise was ready to be picked up.

"Thanks, Bro," said Peter upon receiving the call. "It is always nice doing business with you. I will pick it up right away."

"I will be at *The Junction*."

Peter took his brother to his home in Beau Sejour before dropping Eli off at Khleo's. He then parked and walked into *The Junction*. Imp got up from where he was sitting and joined Peter at the counter. He handed him the cell phone. Peter took it and said, "Thank you. I hope this is no fake."

"That is the real armadillo right there."

"If this works you are likely to get a bonus."

"It works. I tried it. I called my buddy in New York."

Peter laughed at what Imp said but did not reveal his intentions, which never included making calls to friends overseas with that cell phone. All he wanted to do was deprive Khleo of the phone .

NINETEEN

EBITA MANAGED TO RESERVE A room for the night at the Sea View Guest House. The so-called room was in fact a furnished apartment. There were two beds in the room. One was a full size bed and the other was a twin bed. The linens appeared new , clean, and freshly pressed. There was also a dresser with a mirror in the room. The kitchen was equipped with a stove, oven, refrigerator, coffee maker, toaster, microwave and a variety of kitchen utensils. There were central air conditioning and cable television. The apartment was located on the second floor of a three story building and provided a panoramic view of the Caribbean sea.

It took some clever negotiating on Ebita's part to secure the reservation. Management's policy required a three nights stay at a rate of $360.00 per night. Eventually Ebita's offer of $400.00 was accepted for the one night. That came only after she pleaded and pleaded, explaining to the manager that neither she nor Christopher was able to drive the roads of Tobago at nights. They both suffered from night vision blindness and were already exhausted from a day of driving and hiking.

"You are marvelous! Absolutely amazing." Christopher said as they received the keys and were directed to their room.

"It's all because of you," said Ebita. "I wouldn't have negotiated without you because I wouldn't have been here without you."

Christopher sat at one end of a futon that was positioned in front of the television. Ebita went over and sat next to him. She was exhausted, and soon threw her legs up onto the futon while at the same time she rested her head in Christopher's lap. Christopher traced her eyebrows with his fingers and asked, "Are you tired, sweetheart?" She nodded to indicate yes. Then she shifted her entire body in an effort to be more comfortable.

"Perhaps you should lie in the bed," Christopher suggested."

"Why? Am I too heavy for your thighs?"

"No! Not at all."

"Perhaps I should get up. We wouldn't want to miss that sunset."

"My goodness! I forgot about that."

"That could be a once in a lifetime experience."

"Why? Wouldn't you want to come back here?"

"Not in a hurry."

"Why not, hon? Don't you like being with me?"

"I love being with you, Christopher, but there is so much to do in Tobago. The next time we are back I think you may prefer to go somewhere else and try other things."

"That's not unreasonable."

"That being said, let's go," Ebita said. She got up and stretched out her hand to Christopher.

He held her hand and stood up. They embraced, kissed each other and walked out of the room hand in hand. Neither thought of locking the door behind them. They walked to the jetty, put their arms around each other , and strolled to the end. There, they turned around, and behold, there was the sun setting, disappearing behind the forested hills of Tobago's Central Range and leaving in its path an array of brilliant colors resulting from the visible wavelengths of light as they shone over the rain forest. The clouds were in hues of yellow, red and orange, and Christopher loved them.

"Is there anything like it in Mayaro?" Ebita asked.

"Maybe. We are on the Eastern shore. I suppose sunrise might be as lovely but I have never seen it."

"For all the years you lived in Mayaro you have never seen the rising sun?"

"No. I was never up that early."

"You need to do better than that."

"My problem is that I stay up too late reading, so that I wake up later than most other people."

"Excuses! Excuses! Poor excuses. Try again, love."

"It's the truth," Christopher said. He was laughing but Ebita wasn't.

They started walking back to shore when he asked, "Do you know of any restaurants in the village?"

"I do not know for certain but I once heard that there are a few small restaurants here," said Ebita. "We can ask someone at the guesthouse, but why? Are you hungry?"

"I am very hungry."

"I guess a man can't live on love alone?"

"Right now it's hard for me to breathe without your love. I probably couldn't eat without it either, I am so thankful to have it."

"Well, it is all yours from this day on."

"I love you more than you can ever imagine sweetheart, and I vow to stick with you for the duration of our lives."

"That is so sweet, Christopher."

She hugged him tightly. They stood near the shore where they kissed passionately before continuing to the guesthouse. Although he probably wasn't aware of it, Christopher had a look of contentment on his face. For as much as he cared for Khleo, she had never been as passionate with him. He showered her with affection which she acknowledged but seldom reciprocated.

Perhaps she was still struggling with the values she adopted from listening to her parents. The sort of values she had been trying to rid herself of when she became involved with Christopher in the first place. That involvement was contrary to what she knew her parents desired, and it caused her to distance herself from them, although not with complete abandonment. That struggle of trying to abide by her parents unspoken rules and wanting to do what she thought was right in modern society was difficult if not impossible for her to cope with. That, and Eli's sudden return might have been the estranger which led ultimately to Christopher's departure.

They entered the guesthouse and were greeted by a dowdily dressed woman who said, "Good evening!"

"Good evening," answered Christopher and Ebita in unison.

"You are such a lovely couple," the woman said.

"Thank you," Ebita said. Christopher only smiled.

"Look at that smile," said the woman. "I can see that is a smile of contentment and true happiness."

"Thank you," said Christopher. "I am very happy." That made Ebita smile broadly too.

"Stay together. Have a nice evening," the woman said.

"Thanks again," Ebita said.

As they started to walk away, she asked the woman, "By the way, can you tell us of a restaurant in the area?"

"Yes. Just around the corner to your left. It is nothing fancy but the food is good."

They followed the old woman's direction which led them to a small eatery that was operated by a teenage girl. She appeared to be in her high teens although she could have been in her early twenties.

"Welcome to Charlotte Ville," said the young girl.

"Thank you," Ebita said,

"Oh! It smells so good in here," Christopher said. The young girl smiled and asked, "What would you like?"

"What do you have?" Christopher asked as there was no written menu or price list.

The young woman smiled, and in a soft, gentle, Tobagonian lilt said, "We ha rice and peas, crushed plantains and flying fish, bake (a flat bread) and shark, crab and dumplings, and stewed oxtail and rice."

"I will try the bake and shark," Christopher said.

"Let me have the stewed oxtail. However, I would like it with rice and peas instead of plain rice," Ebita said.

"Not a problem," said the young woman. "How would you like the bake, sir? Roasted or fried?"

"I would take the fried bake."

"That will take a few minutes longer, sir."

"No problem. We have time."

"Very well, sir," she said.

She washed her hands, remove a small ball of dough from the refrigerator and started flattening it. When it was flattened as thin as she liked, she punched some holes in it with a fork. Then she dropped it in a frying pan with hot oil. Within three minutes she removed the fried bake which had risen to the point that the inside was hollow. She sliced it around the periphery and stuffed it with a fried shark steak, lettuce and tomatoes.

"Would you like some pepper?" she asked.

"Just a little," Christopher said.

She dipped a teaspoon full of hot pepper sauce and asked, "Is that enough, sir?"

"One drop of that would be fine," Christopher said.

She dropped the pepper sauce on the filling, closed and wrapped the sandwich." It was only then that she turned her attention to Ebita and asked, "Would you like to have a salad with you meal, madam?"

Ebita wondered why she was being called madam but only answered, "Yes. Thank you."

The young woman handed them their prepared meals and Christopher asked, "How much will that be?"

"Forty-two dollars. sir." He took the money from his wallet and handed it to her. "Thank you, sir, and have a blessed day," she said.

There was no place in the little restaurant for them to sit, and although there were picnic tables right outside of the door, Christopher and Ebita elected to take their food up to their room. Before they could get there Christopher's esurience led him to unwrap his sandwich and bite into it.

"Gee Chris! Can't you wait until we get upstairs?"

"Doesn't that tell you how hungry I am?"

"No," Ebita said. She wasn't about to argue with him, although she thought he was behaving like a two-year old.

When they got upstairs, they relaxed on the futon to enjoy their dinner because there wasn't a dining table in the apartment. She turned on the television and asked Christopher, "What is your favorite Saturday evening program?"

"I couldn't say. I do not have cable. More often than not, I prefer to read."

"What are you going to read tonight?" she asked sarcastically. Christopher did not answer. He smiled coyly.

"What was that about?" she asked.

"What ?"

"That evasive little smile of yours," said Ebita. "I know you are not shy."

"I am not shy. I could use a drink though."

"The only thing there is to drink is some local beer." Ebita got up and went to the refrigerator. "Oh, there are two cans of orange juice here also," she said.

"We can mix them," said Christopher. He left his seat and joined her at the kitchen isle. She handed him two glasses with several ice cubes in each. He opened one bottle of beer and emptied equal amounts of the contents into both glasses."

"How did you do that," she asked. She was looking for a bottle opener in a cabinet drawer when he did it.

"How did I do what?"

"Open that bottle of beer."

"With my teeth." Christopher pointed to his pearly white canines.

"You are just too much," said Ebita. "Here is the juice, and here is a can opener."

Christopher took the can of OJ, opened it and filled the glasses that already contained beer. They returned to their seats and he moved the coffee table closer to the futon and rested their food and drinks on it.. They then settled back and ate.

TWENTY

ELLI WAS SURPRISED WHEN HE came home to Khleo's and found that Amanda was there. A feeling of trepidation came over him. He had not forgotten what he perceived as aggressive questioning from her on the way from the airport. He, however, summoned the courage to say, "Hey, Amanda! I see that you are still here."

"In fact, I just got here. We were out most of the evening and just before Khleo got home, some idiot snatched her purse."

"What!"

"Yes! She was mugged."

"How could that happen in quiet, peaceful Mayaro?"

"That was my question exactly when I heard of it," said Amanda. "She is very upset so I told her I will stay for the night." Amanda did not mention that they planned a trip to Las Cuevas the next day.

"Where is she now?"

"She is in bed."

Eli knocked on the bedroom door but got no answer, He knocked again and waited. Still there was no answer. He turned around and looked at Amanda, a quizzing sort of look. "Maybe she is asleep," said Amanda. "Go in."

He pushed the bedroom door as gently as he could and looked inside. Khleo was resting on her side and he could hear her snoring softly. He closed the door and stepped back.

"She is asleep," he said.

"Then you did the right thing. Let her sleep."

"Was she hurt in that incident?"

"Physically, no. Emotionally, she was devastated."

"My God! Did anybody witness what happened?"

"I think one gentleman did and called the police on his cell phone but they did not respond. We went to the station and were told some crap about there wasn't a squad car available. The officer on desk duty said he would communicate with those on foot patrol and ask them to investigate. They never did. We tried to track down the thief but without success. Khleo could not identify the individual because she saw him only after he got her purse and ran off. Even then, he was wearing a hooded sweatshirt which obscured any vision of his face."

"So now he, whoever the hell he is, has her credit cards, driver's license and other important documents."

"No. She recovered her purse with everything in it."

"How?"

"The thief returned it. When we got here from the police station, it was lying on the floor of the veranda."

"Thank goodness for that."

"That's the same thing I said but I also wondered what played on his conscience. Was he just guilt ridden, or did someone force him to return the purse?"

"We may never know."

"In a sparsely populated town like this, where people know so much about others, very soon the truth will be revealed."

"I do hope so. In the meantime, she is safe and resting comfortably. That is all I care about."

"Then, perhaps you should switch off the light in her room," said Amanda. "She is very tired and needs to rest."

"What did you do today?" Eli asked.

"We perused the town and visited the offshore mud volcano just outside of Ortoire village."

"I can understand why you are tired."

"I am not. Khleo is."

Eli got up, opened the bedroom door gently and turned off the light. He closed the door again and rejoined Amanda on the couch. Finally, he was starting to relax. Amanda's focus was no longer on him. She was not asking him dozens of personal questions in rapid succession. Perhaps she had come to terms with the fact that he was Khleo's choice of a mate and if her parents did not object, who was she to be against it. With that in mind perhaps, she asked Eli, "Do you play bridge?"

"I did at one time but since I went to the States, I haven't played any card games."

"Would you like to refresh your game?"

"I wouldn't mind at all."

Amanda got up and removed a pack of cards from the China cabinet drawer. She then said to Eli, "Give me a hand with this."

"With what?"

"This couch. We need to open it up."

"Is it a bed?"

"It sure is."

Khleo could have told me that nights ago, he thought but did not vocalize it. He went ahead and assisted Amanda in opening up the couch bed.

She procured pillows and linens from the hallway closet where she knew Khleo kept them. She made up the bed, then said to Eli, "I am ready for your best game." She handed him the cards and said, "You deal."

While he dealt the cards, she took the remote control and turned the TV on softly. She and Eli then played bridge and poker and conversed from 8:00 p.m. to midnight when Eli started nodding sleepily.

"You are drowsy," said Amanda. "Get some sleep. Maybe

tomorrow you would do much better." She had beaten him at every game they played that night. He, however, was a good sport. She actually enjoyed his company and felt a bit remorseful for the barrage of embarrassing questions she asked him when they first met.

Eli took a pair of pajamas from his knap sack and changed in the bathroom. At the same time, Amanda slipped into a blue, above the knee, night shirt she retrieved from one of Khleo's hallway closets. She was sitting up in the bed with her legs crossed when Eli came back and laid down on the other side. He said only, "Good night." He wondered though, whether his former antagonist was really going to be sleeping in the same bed with him. Neither wanted to awaken or even disturb Khleo, and neither knew whom she may have preferred to have in her bed. So Eli settled down while Amanda sat up, legs crossed looking at television and glancing at Eli every now and then.

After another hour of looking at the television, she pulled the sheet up, rested her head on the pillow, stretched her legs out on the bed, and covered her lower body with the sheet. Her concern wasn't about Eli lying on the other side of the bed. She was worried that Khleo would get up and see her in bed with him. She viewed the situation as just two adults being in the same bed. *We are not sleeping together*, she thought. *In fact, I am wide awake. He is the one sleeping.*

The searing tropical heat in Khleo's apartment made Amanda very uncomfortable. She had become accustomed to sleeping with the air conditioner running in her own place. At her home, she also slept in the nude and kept a powerful fan on to deflect the mosquitoes from her naked body. She was cognizant of the fact that could not happen at Khleo's so she tossed the sheet off her and pulled up the night shirt slightly. That was the first time Eli stirred since he went to bed two hours earlier. He rolled over and hugged her, thinking perhaps that he was in Khleo's bed. Amanda looked at his arm, smiled, put her hand on his, and held it there for 2 or3 minutes. Eventually, she lifted Eli's hand and placed it at his side. He was sound asleep and snoring then. She was still smiling. For some reason, which she didn't understand herself, she was unable to sleep.

After several sleepless hours, Amanda got out of bed and slipped out of the night shirt. She got dressed and was about to leave when Eli asked, "Where are you going so early?" It sounded as if he was talking in his sleep.

"I am going home," she said. He did not respond. Instead, he was snoring again, so Amanda left. Thirty minutes after she left, Khleo was awake. It was 5:00 a.m. and she felt refreshed but anxious. She knew that they were supposed to leave Mayaro by 6:00 a.m., and she hadn't yet packed. *I must hurry,* she thought. *Amanda would be here soon.*

She showered and got dressed in a hurry. Then she packed some clothing and swim wear into a small piece of luggage and set it down at the door. She placed her purse on the luggage with her clothing and waited. Eli never stirred. *He likes to sleep late but I always interrupted him,* Khleo thought. *Today I will let him sleep.*

Amanda got home, showered and got dressed hurriedly too. She then tried to call Khleo. First she called the land line because she had observed that phone on the night table next to Khleo's bed. The phone rang numerous times, then a busy signal was received. Amanda then called Khleo's cell phone. That phone just kept ringing but no one answered. Amanda hung up. *No doubt Eli is awake and keeping her busy,* she thought. *I just have to go over there and get her out.*

She got in her car and drove like a lunatic to Khleo's place. When she arrived and parked in the driveway, Khleo was on the veranda and ready to go. Amanda popped the trunk and Khleo placed her luggage in it. Then Amanda stepped out and said, "You drive."

"Why?" Khleo asked.

"I didn't sleep a wink last night so we both would be safer with you at the wheel."

Khleo did not argue the point. She moved to the driver's seat, buckled herself in and adjusted the mirrors. Amanda meanwhile, settled in the passenger seat and they left town. As they turned onto Manzanilla/Mayaro Road, Amanda asked, "Did you tell him?"

"Whom?"

"Eli! Who else?"

"What was I supposed to tell him again?"

"Did you tell him that you were going to Las Cuevas?"

"No! He was sound asleep when we left. He likes to sleep late and today I just allowed him to sleep."

Amanda was concerned about Khleo's driving skills. She knew that Khleo was a cautious driver. She wondered about the caution though, especially since Khleo drove infrequently. She thought that Khleo might be too cautious because of a lack of driving practice, a lack of experience.

"Are you nervous Khleo?"

"A little. That is because someone else is always driving me around."

"By the time we get to Sangre Grande I am sure you would settle down."

"I think so too. It does take a little getting used to."

Christopher and Ebita had a wonderful Saturday night together. After dinner they were attracted to the melody of a saxophone and the rhythmic sounds of the tamboo bamboo (the act of beating on sections of bamboo while striking them on a solid surface) band. They rushed downstairs and sat together outside. There, they were served pastries and refreshments. The music was loud but the rhythms of soca, Latin, and reggae were tantalizing. At times they danced with each other, with other tourists, or with the locals. At other times they just sat and enjoyed the local beer that was served.

There was a steady flow of warm soothing breeze that blew ashore from over the Caribbean sea. The surf glistened beautifully from the flood lights that shone over the still, turquoise waters. The mood was romantic and Ebita basked in it as the party continued until well after 1:00 a.m. Only then did she and Christopher decided to return to their room. Once there, neither waited to shower affection on the other. They needed no consensus as to who would sleep where. Ebita attempted to move the two beds in the room together and Christopher completed the task. She rearranged the linens and they relaxed in each others arms. It was 5:30 a.m. before they rested quietly and both fell asleep. They slept until noon.

By then Khleo and Amanda had long arrived at Las Cuevas. Unfortunately, they had been unable to find accommodation there. They drove for about 20 minutes to Maracas Bay where they were able to rent a guesthouse. They didn't take the luggage from the car trunk to unpack right away. Instead, they visited the food stalls and procured lunch. After eating, Amanda felt extremely drowsy and said to Khleo, "I have to get some sleep."

"You really should," said Khleo. "Apparently you were up all night."

"Yeah! For some reason I couldn't sleep last night."

"Is it because Eli was on the couch?"

"No. I was comfortable enough with him there," said Amanda. "He slept like a baby."

"Wasn't his snoring bothersome?"

"Not really. He snored but not loudly."

"Now you can get some badly needed rest."

"I hope so," said Amanda. "However, we must go back to Las Cuevas Bay. It gets too crowded here."

"That's fine with me."

They returned to the guesthouse, took their luggage out of the car and unpacked. Then Amanda sat down in an armchair, laid her head back, and closed her eyes.

"Why don't you go to bed, close the shutters and go to sleep?"

"I am going to do just that," said Amanda. "Please wake me up at three o'clock."

"I certainly will."

She did exactly as Khleo suggested and fell asleep as soon as she rested her head on the pillow. Khleo sat on the porch and gazed at the beach and the blue waters beyond. Life guards and bathers moved back and forth. For the first time in quite a while, her thoughts were on Christopher. Her concern was not whether all was well with him but rather how they would get along when classes resumed and they would have to work together, how would they be viewed by their colleagues, and how would the children behave toward her when the gossip and rumors have circulated. She wondered whether she should call him but quickly dismissed that thought. As a result, the fact that her cell phone was missing still escaped her.

TWENTY-ONE

It was 1:05 p.m.. when Peter Aranguez knocked on Khleo's door in Pierreville. Eli answered and said, "Oh man!"

"Oh man what?" asked Peter but before Eli could explain, he asked, "Is Khleo there?"

"No."

"Where is she?"

"I don't know, man. I just woke up."

"It is after one o'clock."

"I know but I went to bed very late last night."

"Ah ha!"

"No! No. It is not what you are thinking. Amanda was here until very late."

"Wow!"

"You have a really dirty mind, Peter."

"Forget about that. Go and get dressed. We are going back to Guaya."

"What for?"

"The picnic, stupid!"

"Oh man! I can't make that. I am really tired."

"Come on Snake, this thing wouldn't be any good without you."

"Right now I wouldn't be good company for anyone."

"Be a sport, Snake. Come with us."

"No Peter. The only sport I am up to right now is in that bed. I am going back to sleep. Good day."

"Shit!" Peter exclaimed as he peered inside the apartment thinking perhaps that Khleo, Amanda, or both were in there with Eli. His suspicion was baseless. Eli was alone. Peter left disappointed but not disheartened. He was determined to carry out his plan with or without Eli or Snake, as he preferred to call him. He returned uncharacteristically sullen to his car that was parked in the driveway, so Paul asked, "What the hell is the matter with you, Bro?"

"That fool, Snake," said Peter. "He changed his mind about the plan."

"He changed his mind?"

"Yes. He said he didn't sleep last night so he was going back to bed."

"Did I miss something? As far as I can recall, there was no plan."

"Shut up little brother. Let me think."

Paul opened the car door and attempted to step out when Peter asked, "Where the hell do you think you are going?"

"I need a drink."

"What are you going to have?"

"A beer."

"Okay. Get me one too."

"You got it," Paul said, as he walked off to The Junction to purchase the beer. He was back in a flash and they sped off on their way to Guayaguayare. Just before reaching Beaumont, Peter remembered that it was imperative for him to know where Khleo was and whether or not she was with Amanda.

"I am going to turn around," he told his brother.

"Why?" asked Paul.

"I need to ask Snake something."

"So why don't you call him?"

"He doesn't have a phone, fool."

"I thought you lent him six hundred dollars so he can buy a cell phone."

"I gave him six hundred dollars. What he did with it is his business but I thought he would be more cooperative because of it."

"You always think that your dirty money can make people subservient to you."

Peter did not respond to his brother's latest statement. He simply made a u-turn and raced back to Pierreville. On arrival at Khleo's, he knocked at the door. Eli answered.

"What the hell is it now, Peter?"

"Easy man, easy. I just want to ask you one simple question."

"Go ahead. I am listening."

"Did Khleo go out with Amanda?"

"Sorry, man. I really don't know. I am not sure when she left here and I do not know where she went or with whom," said Eli, but he wondered, *What business is it of his where Khleo went?*

"Thanks," said Peter as he walked away pondering his next move.

Paul did not question his brother as he re-entered the vehicle and backed out of Khleo's driveway, although, he was wandering whether they would still be going on the picnic without Eli and the ladies, Khleo and Amanda. Peter looked at him and asked, "What's on your mind little brother?"

"Nothing in particular," Paul said.

"Well, if you are wondering whether or not the picnic is on, it is."

"Who else is going?"

"No one."

Paul knew without asking that his brother was up to something shady if not something criminal. He decided, however, to go along because in the past, his brother's schemes were successful. He had no reason to believe that whatever Peter was up to was risky or dangerous. As on previous occasions, he was willing to go along with the hope that it would be another windfall. Peter enjoyed belittling his younger brother but had never questioned his loyalty. He was confident that when he made clear his intentions to Paul, he would have no objections.

When they reached Lagon Doux, Peter informed his brother that they were going to stage a kidnapping in order to collect some badly needed funds. Paul listened intently but as a former police officer he had some concerns. One, he knew the staging area to be a nature preserve in which all of the four known venomous snakes of Trinidad could be found. He also knew that Peter was dreadfully afraid of snakes, even non-venomous ones. He knew also that a kidnapping, staged or not, would be vigorously investigated by law enforcement and the perpetrators, if caught, would be prosecuted to the full extent of the law. So far, they had been successful with their petty crimes, their extortions, and acceptance of bribes. They had never before attempted anything as egregious as what Peter was proposing.

They arrived in Guayaguayare Village and Peter turned right suddenly into Vespry Road. He drove to the point where the road became a dead end. He then took a spade and a duffle bag from the back of the SUV and said to his brother, "Come with me."

"Where are we going?"

"Just follow me. Okay!"

"Okay!"

Together they followed a footpath for about 500 yards. Just off the trodden path to the left, Peter dug a hole about a foot and a half deep and approximately two feet long and a foot and a half wide He then dropped the empty duffle bag in it. Inside the duffle bag, there was an empty plastic bag. He did not cover the duffle bag but tied a white ribbon on a black sage shrub that was close by, then he said to Paul, "Let's go."

"What was that all about?" Paul asked.

"Just keep observing and you will learn little brother."

They left Vespry Road and returned to the Guayaguayare Road. There, they turned right and headed Southwest. When they reached the gate at the Petrotrin Oilfield, the guard on duty approached the car cautiously with his right hand on the weapon he had in a holster before he realized the driver of the vehicle was Peter Aranguez, a friend of his. "Hey, Peter! What are you up to?"

"Nothing special," said Peter. "Just the things I always do."

He is lying, Paul thought of saying but remained silent.

"How are you, Paul?" Mr. DePass, the guard asked.

"I am okay."

"I heard you guys were here yesterday. I am sorry I missed you."

"That's okay," said Peter. "All we wanted to do was check out the possibilities for a hike. For that your colleague was very accommodating."

"He is a good man."

"Very good indeed."

"He said you wanted to visit the nature preserve."

"Just something different to do I suppose."

"If you like the natural world you would enjoy the preserve but be careful," said Mr. DePass. As he walked away from Peter's truck to open the gate he said, "That area teems with snakes."

Neither Peter nor Paul heard what he said clearly and both thought he made some reference to their friend whom they knew as *Snake*. They drove through the gate and over to the Guayaguayare/Rio Claro Road.

The rainfall of two days prior made an already bad roadway even worse. Although they were driving an all terrain vehicle, the drive along that narrow winding, undulating, and unpaved road was rough and dangerous. Those driving conditions prompted Peter to say to his brother, "There is no need for us to drive two or three miles into this forest."

"Why are we here in the first place?" Paul asked.

"You still haven't gotten it. Have you?"

"No. I have not."

"Oh little brother! You are so damn slow."

"So, why don't you bring me up to speed?"

"Listen carefully now! We are going to make that telephone call from in here."

"What telephone call?"

"Oh, that's right. I did not tell you," said Peter. "We are going to call the Karch family and tell them that we have Khleo. She is kidnapped."

"We do not have her," Paul said.

"You know that. I know that. No one else knows that, and they cannot reach her by telephone."

"Why not? Where is she?" Paul asked.

He was uneasy and becoming suspicious that some serious harm had come to Khleo, and that his brother knew of it and was perhaps attempting to capitalize on whatever had befallen her. Peter had never given any detail of his plan to Eli or to his brother until that moment when he said to Paul, "I want you to listen to me very carefully." Paul nodded his head and Peter continued, "It is hardly likely that anyone else would be in here this Sunday afternoon. That is why I chose this remote and secluded area to stage the kidnapping."

"Did you say stage?"

"Yes! If it is staged , we get what we want, which is five hundred thousand dollars, and nobody gets hurt.

"Where is she now? Suppose she is at her parents' when you make the call, what then?"

"I do not know where she is at this moment. However, I doubt that she is at her parents' place. She hasn't been there in two years and at this time they cannot reach her because I have her cell phone right here." Peter pulled a cell phone out of his left breast pocket, showed it to Paul and said, "You see. We are okay."

"We? I never agreed to any of this," said Paul. Then he asked, "Suppose they called her land line?"

"You are such a coward! Her land line is out of commission. Anyway, you are here with me and you now know what the plan is. You are free to leave or you can stick around. However, if you decide to stay, as an ex-lawman, you are aware of the consequences. You would be just as guilty as I am simply by our association. So, what will it be?" Paul did not answer. He was pacing a five feet length of the muddy roadway.

"Say something!" Peter demanded. "Are you in or not?"

"I am in, I am in," Paul said.

"Okay! Then let's make that call."

"Wait a minute," said Paul. "Do you know that your cell phone calls can be traced?"

"I am aware of that little brother. Why do you think I have Khleo's cell phone?"

"Now that is clever. However, if she reported the phone missing, the provider would have disconnected it by now."

Peter felt a bit of anxiety. That caused him to check the phone. "It's working," he said.

"Okay." said Paul. "Make the call.

"Although it is unlikely that we will run into anyone here, we must get off the roadway just in case."

"Okay." Paul said, and they walked about a hundred yards into the woods. Peter Aranguez used Khleo's cellular telephone to call her parents, Mr. and Mrs. Dejongh Karch. He dialed their number. Then said to his brother, "It's ringing."

"Hello!" A female voice answered.

"I want to speak with Mr. or Mrs. Karch,"

"This is Mancilia Karch," answered Mrs. Karch. Peter did not respond immediately so she asked, "Who is calling?"

"Never mind who is calling. We have you daughter, Khleo."

"What do you mean, you have our daughter?"

"She has been kidnapped," said Peter. Mrs. Karch was silent. She did not hang up the phone. She was in shock. So

Peter continued, "Do not contact the police. They can't help you anyway. Just stay by the telephone and we will call you back with instructions."

"Dejongh!" Mrs. Karch called out to her husband. Peter hung up.

Mr. Karch came running in response to his wife's distressed sounding call. "What's the matter Manci?" he asked. He was in the habit of calling his wife Manci. That was short for Mancilia.

"It's Khleo! It's Khleo! She has been kidnapped."

"What?"

"Khleo has been kidnapped. That is what that call was all about. The caller said that we should not involve the police, and that he would call us back with instructions."

"Instructions my ass! He will call back with his demands for money. We are calling the police."

"No Dejongh! Please! No! They will hurt her."

Mr. Karch listened to his wife's plea and put down the telephone. As soon as he did, it rang again. He answered, Hello!"

"Is this Mr. Karch?" Peter asked while his brother was pacing around in the forest.

"Yes. This is Dejongh Karch."

"No doubt your wife told you that your daughter, Khleo has been kidnapped."

"You bloody bastard! If you think ...." Peter calmly interrupted Mr. Karch and said, "It is not what I think, sir. It is what I know. You are going to pay five hundred thousand dollars for her release or you will never see her alive again. We will call you back with instructions." He hung up before Mr. Karch could speak again.

Dejongh Karch took a deep breath as he thought, *We don't see her anyway.* His wife patted his back and said, "Easy Dejongh! Easy."

"We have to notify the police," he said.

"The caller said we shouldn't."

"That is what they all say," said Mr. Karch. "I say the police must be informed." Mrs. Karch who seldom went against her husband's wishes, agreed.

Dejongh Karch took up the telephone and dialed the Mayaro Police Station. Officer Sookram, the officer on desk duty answered, "Mayaro Police Station. Officer Sookram speaking."

Mr. Karch explained to the officer the circumstances which prompted him to call the police. Officer Sookram advised him that when the perpetrators call again he should stay calm, try to appear as though he is willing to cooperate with them. Then try to stall the process. That is, try to avoid paying the ransom for as long as possible. That, the officer said, will give the police more time to act effectively.

"Well, aren't you going to send someone out here to monitor those phone calls?"

"That will be the ideal thing to do , sir, but right now we do not have the manpower."

"Then I will have to take care of it myself."

"That would be foolhardy, sir."

"Foolhardy my ass! The way law enforcement operates in this country is foolhardy."

"Sir! I wish we can do better but right now we do not even have a squad car at the station."

"I will send you a car. My daughter is in danger here. For God's sake, do something."

"That is a very generous offer from you, sir, but it goes against protocol."

Mr. Karch hung up the telephone. He was livid as he stormed out of the house. He got into his car and was about to drive off when his wife came out and asked, "Where are you going, Dejongh?"

"I am going to get some guys and guns. We will find her."

"Where will you begin to look?" asked Mrs. Karch. "Isn't it better to stay here and await their instructions, while at the same time we can make some telephone calls."

"Whom can we call?"

"We can call that young man. What's his name again? The one who teaches in the school with her."

"Do you mean, Christopher?"

"Yes. I think that is his name."

"For your information, he is my number one suspect."

"I know you do not like him but he is a decent young man. Certainly not the type who would do such a thing." Dejongh Karch sucked his teeth, a gesture of disgust used by Trinidadians. He did not respond verbally, so his wife suggested that they call Khleo's friend, Amanda. Mr. Karch was still not responsive, so she pleaded with him, "Dejongh please come back in. At least if you are here when the kidnappers call, I will feel more at ease." He succumbed, stepped out of the car and walked back inside. As soon as they sat down, the telephone rang. Mr. Karch answered, "Yes!" He was gruff.

"Don't you be surly with me," said the caller. "You are forgetting something. I have your jewel, your precious daughter, Khleo. Therefore, I am the one in control here. You have already lost one daughter to Karu. You wouldn't want to lose the other one now, would you?"

Mr. Karch was really angry when he asked, "What the hell do you want?"

"I already told you what we want. I am going to call you back and let you know where to deliver it. Remember one thing though, no police. You deviate and she dies."

The caller hung up and Mr. Karch informed his wife of what was said. "I am calling Christopher right now," she said as she reached for the telephone directory. "What is his last name again?" she asked her husband.

"I don't know. It is either Boyce or Boyz, something like that."

Mrs. Karch first looked up Boyce and found that no such surname was listed. She then looked up Boyz. Christopher was not listed but she saw the name Elizabeth Boyz which she recognized as that of Christopher's mother. She dialed the number and Mrs. Boyz answered.

"Mrs. Boyz, good afternoon. My name is Mancilia Karch, I am Khleo's mother."

"Oh yeah! How are you Mrs. Karch?"

"I am alright. I have been trying to reach Christopher and Khleo but it appears as if I had the wrong number."

"Oh! That is not a problem. I can give you his number."

Mrs. Karch took the cell phone number from Christopher's Mother and called him. "Christopher!" She said when he answered. "I have been trying to reach Khleo and have not been able to get through. Is she with you?"

"No, Mrs. Karch."

Where is she, son?"

"I do not know."

"You two are always together. How is it that you do not know where she is?"

"Khleo has not spoken to me since Thursday." Christopher said.

"That is strange. Did you have a quarrel?"

"No. Some guy named Eli arrived here from the USA and that was it. I became history."

Mrs. Karch smiled, a smile of relief and frustration. Then she asked, "Where are you now Christopher?"

"Right now I am in Charlotte Ville, Tobago. Actually, I came here to relax and recover from the shock."

"Thank you, Christopher. Enjoy your weekend," said Mrs. Karch as she thought, *Thank God that's over.*

"You are welcome. Thanks," Christopher said.

"Normally, I would not ask something like this," said Ebita, "But given the situation, I do have to ask you; who was that?"

"That was Khleo's mother."

"Why is she calling you."

"Apparently they have been trying to reach her but couldn't. I think she called me as a last resort." Christopher had not given

Ebita any detail of his break up with Khleo. He only emphasized that there was no chance of a reconciliation. Ebita had no reason to doubt him so that matter was temporarily put to rest.

The telephone at the Karch family dwelling rang again. Mr. Karch anxiously and hurriedly answered it. The call was from Peter Aranguez, the individual who was faking the kidnapping of Khleo Karch, the family's second daughter. The family was unaware that the kidnapping was being *staged*. They also did not know who the presumed kidnappers were. Given the history of such crimes in the country, they were willing to comply with the demands in order to ensure the safety of their daughter. At the same time, Mr. Karch who has always been known for his toughness, first as a lumberjack, then as a shrewd businessman was not about to give in without some serious efforts of his own to secure his daughter's release without paying one penny to the kidnappers. First, he claimed that it was Sunday and he had no access to that much funds. The Aranguez brothers knew that unlike other businesses in the region, the Karch Lumber and Hardware Distributing Company paid its employees on the second and fourth Mondays of every month. They were aware also that wages at the company were comparable to the national average. So while they were willing to negotiate, they were not about to give in or give up.

When Mr. Karch demanded to speak to his daughter, Peter refused and said, "Don't you dare make any demands of me. I am in control here. I am going to determine who speaks to whom and when. I know that you do have cash on hand to meet your payroll tomorrow, so you better be prepared to pay up or else."

The caller then hung up. That instilled greater fear in Mr. Karch. He nervously related to his wife what had just transpired. She in turn became terrified and pleaded with him to meet the kidnappers demands. By then they were convinced that the kidnappers claims were authentic. Mrs. Karch did not bother to try and reach Amanda as she originally thought she would after she was unable to reach Khleo, and Christopher claimed he didn't know where she was. Mr. Karch on the contrary, wasn't convinced that Christopher Boyz was not at least an accomplice to that heinous act, if not himself the perpetrator. Law enforcement still had not shown up at the Karch family home, and the mood there was somber.

"We cannot handle this alone, Dejongh," Mrs. Karch said.

"You are right. Perhaps we should call Melrose."

"Yes. That is a good idea."

As Mrs. Karch reached for the telephone to call her eldest son, Melrose, it rang again. She answered.

"Put your husband on the line," the caller said rudely. She whispered, "It's him," and handed the phone to her husband who thought the call was from his son and asked in a serious and melancholy sort of way, "How are you, son?"

"Cut the shit, Karch! I am not playing," the caller said. Mr. Karch realized immediately that it was the voice of the kidnapper and he was overcome with fear.

"What do you want now?" he asked.

"Just what I wanted from the very beginning; five hundred thousand dollars."

"I cannot procure that much funds on a weekend."

"I told you I am not playing. Listen to this." Peter had found a recording on Khleo's cell phone. It was that of a shrill, chilling scream of hers. He played it as Mr. Karch listened with tears rolling down his cheeks. "What can we do?" he asked, his voice cracking in the process.

"Drive to Guayaguayare Village. When you get there turn right into Vespry Road. Drive to the point where the road virtually comes to a dead end. Get out of your car and walk ten paces to the left. No! you are a short fella (man), so you may need to walk twelve paces to the left. There you would see a black sage bush with a white ribbon tied around it. About three feet away, there is a freshly dug hole with a duffle bag in it. Inside of that bag is a plastic sack. Place the money in the plastic bag and tie the end. Then place it in the duffle bag and zip it up. Put the duffle bag in the hole and cover it with the loose dirt. Did you get all of what I said?"

"Yes."

"Then do exactly as I told you. No tricks. If you try anything funny, she dies. You got that?"

"Yes, but there is only one problem."

"What is that?"

"I can only muster half of that amount today," said Mr. Karch nervously. "Perhaps you may want to wait until tomorrow."

"No! If you have half of the money, you get half of your daughter back or at best you get her back without an ear, or missing a finger, or even a hand. It is up to you. This essentially is our last call. I will be watching your movements. Be at Vespry Road at four o'clock precisely."

TWENTY-TWO

AMANDA WOKE UP AFTER SEVERAL hours of sleep, but instead of looking for Khleo, she rummaged through her purse and found the telephone number of the sergeant she met at Valencia Police Station the previous Thursday. Impulsively she called the number. When he answered, she identified herself as Amanda Flagg from Mayaro. "You helped me with a flat tire last Thursday night," she said.

"Oh yeah! How are you doing? Did you remember to get that flat spare tire fixed?"

"I certainly did."

"I would imagine that on a gorgeous, sun shiny day like this you are enjoying beautiful Mayaro beach."

"It sure is a lovely day and I am in a bikini enjoying a beach but it is not Mayaro beach by any chance."

"Is it Matura Beach?"

"No! Guess again."

"I am not good at guessing. I was only hoping that you might be at Matura Bay because it is so close to Valencia."

"Were you hoping that I might be at Matura because that is close to you, or were you hoping to see me in a bikini?"

162

"Both."

"Then you can come up here and join us."

"Up here? Us? Where are you?"

"I am at Maracas Bay but very soon we are going over to Las Cuevas."

"Wait! Let me try and understand this correctly. You are vacationing with your boyfriend and inviting me to join you."

"No! I am here with my friend, Khleo. I am sure she would love to see you again."

"Khleo? Is she the young lady who was with you the other night?"

"Yes. You do remember?"

"I couldn't forget. She is very attractive. You both are very attractive."

"Does that mean that you are coming?"

"No. I would really love to come but I am still on duty. I will be here until midnight. If you were at Matura I could skip over there while someone covers for me. As things stand right now, it will take me too long to get to the North coast."

"I understand and appreciate the thought," said Amanda. "I am sure there will be other opportunities for us to meet."

She tried desperately to remember the officer's name but couldn't. She heard it only once that Thursday night when he assisted them with changing the tire. He too did not mention her name in their brief conversation so she assumed that he had the same predicament. As she stepped outside, she noticed that Khleo was sitting on a park-like bench in front of the guesthouse reading one of several books she had with her. Amanda walked over and attempted to apologize for having slept so long and in the process, kept Khleo waiting. Khleo, however, would have none of it. "You were tired and needed the rest , so you should not apologize for that."

"Thanks. I am so glad that you understand," said Amanda. "Now are you ready for Las Cuevas?"

"I certainly am."

"Then let's go."

They made the 15 minutes drive to Las Cuevas Bay. Once there, they found that the beach was a lot less crowded than Maracas. The water was calm, and clear turquoise blue. The sand was golden and compact, and there were lifeguards on duty. Khleo and Amanda did not bother to inquire as to how long the lifeguards stayed on duty because their plan was to stay no longer than three hours on the beach, or to leave when the life guards did, even if that meant leaving before the three hours. Although there were changing rooms and showers available, they had no need for them because they drove to the beach in their swimwear.

Between frequent runs to the surf, The ladies strolled the beach. They enjoyed the serenity, the caves, the flora, and the fauna, and even talked about the absence of palm (coconut) trees as they had become accustomed to on Mayaro beach. So relaxed was Khleo that she never once thought of calling anyone, not even her parents. As a result, she wasn't yet aware that her cell phone was missing. Amanda likewise, called no one she knew. She had no immediate family in Mayaro except for her father, and they did not get along, so she did not feel accountable to anyone. In fact, the only telephone call she made that entire weekend was to the officer at the Valencia Police Station, and they really didn't know each other well.

Two hundred yards away, or thereabout, there was a commotion. People were peering up the beach through their binoculars in efforts to observe what was taking place. Khleo and Amanda who had no vision enhancement devices, decided to run to the scene. Both being former athletes, they arrived there quickly and observed a lifeguard giving mouth to mouth resuscitation to a young man who was rescued from drowning. His female companion was less fortunate. She was still missing as rumors swirled that they had been warned by the lifeguards about bathing where there were red flags. That dampened Khleo's and Amanda's mood and prompted them to leave Las Cuevas earlier than they originally planned.

In Charlotte Ville, meanwhile, Christopher and Ebita were having a rollicking time. The tamboo bamboo band with its saxophonist was again playing. Only that time the entertainment targeted an audience of North American tourists. The crowd was larger than the previous night, many of the patrons were drunk, and very soon there was ruction in the place. Ebita grabbed Christopher's hand and said, "Let's get out of here fast." She had a habit of avoiding crowds, which was the reason she chose to visit Charlotte Ville instead of staying in Plymouth or going to popular Store Bay. She never anticipated that a gathering of thirty to thirty-five people could become so rowdy. She was scared.

When they got up to their room, Christopher tried to comfort her. She was nervous and her tremors were obvious. "Perhaps you should lie down," he suggested. So together they walked to the bedroom and Ebita laid across the bed in her swim suit, a tiny pink bikini. They had not yet gone into the water of Man O' War Bay when the ruckus started, and that was because they had planned to trek the twenty minutes or so over to Pirate's Bay that evening.

Christopher sat at the edge of the bed for about five minutes before Ebita got up. "Where are you going?" he asked.

"I am not going anywhere. I just want to lie straight, parallel to the bed rail." Christopher moved and she rested her head on the pillow and stretched her legs out on the bed.

"Could I get you something, some tea perhaps?" he asked.

"No thanks. Just lie next to me," she requested. Christopher complied and she immediately put her left arm over his back. "How are we getting back to Plymouth?" she asked very softly.

"Why are you whispering?" asked Christopher. "There is no one else here."

"I really don't know. You probably noticed that whenever I am this close to you I tend to speak very softly."

"You are soft spoken generally but in these situations you are always whispering. Anyway, my guess is that we can return the same way we came up."

"Do you mean that we should reverse our approach?"

"Not just our approach, we must reverse the entire journey."

"As you experienced, that was quite a long journey. Not only because of the distance, but also because of the quality of the roadway."

"What else can we do?"

"We can take the Northern Road down. I have never used it myself but it's my understanding that it is a much shorter route to Plymouth from here."

"I have a great deal of confidence in you, Ebita," said Christopher. "You got us here safely and I have no doubt that you would get us back safely. Since you have never used the route, you may prefer that I drive so you can view the beautiful scenery."

"That could be nice but......." Ebita stopped short of saying what was on her mind.

"But what?" Christopher asked.

"This may sound rather selfish......"

"Why don't you let me decide that?"

"Okay! Since you insist, I should tell you that when I drive, you pay more attention to me. When you are driving, your attention is on the road and traffic."

"That is so sweet, in a selfish sort of way I should say."

They turned, faced each other, and smiled. Ebita was much more relaxed as they drew closer together and kissed each other tenderly. As if to ascertain the authenticity of the kiss, they kissed again, and again. Soon they were rolling all over the beds which they had placed together to create a larger sized comfortable sleeping arrangement for two. In the process, they changed positions a half dozen times before they relaxed completely and fell asleep.

Three hours later they were awake. Ebita was up first. She walked out to the veranda and sat down feeling extremely pleased that she had become reunited with Christopher and that they were having a most enjoyable weekend together. Shortly thereafter, Christopher joined her. He walked over, kissed her and said, "You were wonderful this evening , sweetheart."

"Just wait until tonight," she said smiling.

"It couldn't get any better than that. Could it?" Christopher asked with uncertainty and wonderment.

"Why don't you just wait and see."

Back on Trinidad's North Coast, Khleo and Amanda returned to Maracas Bay from Las Cuevas but instead of going to the guesthouse, they decided to visit the food stalls. They were famished and the many local gastronomical delights were mouth watering. They both ordered food which they intended to take back to the guesthouse for dinner. However, instead of going in, they sat at one of the picnic tables overlooking the water. The air was warm, soothing, and refreshingly clean. The smell of their packaged food was tempting. First, Khleo tasted hers. Then Amanda did the same. Soon they were both consuming their dinners outdoors. There was no mistaking, the food, though fattening, was delicious and they indulged themselves. Neither was thinking of Mayaro or the events taking place there. The *staged kidnapping* of Khleo Karch had not yet reached the major news outlets, so they continued to enjoy their getaway with no knowledge of what was unfolding as being newsworthy back home. However, even if it had been made public. Khleo and Amanda still may not have known. Since they arrived at the North Coast, neither had paid any attention to the news. Their car radio was on an all music station and the television in the guesthouse had not been turned on. Neither knew whether it was even operational.

TWENTY-THREE

PAUL ARANGUEZ WAS STILL PACING around in the verdant forest of the nature preserve. Although the foliage was plush and green, the underbrush, as in most forested areas in the tropics, contained a considerable amount of fallen dried leaves, twigs, and small plants. Paul had repeatedly paced an area of roughly five feet in diameter and his old police hiking-type leather boots cleared the debris.

Neither Peter nor his brother, Paul had paid much attention to the flora or fauna of the forest reserve. Paul was too nervous thinking about the consequences of their impending action. Peter on the other hand, was obsessed with his greed and couldn't think of anything else but the Karch family's money. He instructed Paul to wait in the area while he went to Vespry Road to monitor Mr. Karch's movements in delivering the money as he was instructed. Before he arrived there, it dawned on him that his luxurious SUV, the only one of its kind in Mayaro, would be easily recognized by just about anyone in the town. *What can I do?*, he wondered. He then decided that he would park the vehicle and walk. When he reached the Petrotrin gate, he told his friend, Mr. DePass, aka Oxtail, "I will be right back."

Oxtail opened the gate and said, "I would be leaving shortly."

"I wouldn't be long," said Peter as he drove out of the oilfield.

Upon his arrival in Guayaguayare Village, he turned right onto an unsigned road and parked a short distance away from the beach. He then walked back to the main road and started walking toward Vespry Road. As he walked, he looked back periodically. Eventually a taxi approached. He hailed the driver who stopped and asked, "Where are you heading?"

"Vespry Road," said Peter. "It isn't far." He realized that the driver was from out of town.

"Hop in. Just tell me where to stop," said the taxi driver. "This is my first time in the area."

Peter entered the taxi and asked, "Are you visiting friends or family?"

"Neither. I dropped off a passenger here from Sangre Grande," said the taxi driver. "I usually work the Arima /Sangre Grande route."

"Wow! You are a long way off." said Peter. "Okay! Okay!. It is the next intersection. Perhaps you can take me inside. It is not very far."

"No problem."

Peter took out his wallet and handed the driver forty dollars. He seemed puzzled. Peter quickly realized that and said, "It's okay. I really appreciate the ride."

"Well, thank you," the driver said as he received forty dollars for a $5.00 fare. He was at the end of the road.

"Thanks," Peter said. The taxi left and he walked about two hundred yards into the bushes. He climbed a balata tree and waited with a cell phone ready to further instruct or threaten Mr. Karch as he would have deemed necessary.

He didn't have to wait long. Dejongh Karch arrived precisely at 4:00 p.m. He took a small bag from his car, looked around nervously, and spotted the white ribbon on the black sage bush. He walked in the direction of the ribbon and saw the hole. He did exactly as Peter Aranguez had instructed him and left. Peter saw no need to call him on the telephone, so he didn't. As soon as his car was out of sight, Peter came down the tree, walked to the site where he buried the cash and retrieved it. He put the knapsack on his back and calmly forged a path through the bushes to the main road. That way, he avoided walking down Vespry Road. Fortunately for him, he emerged opposite the unsigned roadway where minutes earlier he had parked his SUV.

Peter was prepared. He transferred the money into another backpack of a different color, tossed the old one under some bushes at the sea shore and left in a hurry. When he reached the gate at the Petrotrin Oilfield, his friend, Oxtail was still there. Peter was glad and decided to hurry. He knew that the guards changed shifts at five o'clock. He wanted to get to the nature preserve and pick up his brother before Oxtail was off duty. By so doing, he would have avoided the need to explain to some other guard their reasons for being in the area. Peter rushed to the Old Rio Claro/Guayaguayare Rood in jubilation to meet Paul in the forest.

Paul was elated when Peter explained how easy Mr. Karch delivered the money which he thought was for the release of his kidnapped daughter when in fact, the entire episode was staged. Paul was jumping and prancing joyfully when, for the first time since they arrived at the nature preserve, he stepped out of the clearing where he had created a little circle. Unknown to him or his brother Peter, coiled, and camouflaged under some dried leaves and ready to strike, was an agitated pit viper, a reptile commonly know as *Mapepire balsain* or *Fer-de-lance*. As soon as Paul was within its range the snake struck. It bit him just above his boot on his left calf. He screamed as the snake slithered away quickly. Peter, who was terrified of snakes himself, started screaming and ran off instead of trying to help his brother.

When he reached the SUV, his thoughts were on the money. He took the spade from the back of the vehicle and cautiously started his return to the area where his brother lay bleeding and whimpering in pain. On the way, he used the blade of the spade to mark every tree in his path by making as deep as possible cuts in the tree trunks, and removing some part of the bark.

As soon as Paul saw his brother again, the first words he spoke were, "Get me help fast. Please! Please, Peter!" He pleaded. Because of his training as an elite tactical operations officer in the Police Service, Paul was aware of the consequences of sustaining a bite from the kind of snake he saw. Peter had no such knowledge of snakes, he had only fear, and an obsession with securing the money he had conned from Mr. Karch. In spite of his brother's agony and repeated pleas, he proceeded to dig four holes at varying distances apart, and in no particular order. In one of the holes he placed the backpack containing the money and covered it with dirt. He refilled the other three holes. Only then did he turn his attention to his brother's pleas.

"Let's get out of here," he said . "We are going to the Mayaro Regional Health Center. " Paul's response wasn't audible, so Peter said heartlessly, "Come on fool!"

Paul could barely sit up. He was still conscious and was aware that the snake that charged and bit him was one of four venomous snakes found in Trinidad; one that caused more human deaths than any other on the island. He knew also that the venom was a hemotoxin and that if he did not receive medical attention quickly, he could suffer internal bleeding and severe tissue damage at the site of the wound.

"Please Peter! Help me." He muttered feebly.

Only then did Peter reach out to help. He took his brother's arm and helped him to his feet. He walked slowly as Paul, his arm over Peter's shoulder, hopped to the SUV. Both moving with caution and vigil, cognizant of the fact that other vipers of the same species may be in the area and ready to strike.

By the time they reached the SUV, Paul was having a headache and his body temperature was warmer than usual. He had a slight fever. He vomited a couple of times. The severity of the situation was becoming clear to Peter. Blood was still oozing from the puncture wound when Peter helped Paul into the passenger seat of the small truck.

Paul had always played the role of dumb little brother Peter had bestowed upon him. In reality though, he was considerably more informed than his older brother. When he felt the warmth of liquid on his upper lip, touched it, and saw blood, he realized that he was experiencing some internal bleeding. His boot was also becoming tighter on his left foot where he was bitten, so he asked Peter to help him untie the laces and take off the boot.

"Hurry Peter! Hurry," he entreated his brother. He was aware that without immediate medical treatment, necrosis may occur at the site of the bite and depending on the severity, amputation of the leg may be necessary. He was concerned also about other sequelae such as hypertension, hematuria, and renal failure.

Peter drove hurriedly over the bumpy *Rio* Claro/Guayaguayare Road to exit the forest reserve. When they reached the oilfield gate, Mr. DePass was still on duty. His relief had not yet shown up that Sunday evening. That kind of tardiness was not unusual in that part of the country . Mr. DePass had become quite accustomed to it. As he approached Peter's truck, he noticed that something wasn't right with Paul.

"What the hell is the matter with you?" he asked.

"Snake bite," Peter said.

"My God! I tried to warn you guys about hiking in that snake inhabited wilderness but you rushed off ."

"We didn't hear you," Peter said. He barely remembered the word *snake* rolling off his friend's tongue, which he thought at the time, was in reference to Eli's nickname.

"Do you know the kind of snake that bit him?" Mr. DePass asked.

"No," said Peter. "I didn't see the snake."

Paul in his distress was aware of his brother's ignorance. That was something he had always been conscious of but never once tried to expose it for fear of belittling Peter. On that occasion though, he knew that his life was on the line and he had to do what little he could to expedite and facilitate medical care which was becoming more crucial with every passing minute. He knew the answer to Oxtail's question and decided to respond in a manner that was different from his brother's. Although the reptile was swift in its attack, Paul saw it clearly and was able to tell Oxtail (Mr. DePass), "It was a Fer-de-lance."

"Oh my God!" Lamented Oxtail. "You may get to the *Mayaro Regional Health Center* and there may not be a doctor on duty. If you are lucky and there is an experienced physician on duty, the Center may not have the appropriate anti-venom. On the other hand, if there is one of those new, foreign graduates on duty and anti-venoms are available, he or she may not know the right one to use." *We are losing valuable time here*, Paul thought. Then Oxtail said, "Here is what you do, Peter. When you get to the village. Guayaguayare Village that is, stop at Aunt May's, the snake woman. You know her, don't you?"

"Yes. I certainly do," said Peter. "Thanks."

Peter rushed off to Guayaguayare Village where he stopped at Aunt May's house which was located on the main road. He pulled up into the driveway. Aunt May was coming down the step and intuitively realized that there was an emergency. She moved her aging but agile body toward the passenger door of Peter's SUV and opened it.

"Give me a hand with him," she said.

Peter hopped out and rushed around to assist the old lady in taking his brother inside. She looked at the wound and said, "Fer-de-lance." That was either a lucky guess or she knew from the pattern of the puncture wounds the fangs made.

"Did you see the snake?" she asked Paul.

"Yes," he answered. He was almost inaudible. At the same time he shook his head in the affirmative.

"Can you describe it?"

"It was large, aggressive, and swift. The head was lance-shaped and it had diagonal stripes and various shades of brown diamond shaped scales," he said softly.

"*Bothrops asper,*" said Aunt May. Again Paul shook his head indicating the affirmative. Aunt May realized that Peter had no idea what the name meant so she looked at him and said, "*Mapepire balsain.*" Peter had no concept of genus or species but he recognized the name *Mapepire* and understood that his brother's life was in considerable danger.

Paul was lying down on a twin bed in a quasi emergency room set up in what was once a garage at Aunt May's house. There were several large glass jars perched on shelves in the room. Each jar contained some sort of liquid into which different dead snakes were submerged and apparently preserved. Other jars with similar liquid contained either dead scorpions or dead centipedes, and one jar was filled with dead tarantulas. All of the jars were meticulously labeled with the genus and species of the organisms they contained.

Aunt May pulled open a drawer in which she kept clean glassware and removed a small container, a three ounce glass. She removed the jar labeled *Bothrops asper* from the shelf, opened it, and meticulously withdrew some of the fluid in a disposable plastic syringe. She carefully checked the syringe to be certain that the amount of fluid she withdrew was exactly 20 cc. She squirted the fluid into the small glass and handed it to Paul. "Drink this," she said.

Peter was squeamish, squinting, and *making funny faces* but Paul drank the concoction without question. When he was finished, Aunt May said to Peter, "Let him lie down for ten to fifteen minutes. He should feel better. You can then drive him to the Health Center. They should be able to take care of that wound."

Paul lay flat on his back. He was still in an awful lot of pain and blood continued to ooze out of the wound. Aunt May left the room and returned with a flat plastic container. She handed it to Peter and said, "Hold it for him to vomit into." Peter squinted and Aunt May said, "Don't be a fool young man. Your brother needs help." Peter then complied.

Ten minutes after Paul drank Aunt May's concoction the bleeding from the bite wound lessened. The pain he felt was less severe but he developed a skin rash on his legs and lower torso. He was shivering and complained, "I am cold."

"That's an indication the anti-venom is working," said Aunt May. "Soon he should feel well enough to travel."

That was the first time Aunt May ever indicated that the liquid she gave Paul constituted an anti-venom. Peter had no reaction although she directed her statement to him. That caused her to shake her head as if to say, *What a sorry fool.*

Peter was acting silly because he was afraid. As much as he took pleasure in deriding his younger brother, he grew to depend on him. They were close and did so much together that Peter, faced with the reality that Paul could die from the snake bite was frightened. He was domineering because he recognized his own intellectual imperfections and thought that by acting as a bully it wouldn't be noticed. He was wrong. His brother saw right through the camouflage, as did most other people.

After about 20 minutes Paul sat up. He looked dazed and was still whimpering but asked Peter, "Can we leave now?"

Peter looked at Aunt May in a quizzical manner and she said, "You can. In fact, you should try to get him to the Health Center quickly."

Aunt May knew that her remedies had helped hundreds of people over the years but she never pretended that it was a sure substitute for conventional medical care and said to Paul, "If or when you see a doctor, remember to mention that you were treated briefly by a herpetologist."

"I will," Paul said. *Herpetologist, herpetologist,* he repeated the name to himself in an effort to remember it.

"That's good. May God bless you, son."

As soon as Aunt May spoke, Peter walked over and asked, "How much is your fee, Aunt May?"

"I never charge a fee, son, but I will accept a donation."

"How much of a donation?"

"That is entirely up to you, son."

Peter took five blue notes (TT$500.00) from his wallet and handed them to Aunt May. "Thank you," she said. "You are a very generous young man." Peter did not respond to that. He simply smiled, a joyful sort of smile. He was pleased that his brother was improving even before he was seen by a physician. Aunt May recognized Peter's loss for words and said, "You must drive safely now. Any anxiety could increase Paul's risk of hypertension given the present circumstances."

With a little help from Aunt May, Peter got his brother into the SUV and they left the village. When they reached New Lands, two police vehicles went speeding in the opposite direction.

"They are late," said Peter laughing. "The loot is gone. Old man Karch was pretty fooled. That's for all of the hard working, underpaid people he has taken advantage of."

Paul paid no attention to what Peter said. He was in too much distress to think of such things. He remained almost motionless in the reclined seat as Peter continued to rant.

"We are making a stop at Indian Bay," he said. "I have to get rid of these boots." That brought a reaction from Paul who had always questioned the authenticity of the name.

"Do you mean the Glassy Beach?" he asked.

"Call it what you want. We are going to stop there briefly."

"Okay," Paul said. He was in no mood or condition to argue with his brother.

Peter pulled off the road and changed shoes. He took off the size twelve boots he was wearing and put on a size ten designer brand-named sneakers. He had stolen the larger size boots just to carry out his crime. By the time they reached the bridge over the lagoon that emptied into the so-called Indian Bay, Peter's thoughts were on other things.

"Aren't you going to stop?" Paul asked.

"Shit! Yes," said Peter. He stopped abruptly just beyond the bridge. He backed up the SUV, stopped on the bridge, reached back, took the pair of boots and tossed them out the window into the lagoon. He then sped off feeling confident that no one had noticed.

TWENTY-FOUR

OFFICER SOOKRAM AND ANOTHER OFFICER, presumably a member of the National Protection Agency (NPA) who was in plain clothes, were at the home of Mr. and Mrs. Karch to investigate their report of the kidnapping of their daughter, Khleo. Mr. Karch was very upset that it took law enforcement so long to respond. His wife, however, was glad they came. Some members of the Press were also present but they were not allowed inside the house for fear that too much detail of the alleged kidnapping may be released.

No one was able to say where or when Khleo was taken hostage. It was Officer Sookram's hope that the perpetrators would call again while he was at the family's home but that never happened. Instead, there was a call from the Police Commissioner which puzzled Officer Sookram. He wasn't aware that the commissioner was informed of the incident by anyone from the local precinct. He wasn't surprised though. After all, Mr. Karch had been a prominent citizen who was politically well connected. He could have called the commissioner himself, or the local legislative representative could have made the call on his behalf. The speculation was rampant. Nevertheless, the Police

Commissioner asked to speak with one Jennifer Nightlife of the Old Time News. How did he know that she was on the scene, was anybody's guess.

The police officers who rushed to the scene of the payoff at the end of Vespry Road, took photographs of the area. They examined the footprints at the scene and found that there were two different sets of approximately the same size. They measured and photographed the prints. They knocked at ever door along Vespry Road and spoke with the inhabitants. No one remembered seeing anyone lurking in the area. One person made mention of a taxi leaving the area around 3:45 p.m. but could not describe the car or its driver. That witness saw the vehicle only when it was leaving and never felt a need to record the license plate number because in the words of the witness, "Taxis come and go all the time."

The investigating officers either did not see the white ribbon on the black sage shrub, or they saw it and didn't think that it was relevant. It might not have been useful to their case anyway, because there had been intermittent convectional rainfall since the ribbon had been tied there. As it turned out, there really wasn't another witness to interview that would have help their case, so the police left.

Back at the Karch family home in Pierreville, the police and the press core were gone. In their place was a gathering of family and friends. Everyone wanted to know what the kidnappers demanded. Mr. Karch made no secret of it. However, when asked by a friend how much of the amount demanded he paid, if he did pay, he refused to comment.

As more and more people gathered in the living room in a show of sympathy, Mrs. Karch turned on the television. The Pastor of The Universal Christian Ministries, who had fallen out of favor with Khleo's friend, Amanda, because of his sexual advances toward her, dropped in. He was scheduled to leave for St.Kitts the next day and wanted to express his sympathy. The shop steward of Karch Lumber and Hardware Distribution

Company also came. He had a proposal from the workers to forgo one fortnight of pay in a show of gratitude, sympathy, and help to Mr. Karch and his family.

The outpouring of goodwill brought tears to Mr. Karch's eyes. He was thankful and humbled, hoping and praying only for the safe return of his daughter. Just then the news of Khleo's kidnapping was being broadcast as a breaking news brief on television. Everyone listened intently but nothing new was revealed, only what the reporters learnt from the Karch family and the Mayaro Police.

Shortly after the news brief, the telephone rang. Mrs. Karch answered and asked the caller to hold on. She then said to Mr. Karch, "Dejongh, please hang up after I take it in the bedroom." She had forgotten that she could have put the caller on hold herself. Anyway, Mr. Karch held the line until he heard his wife's voice . He then hung up the phone.

"Hello!" Mancilia Karch answered.

"Mrs. Karch! This is Christopher. I just heard the news on television and I am so sorry."

"Thank you Christopher, my dear. We are all praying for her safe return."

"I will join you in doing the same. In the mean time, I will try my best to get a flight out of Tobago tonight or first thing tomorrow morning."

"Thanks so much , Christopher. You are just so good with her. You are truly wonderful, a blessing indeed," she said hypocritically.

Christopher was crying by the time he got off the telephone. He looked at Ebita who had watched the same report he did and overheard his side of the conversation with Mrs. Karch. She was crying too, although not for the same reasons as Christopher.

"Are you going to leave me here and return to Trinidad?" she asked. Christopher did not answer so she continued her line of questioning, "You are still in love with her, aren't you?" There was still no answer from Christopher. He was confused, very confused to say the least, as Ebita said, "That's okay! I got it." Suddenly her mood shifted from sorrow to anger.

"Please don't be angry with me," Christopher pleaded.

"I am not angry with you. I am angry at myself for thinking that you were any different from the rest."

Christopher was in a quandary. During the time he was with Ebita in Tobago he had gotten to know more about her than he knew for all the years they were at the university together. That weekend on _Paradise Island_ had taken them from being good friends to being lovers. The Karch family distress, however, brought out something he no longer thought he had; deep feelings of love and caring for Khleo. _Could I suppress those feelings?_ he wondered. _For whatever her reason, Khleo clearly made her choice. It was Eli. Why should I give up the good thing I have found in Ebita now?_ Christopher questioned himself. Then without hesitation, he walked over to Ebita, hugged her and said, "I love you, darling."

"I love you too, but right now I am just scared; very, very scared, Chris."

"Please don't be, hon. What I feel for Khleo, or what you thing I feel, is nothing more than sympathy. It is a deep heartfelt sympathy. It is in no way the emotion we call love."

"Are you saying that you do not love her."

"I am saying that I am not in love with her." Ebita pondered Christopher's response for a moment. Then she asked, "Would you mind if I go with you?"

"Not at all."

"Not at all, meaning you wouldn't mind if I go with you. Or, not at all, meaning I shouldn't go with you?"

"Sweetheart you are welcome to join me. Mayaro is always a wonderful place to visit. I am sure we can have lots of fun there together."

"Thanks. I have one more question though."

"What is it?"

"Can we leave on Tuesday instead of tomorrow?"

"Sure!"

By then Peter Aranguez reached the Mayaro Regional Health Center and assisted his brother into the Emergency Room. Paul was triaged by the charge nurse on duty and immediately rushed in to see the doctor, a Cuban physician who was on contract with the T & T government and assigned to Mayaro as the District Medical Officer (DMO). He checked Paul's vital signs, checked his eyes and determined that there was some capillary bleeding. He looked at the open wound which had stopped bleeding by then and in a halting Spanish accent said simply, "Bushmaster." Peter gave the doctor a blank stare. He had no idea what a Bushmaster was and he knew even less of the differences between the *Mapepire balsain* and the *Mapepire zanana*. Paul, on the contrary, shook his head to indicate the negative in response to the doctor's suggestion. The doctor realized that Paul might know a thing or two about snakes so he asked, "Are you familiar with the venomous snakes in this country?"

"Yes," said Paul. "There are four venomous species in Trinidad and none in Tobago."

"What are the venomous species?" asked the physician, himself a herpetologist.

"Here we have two Coral snakes, the Fer-de-lance, and the Bushmaster."

"So you think that you were bitten by a Fer-de-lance?"

"I think so, although there is some confusion as to which species of the Fer-de-lance is found in Trinidad."

"Is that so?"

"Yes! Some think it is *Bothrops atrox*, others argue it is *Bothrops asper*. The two species are very close."

"What do you think?"

"I believe it is the *B. asper*."

"So you think that you were bitten by a *B. asper*?"

"Yes, sir."

The doctor was glad to have a patient who could be proactive in his own care and said, "Bueno, Senor! You are in luck. We have a combination antiserum of both species."

Paul smiled and said, "I should tell you Doc., that I received some antiserum from a herpetologist in Guayaguayare."

"Was that Aunt May?"

"Yes. Do you know her?" Paul asked with amazement in his voice.

"I met with her several times. She is very knowledgeable," said the doctor. "What she gave you obviously helped. What we will give you here will only complement what you have already received."

"Thanks, Doc."

"Muy bien! Keep in mind that the discussion about the Fer-de-lance will continue for a while. Some people believe that there is only one true Fer-de-lance, the *Bothrops lanceolatus*, and it is found in Martinique.

The Cuban national whom the locals referred to as Dr. Companero was right at home in Mayaro. While he was speaking with Paul, a former patient came in with a basket of goodies for him. It consisted primarily of fruits. In that basket were ripe bananas, mangoes, a pineapple, ripe cashews and golden apples. There were also some star apples and a sour sop. The doctor was delighted and offered to share his care package with Paul who politely declined to accept.

It was obvious that Paul was feeling better but the doctor said, "We have to get that wound dressed and keep you here for twenty four hours or so to observe your progress. That came as no surprise to either Peter or Paul. Quite frankly, they were both relieved to hear it, since both lived alone. Paul wasn't yet able to resume caring for himself and Peter certainly wasn't up to the task.

As Paul was wheeled out of the examination room, Peter attempted to leave and said to his brother,

"I will see you in the morning."

"Wait a few minutes, sir," said one of the nurses present. "We want to give you his personal effects. Please take a seat in the lounge."

It wasn't long before the nurse went to the waiting area and handed Peter a plastic bag containing Paul's belongings. He took the bag, said, "Thank you," and left.

TWENTY-FIVE

ELI STAYED AT HOME ALL day and spent most of the time sleeping except for the occasional periods he spent looking at television. Sadly though, he had not seen the news flash about Khleo's kidnapping. He learnt about it from the police when two officers came to the door to questioned him as a person of interest. Small town gossip reached the police as information about a young man who was deported from the USA and was staying at Khleo's place prompted them to investigate.

There was no one who could verify Eli's whereabouts for that entire Sunday in August of 2005. For reasons he could not explain, he isolated himself all day. He needed to appear credible when explaining to the officers the kinds of activities he engaged in. That seemed like an insurmountable task since he slept most of the time. His credibility was already an issue with law enforcement. The officers were suspicious about him because of the circumstances under which he left Trinidad a decade earlier, and more recently, because of the events that surrounded his return from the USA.

He was genuinely distressed to learn of Khleo's kidnapping but the burden of proof of his innocence as the culprit or as a co-

185

conspirator was on him. He was questioned about his relationship with the Aranguez brothers and what, if anything he knew about the purse snatching to which Khleo was a recent victim. He had no explanation as to why the telephone at the house was out of commission or why Khleo's cell phone was used to call her father to demand a ransom. *Could Khleo be a party to her own kidnapping? Was Amanda involved?* he wondered.

"We would have to ask you to come with us," said the senior officer.

"Why? Am I a suspect?"

"Not particularly. In cases like these, however, everyone is a suspect."

"My God!" Eli exclaimed as he got into the police cruiser with the two officers. Hs eyes were filled with tears.

"Do you know Ms. Amanda Flagg?" asked the officer.

"I sure do. She is Khleo's best friend.

"Where is she now?"

"I don't know," said Eli. "I believe she and Khleo went some place together."

"You believe! What do you mean, you believe? Didn't they tell you where they were going?"

"No."

"Incredible!"

"Incredible as it sounds, it is true."

"We need to speak with Ms. Flagg," said the senior officer to his partner. "Do you think her father might know something?"

"I doubt that. Those two do not get along. They don't even communicate."

"Isn't he the same person called Pastor Flagg?"

"That makes no difference to Amanda."

When they arrived at the police station, the officers ushered Eli to a room with one table and two chairs. He was given a copy of the local paper and told that he can use the telephone that was on the table to make local calls but that he was limited to two calls.

"Why do I need to call anybody from here if I am not under arrest?"

"Suit yourself, man," said the junior officer. "We are only trying to help."

"Thanks, but I will be fine," Eli said.

Eli was left alone with a newspaper in an interrogation room as the officers rushed off in response to an emergency call. He read the paper and for the first time saw a news report of Khleo's kidnapping. His feeling of shock and dismay surfaced again; just as when he was first told about it by the police. "Why would they suspect me?" he asked himself repeatedly without ever getting an answer. He bowed his head over his crossed arms on the table and could not hold back tears. He cried and cried, and on occasions wiped the tears away with his bare hands. Suddenly he heard footsteps approaching the door so he sat up, blew his nose and waited. *I am innocent,* he thought. *I know it but innocent people have been charged, convicted, and even executed before.*

The footsteps stopped at the door. Eli turned his head and saw the same two officers who brought him to the police station earlier standing there with a drunken woman in handcuffs.

"Why are you still here?" asked the senior officer.

"No one told me that I could leave," Eli said.

"Oh man! The officer at the desk was supposed to complete the paper work and let you go. Leave now," the officer said sternly.

Eli smiled and said, "Thank you." He looked up and muttered, "Thank you, God," and left, apparently with renewed faith in a higher power.

As soon as he was out of the precinct he started looking for a working pay-phone, something that is not always easy to find in Mayaro where everyone has a cell phone. Just when he was about to give up, he tried a public telephone on Plaisance Road. It had a dial tone. He pulled out his address book and dialed Amanda's home phone. It rang but no one answered. There was no opportunity for Eli to leave a message. Amanda did not have her voice mail service activated. Unfortunately for him, he did not have her cell phone number and could not obtain it since cell phone numbers were not publicly listed. He thought of calling Peter but then decided against it. He was not aware of Paul's encounter with a viper, a rather unfortunate incident, but did not consider calling him anyway, for the simple reason that of the two brothers, Peter was the one with whom he was friendly. Paul remained merely an acquaintance.

Eli made a bold decision and dialed Khleo's parent's home phone number. A female voice answered, "Hello! You have reached the Karch family home, Caroline speaking."

"Is that him? Is that the kidnapper?" asked Mrs. Karch. They had not heard from the kidnapper since Dejongh Karch paid the ransom. "No, Mom," said Caroline as she continued to speak with the caller. "I am sorry about that," she said.

"That's okay, Caroline. This is Eli Ebbs......."

"Oh my God! Oh my God! Eli! I did not recognize your voice. How are you?"

"I am fine," said Eli. Although he found it strange that Caroline would be so excited to hear his voice given the circumstances. He asked, "How are you?"

"I am not at my best. The entire family is struggling. Perhaps you have heard of Khleo's kidnapping, with all of our major print and television news groups having web sites these days."

Eli found himself in an awkward situation. Caroline assumed that he was still abroad, when in fact, he was back in Mayaro at Khleo's place. Her family meanwhile, was distressed and concerned for her safety, supposedly in the custody of her kidnappers. *What is the best way for me to handle this?* he wondered. Then he said quickly but calmly, "I only recently learned about it, but not from the internet. I am here in Mayaro and read about it in the local paper just about twenty minutes ago." He did not say that he was at Khleo's place. He was hoping that as the conversation with Caroline progressed, there would be an opportune time for him to let her know that he was staying at Khleo's. He firmly believed, rightly or mistakenly so, that her parent's already knew that.

Caroline was urged to free up the line if she wasn't speaking to the kidnapper. "If it's not him hang up," her father said bluntly. She in turn asked Eli, "Can you call us back later?"

"I shall do my best."

"Thanks," said Caroline. "I am sorry. I didn't mean to be rude but we are awaiting word from her captors so I am asked to keep the line open."

"I understand," Eli said to end the conversation.

Peter Aranguez took his brother's belongings home with him. He placed them on the couch in the living room and went to the kitchen to brew some coffee. As the percolator dripped, he paced the floor. He was worried, not so much that he would be detected, his concern was more about the money. He knew that law enforcement had unearthed graves of kidnapped victims in the forest before. The freshly dug holes, he feared, though covered, could be mistaken for graves and dug up by the police who may be in search of victims. He was not too worried about them looking for Khleo per se. Although he didn't know where she was, he felt certain that she would show up as soon as the weekend was over. The family would realize then that they were conned and the police, if they were ever searching for her would end their search. The likelihood of them putting more resources and manpower to the task of discovering who *staged* the kidnapping, he felt was unlikely. Peter understood that with the state of crime and chaos in the nation, it was incongruous for law enforcement to utilize resources in the pursuit of shadowy captors when there were no victims other than an individual who was duped into giving up his money. Had it been a corporation, the situation would have been quite different.

The events of the day had taken their toll on Peter. He felt lethargic, fearful, and unable to think clearly. He threw himself on the couch without clearing his brother's belongings from it. Within minutes he fell asleep. That's where he spent the night.

The Karch family received no further calls from the kidnapper. They did not hear from Khleo, and the many well wishers who were gathered at their home left for the evening. Caroline stayed but her husband, Karu was not there. He did call earlier to express his sympathy but as a matter of principle he did not show up. Long before he and Caroline became engaged, he made a concerted effort to stay away from the Karch family home. The hatred Dejoghn Karch displayed toward him and the despicable remarks he made about him, left Karu disillusioned, bitter, and with little or no respect for Mr. Karch.

Khleo's family grieved and hoped for her safe return. They understood that the odds were not good for a victim to be reunited with family even after a ransom had been paid. While they prayed and pined, Khleo and Amanda were living it up at a beach party in Las Cuevas. At about 10:00 p.m. when there was an intermission, Amanda called the sergeant at the Valencia Police station in a failed effort to encourage him to join her when his shift ended. He was cordial and polite but hesitant. He simply wanted to go home after his tour of duty ended at mid-night. Amanda sensed the uncertainty in his response, so as soon as the steel band resumed playing, she shouted above the sound of the music, "I will call you tomorrow." Having said that, she hung up. The party went on late into the night but Khleo and Amanda left before it ended.

When they arrived at their guesthouse it was 12:31 a.m. Amanda said to Khleo, "I am so disappointed."

"Disappointment? You had me fooled. I thought you were having a really good time."

"I did have a good time. My disappointment is with *the pretty boy* sergeant at Valencia Police Station."

"That I do not understand," said Khleo. "Why would you even be concerned about him when so many fellas

(men) were enjoying your company and dancing with you all night long?"

"They were also dancing with you."

"True, but I am not complaining."

"Well Khleo, you know me. I want what I want and nothing else."

"You mean who you want?"

"Okay! Whom do I want? He is the one Khleo, he is the one."

"How do you know that? You don't even know the man. You only recently met him."

"Intuition my dear. It is a woman's sixth sense."

"How can you be so obsessed about that guy when you are engaged to Quin."

"Please Khleo! Don't even go there. Don't you get me started."

"You can say what you want to say. I wouldn't be bothered by it."

"Seriously though, where is Quin now? When last I saw him, or even heard from him?" Khleo did not answer so Amanda continued, "Just like you, I have needs, but you would not understand that because your needs are satisfied one way or the other."

"Why are you getting upset?" Khleo asked.

"I don't like your self-righteous attitude."

"How am I being self-righteous?"

"It is funny that you would ask that when you just dumped Christopher for Eli whom you had not seen in ten years."

"Okay! Now I understand. You are jealous."

"Jealous! Come on. Give me a break."

"Fine! Have it your way." Khleo walked away with her hurt feelings.

"I am sorry. None of this is directed at you personally. I just don't like the way my life is going."

"Most people would say that you have a great life."

"That is because most people don't know."

"Anyway, I am going to bed. Have a good night."

"Good night."

TWENTY-SIX

CHRISTOPHER AND EBITA AWOKE EARLY Monday morning and went down to the beach to view the sunrise before breakfast. They stood on the jetty in awe of the spectrum of vibrant colors over the horizon as the rising sun shone on the waters of the bay. The water was still except for a gentle ripple at the surf.

"It is so peaceful here," said Ebita. "The ideal place to find solace and relaxation."

"I hope you found both," Christopher said.

"I certainly did. Did you?"

"I found more than that."

"Really?"

"Yes. I found peace, a vision, and love. I found you my dear. You are all that."

"Oh! That is so sweet."

"It is you who are so sweet, Ebita. I feel rather fortunate to have met you again at this juncture in my life."

"I am extremely grateful myself," said Ebita. "This has been, by any standard, the best weekend of fun that I have ever had. Thanks to you, Christopher."

"You are welcome, honey."

Ebita was relaxed. Christopher, however, was still thinking about Khleo. *Has she been heard from?* he wondered. He thought of calling her parents but was concerned that he might again upset Ebita in the process. So after some careful deliberation, he dismissed the idea and asked her, "Are we going to visit Flagstaff Hill?"

"Not if we are using Northside Road to return to Plymouth."

"What's the difference?"

"We should have stopped at Flagstaff Hill on our way here. To do that now we will have to reverse course. I seriously doubt that you would want to do that."

"Why? Is that so bad?"

"Perhaps it is my superstition. I prefer to move forward."

"How is that superstitious?"

"I don't like looking back. You do recall what happened to Lott's wife?"

"Who is Lott?" Christopher asked, and Ebita started laughing hysterically at the question.

"You really don't know, do you?"

"Why do you think that I am supposed to know who was Lott's wife, when I have never even heard of Lott himself?"

When she composed herself, she explained the biblical story of the cities of Sodom and Gomorrah and the events leading up to Lott's wife becoming a pillar of salt. At that point, it was Christopher who was laughing. When his laughter subsided, He said, "What a fable, Ebita! It's a funny one too."

"There is nothing funny about it," said Ebita. "It is written in the bible."

"Yeah! Right."

Ebita did not immediately respond to what she thought was Christopher's sarcasm. On the contrary, she was thinking far ahead as she wondered, *How do I change his religious persuasion, for our children's sake at least?* Then she said, "You might be doubtful Christopher but remember that with God all things are possible."

"Okay Ebita. You are right," Christopher said in resignation.

"No! Think about it. Do not just accept my word without protest," said Ebita. "We are the perfect example. Just when we had given up on the possibility of ever seeing each other again, he brought us together."

"I must say, you are a woman of strong faith."

"Thank you."

They turned around, held hands, and walked off the jetty as the rising sun came up over the horizon. It was 6:45 a.m., and unusual for them to consider having breakfast at that time, but they wanted to get an early start on their trip back to Plymouth because they intended to use a route that was unfamiliar to either of them. They returned to the little one door restaurant operated by the young Charlotte Ville woman and ordered the same menu as they did on their first morning in town. Just as before, they returned to their suite to enjoy their meal.

After breakfast, while Ebita packed, Christopher checked on the car to be sure the fluids were adequate. Everything was fine. The gas tank was still more than half full, the tires were well inflated but the car was covered with dust. A grounds man who observed Christopher's concern, offered to wash the vehicle for him and he accepted. He paid the grounds man in advance and returned to the suite to pack. His packing was easier and faster than Ebita's. He had only one small bag, so within a very short time he was finished packing and ready to go.

They left Charlotte Ville at 8:00 a.m. and traversed the rugged winding Northside Road. Christopher drove while Ebita reclined and rested. She was in awe of the lush, green vegetation, and the fresh, clean air that blew into the open window. Her only complaint or regret was the fact that they did not visit Man O' War Bay.

"We really should have visited Man O' War Bay," said Ebita.

"I understand it is a relatively long stretch of compact yellow sand that is washed by clear calm turquoise waters."

"You are really lamenting that missed opportunity, aren't you?"

"Of course."

So why didn't we go?"

"I don't know."

"Well, don't worry about it. From what I have experienced here, I am sure we will encounter some fun things ahead."

"I hope you are right, but even if you are not, we are going back to Plymouth which is itself a wonderful place to be."

"I couldn't agree more."

Khleo and Amanda were leaving Maracas Bay just about the time Christopher and Ebita reached Moriah, a sleepy little enclave where the Northside Road ended. By then it was 9:00 a.m. That was when Khleo decided to call her parents and realized that her cell phone was missing. She wondered whether it was stolen while they were on their weekend retreat or whether it was removed from her purse when she was mugged in Mayaro. Don't worry," said Amanda. "Use mine to call your parents. Then call the telephone company and report that your cell phone has been stolen."

Khleo took Amanda's cell phone to call her parents. At the same time Amanda turned on the car radio and kept the volume low. She fiddled with the tuner until she found a news station. It was the first time that the car radio had been off the all music station since they left Mayaro to go to Las Cuevas. Khleo dialed her parents' telephone number. Her sister Caroline answered. "Hello! The Karch family residence..........,"

"Caroline!" Khleo said excitedly on hearing her sister's voice because they had not spoken to each other for quite some time. Caroline was just as excited, although for different reasons. She shouted joyfully, "Khleo! Khleo! You are safe. You are alive. Thank God."

"Caroline, please calm down."

"Calm down? Girl! We have been so worried about you," said Caroline. "Have they released you?"

Before Khleo could respond to her sister's shocking question, she heard Amanda shout, "What the hell!" Amanda's exclamation was also audible to Caroline, although barely so. Amanda sat stunned as Caroline yelled, "Khleo! Khleo! Are you okay?"

"Yes. I will call you back," Khleo said as she hung up the telephone abruptly.

Mr. Karch was on his feet. His wife rushed to his side and both waited as a stunned Caroline tried to explain that the call she received was from Khleo.

"Did they release her?" asked Mr. Karch.

"She didn't say. There was no time."

"Did you speak with her captors?" Mrs. Karch asked.

"No," said Caroline with tears streaming down her cheeks. She was respite in the thought that a wonderful life could suddenly become so tumultuous and uncertain. That thought almost instantly gave her a great appreciation for family and friends. Right there and then she vowed never again to stay away from those with whom she was close.

"Well, thank God she is alive," Mr. Karch said.

"I do hope they let us speak with her real soon," Mrs. Karch said.

"My hope is that she will be home soon," Caroline muttered.

Khleo meanwhile, looked at Amanda and asked, "What the hell was that?"

"They were reporting that a warrant has been issued for the arrest of Khleo Karch, aka KK, of Pierreville, Mayaro."

"I haven't done anything but spent a weekend at Las Cuevas and Maracas. Is that a crime?"

"It wasn't when you were underage and was there with Snake, so it couldn't be now."

"Stop kidding, Amanda. This is serious."

"The report said you are sought as being culpable in a *staged kidnapping* of yourself."

"I heard what the damn report said. What I want to know is why?"

"That I do not know. I imagine though, that we will soon find out."

Khleo decided to make a few calls. First she tried calling Eli. The telephone at her apartment kept ringing but no one was answering. She knew that she never disconnected the service although it wasn't used.

"He is not answering the phone. Where could he be this early in the morning?"

"Why are you asking me that? I am not privy to your man's habits and routines."

"I am not asking you anything. I am only thinking aloud."

"Good! Because I certainly do not have the answers."

"I am going to call Christopher."

"Suit yourself." Amanda said.

She couldn't believe that Khleo would have the nerve to call Christopher after treating him the way she did. Nevertheless, Khleo dialed Christopher's number. The cell phone rang in the glove compartment and for safety, instead of reaching over to get it, Christopher said to Ebita, "Please answer that."

"Hello!" She answered. Khleo listened, waited momentarily, then hung up without saying a word. Amanda looked over at her. She was glum so Amanda asked, "What just happened there?"

"Some woman answered the damn telephone."

Oh! Oh!"

"Why would he let someone else use his cell phone?" Khleo asked , but before Amanda could comment, she continued, "A cell phone is so personal, almost like a toothbrush."

"If I recall rightly, you have used his cell phone many times. You have just used my cell phone. So what is the big deal?"

"Why do you always have to be so logical about everything? Here is your cell phone." Khleo handed the phone to Amanda.

Then said, "The only reason I used your damn phone is that mine is either lost or stolen."

"I know that."

"So why do you feel the need to rise up to Christopher's defense?"

"You cannot always have it your way, Khleo."

"Say whatever you want to say."

Khleo Karch was obviously distressed and did not want to continue a tit-for -tat with her friend. They both knew that the accusation heard over the air was false and both were cognizant of the fact that even so, the implications could be dire. Khleo, however, was much more concerned. After all, it was her good name that was being tarnished. She was concerned about her job and how she would be looked upon both by people in Mayaro and around the nation.

The national Protection Agency (NPA) released a description of the alleged suspect together with an advisory to the public that she might be armed and dangerous, and should not be approached. '*Should you see this individual, please alert your local police precinct,*' said the reporter. '*Do not attempt to approach this individual. I repeat; Do not approach this individual.*'

That announcement brought Khleo to tears. Her crying became more and more intense, to the point at which she was inconsolable. Amanda's efforts to comfort her were futile. In a last desperate effort to help, Amanda suggested that they stop at the police station in Valencia and speak with the sergeant they recently met. That suggestion was immediately rejected by Khleo. Amanda could not think of anything else that she could suggest that will help Khleo's emotional decline. There was a brief period of silence during which the two friends did not converse. That period of silence was soon broken after a news report suggested that, "Alleged self-kidnapper, Khleo Karch, was traveling with an accomplice named Amanda Flagg. Both are believed to be teachers at Mayaro Elementary Public School and may have already left the country."

"What crap!" Amanda exclaimed.

"It has to be taken seriously," said Khleo. "Just what can we do?"

"I don't know but I am not going to sit back and take it."

Amanda pulled up to the curb and parked just before reaching Valencia. That unusual move prompted Khleo to ask, "What are you going to do?"

"Call my attorney," said Amanda. "When they start messing with me they ought to know that I will sue the pants off their backsides."

Amanda took out her cell phone, dialed a number and asked to speak with Mr. Kavaanah. She was told that he was in court and should be back in the office by 3:00 p.m.

"Who is Mr. Kavaanah?" Khleo asked timorously.

"He is really Clifton J.W. Kavaanah of the law firm, Kavaanah, Regis, and Johnson. I am sure you have heard of them."

"I can't say that I have."

"Well, you will have an opportunity to meet him this afternoon."

TWENTY-SEVEN

WHILE ON HIS WAY TO pick up his brother who was being discharged from the Mayaro Regional Health Center, Peter Aranguez heard the news that Khleo Karch was viewed as a suspect in her own kidnapping. He was delighted at the thought of someone else being accused, and may possibly be charged and convicted of the crime he and his brother committed. Paul was sitting up in bed with his legs stretched out when Peter walked into the room. There was no one else there. The patient who occupied the other bed during the previous three days was discharged two hours earlier. Paul too was being discharged. In fact, the doctor had already signed the necessary papers that would have allowed him to leave. The only reason he was still there, was his inability to walk well enough on his own.

Peter helped his brother off the bed and handed him a pair of crutches that was assigned to him. Paul asked Peter to wait a while because he needed to get dressed.

"Damn!" Peter exclaimed. "I forgot to bring your clothes."

"What! Did you expect me to leave here in hospital pajamas?"

"I am sorry. I will be back with your clothes in twenty minutes."

He left the hospital in a hurry but instead of going to his home in Lagon Doux where he left Paul's clothes the day before, he headed to Paul's house in Beau Sejour. The brothers always carried keys to each other's fabulous homes. Peter wanted to get some clean clothing for his brother. The clothes he left on the couch were soiled and damaged, especially the pants leg that was pierced by the fangs of the Fer-de-lance.

Peter entered Paul's house and opened a small room that was used as a walk-in closet. He stood just inside the door unable to decide what he should select for Paul to wear. The closet was filled with expensive designer clothing and shoes. After about five minutes, Peter settled on some baggy jeans, white sneakers, and a light summer print shirt, the type older male tourists wear when they visit the Caribbean islands. For some reason he forgot to get his brother clean socks and underwear. He never realized his error until he was back at the hospital. Paul did not want to be a bother, so he said to Peter, "I can get home with what I have."

"Dirty underwear?"

"They are not dirty."

"You have worn them for twenty-four hours now."

"I am going directly home," said Paul. "Where else can I go?"

Peter was eager to get out of the Regional Health Center. He did not want those who knew him and or his brother to engage either in conversation. His concern was that there might have been questions about the circumstances surrounding Paul's unfortunate encounter with a fer-de-lance. Therefore, as soon as Paul was dressed, he rushed him home. Once there, he disengaged his brother's telephone. The land line, that is. He realized then that he was still in possession of Khleo Karch's cell phone, something he knew could be incriminating, in light of all the buzz about her kidnapping, or *staged* version of it.

Without saying anything to Paul, Peter took a swim trunk off a clothes line in the backyard and changed into it. He then procured a towel from a linen closet and headed to the beach. Once there, he waded out into the water and stood in water that reached above his waist. He then tossed Khleo's cell phone as far into the Atlantic ocean as he possibly could have. Once he had gotten rid of the cell phone, he turned around, dove in the shallow water and was washed ashore by a huge breaking wave. He was grinning from ear to ear at the thought of being able to dispose of a vital piece of evidence in any case that may possibly be made against him and/or his brother.

After towel drying himself, Peter Aranguez placed the damp towel on the driver's seat of his luxury SUV, sat on it and drove from the beach at Beau Sejour back to his brother's place. Paul had fallen asleep shortly after Peter left, and Peter made no effort to rouse him. Instead, he got dressed, pulled the front door closed behind him, and left. He did not lock the door. He just didn't feel the need to. Home invasions were extremely rare in Mayaro.

Peter arrived at his home in Lagon Doux and threw himself down on the couch. He didn't bother to move his brother's dirty clothing. He simply kicked them off. Before long, he too was fast asleep. It was not at all unusual for people to sleep during the day in that hot tropical paradise.

Khleo and Amanda were approaching Manzanilla when they heard another breaking news report on the radio. *'There still has been no sighting of Amanda Flagg and Khleo Karch, the two school teachers from Mayaro who are the alleged perpetrators of a kidnapping hoax. Some believe that they have already left the country. However, if they have not, they are known to be armed and dangerous. If you see these two individuals, do not approach them. Contact the nearest police station immediately,'* the announcer said. Instead of screaming, Khleo shook her head in disbelief. She was crying again. Amanda was blurting out expletives at the radio reporter. She had not shed a tear over the accusations. She was defiant. "I know we are innocent. You know we are innocent. So nobody is going to railroad us; not the police, not the NPA, nobody!" She told Khleo. "We will investigate this thing ourselves if we have to."

"I do not have that kind of skill," Khleo said.

"Yes! You do. Every teacher does," said Amanda. "You deduce correct answers from students by skilful questioning all the time. You just need to apply that same technique to the adults we may suspect and feel the need to interrogate."

"Interrogate? Isn't that what the police and NPA do?"

"Yes! Of course. They do it threateningly. We will do it with persuasion and charm."

"You are forgetting something, Amanda."

"Just what might that be?"

"You are forgetting that those children in the classroom are obliged to listen to us," said Khleo. "The grown-ups we may want to question, or interrogate as you say, can simply brush us off."

"Now, you are forgetting something."

"What?"

"You and I have the perfect investigative tool."

"What could that be?"

"It is called charm, Khleo. Charm! It works every time. I have never been brushed off by any male of the species and neither have you. It works perfectly if we approach the task with definite goals and strict limits."

"Definite goals and strict limits," Khleo repeated, uncertain as to what exactly Amanda meant but she did not ask.

"So what do you say? Are you up to the task?"

Khleo wasn't sure but she said, "Yes."

"You said yes without any conviction," Amanda said.

"Conviction?" Khleo asked.

"Yes, girl. You need to be upbeat about it, convinced that it can be done."

"I know the meaning of the word."

"So what is the problem?"

"I have no faith in the system."

"Why don't you?"

"Look! If they arrest us and hold us in jail, we would have no opportunity to do the things you think we are capable of doing."

"You know what your problem is, you lack self-confidence. They have no evidence to justify holding us."

"More often than not, law enforcement people do not need to justify their action. You and I have seen many of their egregious acts of injustice."

"While that is true, we have to stay focused and remain convinced that we can make a difference. It is our good name and our character that are being sullied. Our lives are at stake here." Khleo nodded affirmatively but remained doubtful. *Whoever masterminded my staged kidnapping, already got my father's money,* she thought. Then she said to Amanda, "Dad may not even have money left for my bail."

"All the more reason we have to act on our own and act fast."

"Hmm!"

"Is that all you have to contribute?"

"Let me think about it. Will you?"

It was noon when they arrived at Khleo's place. Amanda parked in the driveway and they both went in. Eli was lying in the couch. He stirred only when Amanda said, "Eli! Good afternoon. We are back."

"Back from where?"

"You mean Khleo didn't tell you?"

"Tell me what?"

"She really didn't tell you that we were going to Las Cuevas?" Amanda asked and looked at Khleo as if to validate the question. Khleo looked at Amanda with disbelief but did not comment.

"No," said Eli. "The only thing I know is what I heard on the news."

"That's not good," Khleo said.

"Not good at all," Eli said.

He went on to explain how he was escorted to the precinct, questioned by the police, and released. He also mentioned his effort to reach her parents but in the process was only able to speak briefly with Caroline who was glad to hear from him but was forced to cut the conversation short.

"Why would she cut you short?" Khleo asked.

"I heard someone in the background asking her to keep the line open in the event the kidnapper or kidnappers should call."

It was obvious that Eli was terrified. That was his reason for not leaving the apartment since the police told him at the precinct that he was free to leave. He did not hear from his friends, the Aranguez brothers. So he was unaware of Paul's unfortunate encounter with the venomous snake in the nature reserve at Guayaguayare.

"Listen Eli! We have a plan and we are hoping that you would join us," Amanda said.

"You want me to join you? Are you aware that there is an APB (all-points bulletin) out on you?"

"Yes! We know. However, we also know that we are innocent and we intend to prove that."

"Our intention is not just to prove our innocence but to determine who the culprits are," Khleo said.

"Just how do you plan to do that?" Eli asked.

"We plan to vigorously investigate this ourselves," said Amanda. "In recent years law enforcement has been slow to act on such cases. That is why we need as much help as we can get."

"Hmm!" Eli murmured.

"Are you with us or not?" Khleo asked.

That question from Khleo clearly placed Eli in a bind. He could have said no but that might have caused her to ask him to leave. He had no place to go. Reluctantly, he said, "Yes." He was aware of the fact though, that he could be targeted for serious bodily harm or even death at the hands of the perpetrators, whoever they may be.

"That's good," said Amanda. "We should start this evening."

"Not so fast!" Said Eli. "Where are we starting? What do we have to work with? This requires some planning."

"We have all afternoon to plan, and plan we will. However, we must first make some phone calls," Khleo said.

"The telephone is not working."

"We know that. Since Khleo lost her cell phone, we are going to use mine. I am going to charge it up for an hour or so."

TWENTY-EIGHT

CHRISTOPHER AND EBITA ARRIVED AT her condo in Plymouth, Tobago, at 12:30 p.m. They were both relaxed, refreshed, and happy after a most enjoyable trip around the island and an overnight stay in Charlotte Ville. If the thought of Khleo Karch's kidnapping was on Christopher's mind, he gave no indication of it. Ebita did not mention it, and neither of them heard the news in which Khleo and her friend, Amanda were implicated, though falsely, as participants in the kidnapping.

As they relaxed on the veranda overlooking the calm turquoise waters of the bay, the warm tropical breeze felt very soothing on their faces. Both felt sleepy and struggled with the temptation of going to bed or walking down to the shore. Eventually, they settled on the latter. They changed into their swim wear, grabbed two beach towels and headed out of the condominium.

They strolled up and down the beach before they settled down to relax under a spreading grape tree, sea grapes, as the plant is known locally. Christopher leaned against the tree trunk and Ebita rested her head in his lap. It wasn't long before they fell asleep. Neither slept soundly and very soon they were up and racing each other to the surf.

The weather was fine, with a mid-day temperature hovering around 25 degrees Celsius. The water was warm and inviting. They waded in and stood where it was waist deep. The water was so clear, they looked down and saw their feet. Ebita, nevertheless, refused to go any further in. Like Christopher, she was not a very good swimmer. So they agreed on an imaginary line beyond which they would not go. She held Christopher's hand, looked in his eyes and said, "I love you so much, darling." She said that several times before but somehow, on that occasion, there was a specialty in her voice that made it sound even more sincere. Christopher's response was to ask, "Is this Crusoe's Island or Paradise Island?"

"It is Tobago, the smaller of the twin island nation of Trinidad and Tobago."

"True! Although, right now it feels like paradise because you are here with me. I am so fortunate."

"The fortune is all mine, and I couldn't be any happier. Thank you, darling."

Without further discussion, they held hands, walked out of the water, and strolled up the beach on their way back to the condo. Once there, they showered, dressed, and headed out for a late lunch at the restaurant where they ate on the first night when they arrived in Plymouth. There was an entirely different staff on duty. Not one familiar face did they see. It became obvious to them that the little restaurant operated on a shift system. They were disappointed but not dissatisfied. The new crew was courteous and professional, and the food was good. They enjoyed their lunch and returned to their temporary residence.

As soon as they entered the condominium, their cell phones rang simultaneously. Ebita walked to the veranda to answer hers. Christopher stayed in the living room to take his call. It was Amanda on the wireless.

"Christopher! This is Amanda," she said.

"What's up, Amanda?"

"Nothing but trouble. Perhaps by now you have heard the news."

"Of Khleo's kidnapping? Yes."

"Oh! Oh! I guess you haven't heard it all."

"Oh my God! What more is there?" Christopher asked. His thoughts were racing. *Perhaps there was a huge ransom demand. Her wealthy parents paid it but her captors did not release her.* He soon realized that his thinking was wrong as Amanda revealed, "We are alleged to have staged Khleo's kidnapping."

"We?" Christopher asked with concern that he too might be a suspect, although he knew that he could account for his whereabouts from the time he got into the taxi in Mayaro the previous Thursday until that Monday afternoon when he was speaking with Amanda.

"Yes. Khleo and I. That has been all over the airwaves," said Amanda. "Where are you that you haven't heard?"

"I am in Tobago."

"No wonder you haven't heard anything. You are too busy enjoying your life in paradise."

"It's funny you said that. I was of the opinion the three of you weren't allowing me to get in the way of your life pleasures, so I had to find ways to pleasure myself. Tobago turned out to be the ideal place for hiking, snorkeling, swimming, and enjoying the local food and festivals.

"I take it that you are not alone."

"That is irrelevant."

"Right now it certainly is. The reason I am calling is to solicit your help."

"What do you need my help with?"

"Well, we are not the perpetrators of what has become known as the staged kidnapping in Mayaro. We are innocent."

"So, how do I fit in?"

"I am not quite sure yet but we can use all the help we can get."

"I believe that you have all the help you need from Snake, or Eli, or whatever the hell his name is."

"I know that you are hurt and angry, but please, consider how this accusation could impact us negatively."

"Why didn't you think of that when you encouraged Khleo to hook up with her ex, Snake?"

Christopher was becoming angry and Amanda realized it. Still she persevered. She was willing to risk his wrath if in the end she got his help.

"Christopher!" She said, "Don't hang up. Please listen to me."

"Okay! Speak up."

"As it stands, the police did not investigate this case diligently before leaking news to the media that we are the prime suspects."

"What does that have to do with me?"

"Not much. Perhaps nothing at all, unless......." Amanda hesitated so Christopher asked, "Unless what?"

"Unless you are also on their list of suspects."

As far as Amanda was concerned, since she and Khleo were named as suspects, no one could be ruled out. Consciously or unconsciously, while she was seeking Christopher's help, she did not remove him as a suspect on her own short list of people she thought of as *people of interest* who might seek to profit from a *staged kidnapping* of Khleo Karch. Christopher meanwhile, was trying not to show too much concern.

Ebita walked into the living room, looked at Christopher's expression as he spoke with Amanda and asked, "Is everything okay, sweetheart?"

"Yes," he said. Then he asked Amanda, "Can I call you back?"

"Please do."

Ebita's expression was neither joyous nor sorrowful. She was stoic. The phone call she received was from her stepmother who wanted to inform her that her father's will was going to be probated the next day. She explained that to Christopher. Then she asked, "Would you believe that she had the nerve to ask me if I would like to be present?"

"Wait a minute! She wants you to be in Probate Court, in Barbados tomorrow, and notifies you today?"

"That's the kind of person she is. She never wanted me there in the first place."

"You can't say that you weren't notified, can you?"

"You get the gist," said Ebita. "One thing I can say is that my father saw to it that I got a first class education that no one can take from me."

Ebita was very upset. The rigors, heartbreak and distresses of her childhood came rushing back to her. She was crying so Christopher said, "Rest your head in my lap, dear. You seem stressed."

"I am." She rested her head in Christopher's lap and stretched her legs out on the couch. It wasn't long, however, before she got up and said, "I will sit outside for a while."

"Okay." Then I will return Amanda's phone call."

"That's fine."

Ebita walked to the veranda and sat down. Christopher dialed Amanda's home telephone number but no one answered. He left a brief message simply to identify himself as the caller. He then dialed her cell phone number. Still, he received no answer. Once again he left a brief message. As soon as he folded his cell phone to end the call, it started ringing. It was Amanda calling.

"Hello!" He answered.

"Hey, Chris! Do you want to speak with Khleo?"

"Why would I want to do that. If I had any reason to speak with her I would have called her."

"Well, excuse me, sir," said Amanda. "Apparently you don't know."

"Don't know what?"

"That her cell phone was stolen and her land line is out of commission."

"How was I supposed to know that?" asked Christopher. "She has made no effort to speak with me since Snake arrived in Mayaro."

"Did you ever try to reach her?"

"No."

"Well, there is your answer," said Amanda. "Anyway, when are you coming home?"

"Tomorrow. Why?"

"We really need your help."

"In what way can I help that Snake cannot?"

"In every way Christopher. In every way I can think of."

Christopher wasn't objecting to helping Khleo and Amanda. He simply resented the fact that Eli Ebbs, a deportee from the USA with a tarnished reputation, had replaced him as Khleo Karch's constant companion. In spite of that, he had no aversion to helping his fellow teachers in any way he could have. His concern though, was for Ebita. He had agreed for her to accompany him to Mayaro when they returned to Trinidad the next day, Tuesday. He did not want to inflict any further harm to her already fragile emotional state of mind. She was still trying to cope with the loss of her father and the greed of her stepmother. The last thing she needed , he thought, was to see him interacting with his ex-lover, Khleo Karch. With that in mind, he told Amanda, "I can take a look at what you might want me to do but not before Friday or Saturday."

"Why Friday or Saturday?" asked Amanda. "Didn't you say that you would be back here on Tuesday?"

"That is true. However, I have previously planned engagements that will keep me busy through Thursday."

"All right, Christopher," said Amanda dejectedly. "I suppose we will take whatever time you can offer."

"Thanks for understanding."

"Thank you."

After speaking with Amanda, Christopher joined Ebita on the veranda. To his delight, she seemed more relaxed, and they were able to converse amicably about everything that was of interest to both of them. Ebita was excited about the prospect of visiting Mayaro, a place she heard so much about, even before her first visit to Trinidad. Christopher was cautious. He did not want her to be disappointed when she arrived at the sea side resort he called home. He was well aware of the attractiveness of beaches in Barbados, so he decided to caution Ebita.

"We have a lovely beach but the water is rough," said Christopher. "Ours is not exclusive to tourists and tourism. The beach area is integrated with residence of the locals and resort facilities."

"That is of no consequence to me, Chris. I do not plan to go swimming."

"Also, we do not have beautiful waterfalls, a botanical garden, nor a bird sanctuary."

"What is there?"

"Who is there? would be the more appropriate question," said Christopher. "The beauty of Mayaro is in its people."

Ebita laughed and asked, "Is it because you live there?"

"No! Seriously, the people of Mayaro are warm and friendly. They are respectful, mannerly, and generous."

"My dear, Chris, why don't you let me be the judge of that when we arrive there tomorrow?"

"Okay."

TWENTY-NINE

KHLEO, AMANDA, AND ELI SET out to investigate the staged kidnapping. Amanda, the autocratic, loquacious, school teacher, assumed the leadership role. She assigned specific areas of the district to herself and the other two novice investigators, none of whom had any experience in the task they were about to undertake. Khleo and Amanda were determined to succeed. It was their reputations that were being tarnished. Eli was reluctant but felt constrained and could do no less. He was, for the time being at least, solely dependent on Khleo for his day to day needs.

Amanda decided she would cover all areas north of the Naparima/Mayaro Road (NMR) from Peter Hill to Plaisance, and along the Manzanilla/Mayaro Road (MMR) to as far as Cocal. She assigned Khleo the area south of the NMR from Pierreville to Plaisance, and along the Guayaguayare/Mayaro Road (GMR) to New Lands. Both assigned areas were to include all residence between the main roads and the beach. Eli was assigned the area from Pierreville to Chrysostom Trace, and including Inner-Mafeking and all other points between.

Amanda demanded that the assigned areas be canvassed as if

a population census was being undertaken. Khleo and Eli were wondering how on earth they were expected to accomplish that but neither wanted to ask Amanda. Only Amanda had a vehicle and she anticipated what the others may have on their minds but were reluctant to say.

"You are probably wondering how you are going to accomplish this without a car?" asked Amanda. "Well, the answer is simple. We will walk. It is the only way we can be sure that we get an opportunity to speak with everyone within the given radius, perhaps even the perpetrator or perpetrators themselves."

Khleo suggested that they need some sort of recording device to be able to do the job well. That is, to be able to recall what they were told and convey the information to police.

"Use your cell phones," Amanda said.

"What are you talking about?" asked Khleo. You are the only one among us with a cell phone,"

"Forgive me. I totally forgot," said Amanda. "That being the case, we must go over to Bhagnan's Store and purchase a couple of tape recorders for you."

Eli rolled his eyes but said nothing as he and Khleo followed Amanda to the local Department Store where they purchased three small tape recorders, three note pads, and pens and pencils.

One major concern that played heavily on the minds of the three friends, was whether they could have proceeded with their planned investigation without being corralled by law enforcement. After all, the press had revealed the names of the two women as people of interest in the *staged kidnapping*, and Eli, aka Snake, was at one point, questioned by the police and released." Nevertheless, they headed out to their designated paths.

Although they were well known in the community, Khleo, Amanda, and Eli soon discovered that people were reluctant to speak with them about the case. Most people knew nothing more than what they read in newspapers, heard on the radio, or saw on television. Most knew that the motive for the crime was greed; the need to acquire some portion of the perceived wealth of the Karch family. It mattered little to the perpetrator or perpetrators that such an acquisition was ill-gotten. He, she, or they, firmly believed that the Karch family possessed wealth. They had not taken into consideration that Mr. Karch once worked hard as a lumberjack, saved penny by penny from his earnings, and borrowed additional funds to get his hardware and lumber business started. It never occurred to them that even as the business was thriving, Mr. Karch was still struggling to meet the pay roll, meet day to day business expenses, and achieve a marginal profit. That profit has been his personal income; the income he used to educate his children and live comfortably, certainly not ostentatiously. He wasn't a pauper, but he was by no means a wealthy man. He was, however, perceived as such.

After two hours of canvassing the neighborhoods, the group returned to Pierreville and gathered at Khleo's place to compare notes and assess their progress. Amanda seemed to have been the most successful. Although, none of the others was aware of it, one of the homes she visited in Beau Sejour, along the Manzanilla/Mayaro Road, was that of Paul Aranguez. He was up and about after his encounter with a viper in the Guayaguayare, Trinity Hills Nature Preserve, but he was not completely back to normal. Amanda wasn't aware of the snake bite incident and saw no need to question Paul about his health. The brothers were known to be robust individuals who, when not body-building, enjoyed hunting or went deep sea fishing for sport. Like everyone else in town, it probably would not have struck her as being odd if she knew that Paul was bitten by a fer-de-lance. She was unaware, nevertheless, that she had spoken to one of the perpetrators.

Neither Khleo nor Eli had anything of significance to report. They all agreed, however, that their initial effort was a success in that there was no interference from law enforcement. The police, for the most part, acted as if no crime was committed and they; Khleo, Amanda, and Eli were no different from any other citizen. It was almost as if they did not exist.

Khleo and Eli complained about back and muscle aches. Amanda was hurting too but did not complain. Instead, she said, "Listen guys, it is already 6:00 p.m. Perhaps we should think of getting something to eat and just relax for the rest of the evening." The others did not disagree. On the contrary, they agreed on having pizza for dinner. They called the Brick Oven Pizza Parlor and had a large pie delivered to them. As they ate, Amanda reassessed the situation. She knew that she wasn't going to sleep on the couch bed with Eli again. She thought of alternative arrangements Khleo might suggest, and none met her fancy. Finally, she decided that she would leave Khleo's place at about 9:30 p.m. and return to her own apartment. She made that known and neither Khleo nor Eli objected.

They chatted about a variety of topics but their main focus remained that of determining who the perpetrator or perpetrators were of the staged kidnapping of Khleo and the extortion of money from her parents. The laconic Mr. Eli Ebbs had little to say but he was the perfect audience of one for the loquacious Amanda and sometimes glib Khleo. He listened attentively and that somehow, changed Amanda's attitude toward him. She became less suspicious, less belligerent toward him, and more inclined to embrace him as a friend. Was that genuine or was it because she needed all the help she could muster, not just to find who was culpable, but to restore her good name?

"What are people saying about us?" she asked, directing her question to both Khleo and Eli.

"Everyone I spoke with was sympathetic," said Khleo. "No one had anything negative to say."

"What have you heard , Eli?"

"Nothing of consequence. People seemed more concerned about when I arrived and when I plan to return to the USA."

"You need to be more proactive, Eli. Steer the conversation the way you want it to go and spend less time reacting to people's fascinations."

"Amanda, I believe that people are more likely to reveal what they know if they are comfortable with you," said Eli. "That is never achieved by brushing people off."

"You may have a valid argument but that means you will have to spend more time with each person to whom you speak."

"If that is what it takes, then that is what I will do."

"Okay, Eli. Do it your way. You will achieve a great deal that way."

Eli wasn't at all perturbed by Amanda's sarcasm. He was confident in his belief that being aloof had no place in dealing with people he grew up with. In his own laconic style, he replied, "I will." There was no further comment from Amanda, and Khleo added nothing to that topic. Instead, the discussion focused on what people in the assigned areas had to say. As it turned out, neither Khleo, Amanda, nor Eli learnt anything new. Most people were reporting what they read in the newspapers or heard on radio or television. Some, however, had their own twist to what was reported.

Amanda suggested that if they encountered anyone who, perhaps heard something that was not previously reported, they should not hesitate to meet with the individual or individuals again. The objective she explained was to put people at ease, then skillfully deduce from them what was needed. That seemed contrary to what she said minutes earlier, and it made Eli wonder whether Amanda thought that any of them could go around Mayaro acting uppity and still get people to cooperate. Nevertheless, he made no objection, and neither did Khleo.

It was approaching 9:20 p.m. when Amanda said, "I think I should be on my way now."

"Not before we had some coffee," said Khleo. "It will take only a few minutes to brew."

"Okay," Amanda said as she sat back.

Khleo went to get the brew started and Eli took that as an opportunity to say to Amanda, "I don't think that I am capable of walking as far again tomorrow."

"What is the matter?"

"My entire body aches, but my calf muscles are particularly sore."

"So, do you need a cane?"

"I am not kidding Amanda. For the last ten years I have not done that much walking."

"For the last ten years you have done nothing," Amanda said rudely.

"You can be as hostile as you want to be. If tomorrow morning I should feel the way I do now, I will not go trekking on to Chrysostom Village."

"Khleo might enjoy hearing that."

"What will I enjoy hearing?" Khleo asked as she walked into the room with the coffee.

"I will let Eli address that," Amanda said .

"I was telling Amanda how difficult I think it would be for me to walk again tomorrow."

"I know. I feel the same way," Khleo said.

"Hmm! Amanda murmured.

"Listen! Let's have some coffee, get some rest tonight and see how we feel tomorrow," said Khleo. "If we are still aching, we will rent a car."

"One car?" asked Eli. He was wondering how he would get to Chrysostom and Khleo to New Lands at the same time with one car.

"What! Do you want her to rent two cars?" asked Amanda. "Why can't your buddies drive you around?"

"Who are my buddies?"

"Eli, please! Don't play dumb. They are the Aranguez brothers of course."

"They are not my pals. You are well aware that I barely know them."

"Would you two just stop. Please!" Khleo pleaded.

"Certainly. I am leaving right now. I will see you tomorrow evening," Amanda said and left without having her coffee.

"She is really teed-off," said Khleo. "She behaves like that sometimes when things don't go the way she wishes."

"That's just too bad. I am not her child."

"That is precisely her problem. She treats everyone as she does her kindergarten pupils."

THIRTY

CHRISTOPHER AND EBITA RETURNED TO the condo in Plymouth after having dinner at the small restaurant where they had dined previously. Ebita was much more relaxed by then as she conversed quietly with Christopher. She spoke extensively about her love for her father, the sacrifices he made to educate her, and the void she felt in her life since his passing. She became emotional at times when she spoke of the injustices she had suffered at home from her stepmother. The horrific acts of cruelty she suffered were never before revealed, not even to her beloved father. That was an indication of the level of trust she placed in Christopher.

As she chronicled her childhood ordeal, Christopher listened attentively and at times became emotional, shedding a tear drop or two and in the process, revealing his softer, gentler side. Through it all, Ebita remained calm and very proud of her upbringing in Barbados. Christopher promised once again that she could depend on his continued love and support. She smiled and said, "I am confident of that Christopher. It is, perhaps, the reason the good Lord brought us together again."

"Perhaps it is."

"I am so happy with you, Chris. I can hardly wait to meet your parents."

"Oh my!"

"What is the matter?"

"I forgot to let them know that we will be visiting them tomorrow."

"Oh, Christopher! How could you?"

"You and I became so engrossed in whatever we were doing, I seldom thought of anything or anyone else."

"That is very flattering but you cannot surprise your parents like that."

"You are right," said Christopher, but he made no immediate effort to call home.

"Don't you think that you should call them now before it is too late?"

"It is never too late for me to call Mom. However, I will call right away."

Christopher took out his cell phone, called home, and informed his mother that a friend was coming home with him for a weekend's visit. He introduced Ebita to his mother, Mrs. Elizabeth Boyz. They spoke briefly but pleasantly on the telephone. However, Christopher's father, Mr. Stanford Boyz, was already asleep. Mrs. Boyz assured Ebita that she would convey the news to her husband and that she, Ebita was welcome to stay with them for the entire month if she so desired. Ebita thanked her and returned the phone to Christopher who continued speaking with his mother for the next hour. The conversation was interrupted intermittently only by bursts of laughter from Christopher. His mother was laughing too but the sweet sound of her expressed happiness was music only to Christopher's ears. In a strange sort of way, Ebita felt a little left out. Nevertheless, she also felt a heightened admiration for the relationship Christopher had with his mother.

When he eventually folded his cell phone to end the

conversation, Ebita suggested that they complete their packing so there would be no need for them to rush the next morning.

"Are you forgetting something?" Christopher asked.

"What?"

"I have already packed."

"That is not fair."

"What isn't fair?"

"Men can travel so lightly while we ladies have to take so much with us."

"These are some of the little things that define us darling. I doubt whether you would want to trade places."

"I am happy just the way I am, more luggage and all."

"Can I help you pack?"

"Good idea. Let's get it done so we can go to sleep."

"Go to sleep, or go to bed?"

"What is the difference?"

"I would have to show you after we have completed the packing."

"You stop now," said Ebita. She was laughing and so was Christopher.

When their laughter stopped, they got the packing done as they conversed and looked forward to the trip back to Trinidad. Christopher was trying his very best not to mention Khleo Karch in the conversation for fear that it might upset Ebita. She, on the contrary, could not resist her need to know what the situation was with Khleo and her family so she asked , "Did Khleo's family meet the kidnappers demand?"

"I think so. I believe they paid the ransom."

"Is she okay?"

"That I cannot say with certainty," said Christopher. "As you perhaps noticed, there was no follow up of that incident in the press or on television, and I have not been in constant communication with anyone from home."

"Yes. There are always other breaking news and generally,

there is a tendency for interest in these cases to wane after the ransom had been paid."

"That is quite true."

"What will happen now?"

"I do not know," said Christopher. "What I can tell you is that Amanda, Khleo's best friend, has asked me to help in tracking down the perpetrators."

"Doesn't the situation make it more difficult for private citizens like you and Amanda to help?"

"If you are referring to the fact that the ransom has been paid, yes. It might."

"What can you do?"

"I don't know."

"Then how can you help? You are not trained in law enforcement, are you?"

"I am not sure how I can be of any help but Amanda claims that she has a plan."

"Was she ever a police officer?"

"No."

"Were you ever a police officer?"

"Didn't you ask me that before?"

"I did but you didn't answer."

"Well, quite frankly, I was never trained in law enforcement."

"It is my hope that Amanda's plan is not one that would get you or anyone else seriously hurt or killed."

Christopher did not respond to Ebita's last statement. He was worried. His concern was not just about Khleo but for his own safety as well. His hope was that by the time he and Ebita arrived in Mayaro, the saga would have come to a happy ending. He was aware that the kidnapping was *staged*, that Khleo was safe, and that Amanda's intent on tracking down the culprits was to restore her good name. Her effort did not go unnoticed. Most people believed that the young elementary school teachers were innocent of the crime for which they had become the prime suspects.

Although there had been doubters, Khleo Karch and Amanda Flagg knew that they were innocent. Two other people in town also knew the facts of the case. Facts that would have cleared Khleo and Amanda of any suspicion, restore their dignity, and their faith in the judicial system. It was not conceivable that those knowledgeable individuals would ever have come forward. In fact, the buzz about the investigative efforts of the trio; Khleo, Amanda, and Eli reached Peter Aranguez. He immediately rushed to his brother's home. There he learnt that Amanda Flagg had questioned Paul. Although her questions were of a general nature and she did not ask how or where Paul was bitten by a venomous snake, the mere fact that she spoke to Paul made Peter very worried and nervous. Immediately, he started thinking of ways to divert attention from the case, from himself, and from his brother.

Peter called his friend Imp and concocted a story that Amanda Flagg was influencing Khleo Karch to pressure Eli Ebbs, aka Snake, not to associate with him and his brother. He somehow managed to sound convincing enough for Imp to ask, "What would you like to happen to her?"

"What can happen?

"Quite a lot, Bro," said Imp. "What do you want?"

"I would leave it up to you. However, you must keep in mind that no one must be physically harmed."

"I know the perfect solution but it could cost you a great deal."

"How much?"

"Five thousand."

"Five thousand dollars?"

"That's my price for a job I would like to do myself." Imp did not tell Peter what he intended to do. Peter, therefore, was unable to estimate the cost.

"That's a lot. Let me think about it."

"Take your time. I am not going anywhere."

"Okay. I will call you tomorrow."

"Bye."

Imp was thinking of the worst possible crime that could ever be perpetrated against a woman. He was certain that he could have pulled it off and place the onus of responsibility for solving the *staged kidnapping* back on the police who didn't seem to care very much. Amanda, he thought, would be much too concerned about her own emotional and physical distress to continue her quest to identify the perpetrator or perpetrators in the Khleo Karch's *staged kidnapping* case.

That Monday night Imp was so excited about the possibility of earning $5000.00 in one evening that he decided to celebrate his good fortune before the job was even assigned to him. He picked up a friend, drove over to the bar and grill known as *The Junction* where he ordered drinks for two. Soon two other acquaintances walked in and greeted him and his friend. He ordered drinks for them also. The rounds of drinks amounted to eight when the bartender informed them that he could no longer serve them.

"Why not?" asked Imp. "Do you think we cannot afford it?"

"No! it is company policy."

"What is company policy? Imp asked. His speech was slurred, he had stopped smiling. Instead, he had a fleer on his face, his hands seemed feeble as he waved them in the air threateningly. His glass of scotch spilled over onto the carpet.

"The policy is that we stop serving any patron who appears to be drunk after the eighth drink."

"After… after… the eighth drink?"

"Yes, sir."

"Let me speak with your boss."

"You are speaking to him."

"How much do I owe you?"

"That would be seven sixty-five, sir."

"Seven dollars and sixty-five cents?"

"Seven hundred and sixty-five dollars, sir"

"Oh!"

Imp handed the bartender TT$800.00 and left with his friend. He did not wait for his change. To him, that was a generous tip, an amount he felt he could easily part with because in a day or two he expected to collect a windfall from a new job he had to do for Peter Aranguez. He knew Peter to be a good and dependable client, one who always paid promptly once the job was done.

Imp's friend was a licensed chauffeur but he did not have a vehicle, so Imp offered to take him to his home in Grand Lagoon. He gladly accepted the ride. As they left *Pierreville*, Imp was driving erratically and very fast. That was not unusual in Trinidad & Tobago. Men drank and drove constantly. Often the results were tragic. That Monday night was no different. For much of the journey, the traffic was light and Imp was able to drive extremely fast. Although his luxury car swerved considerably, he drove at speeds of 70 to 80 mph. As soon as he crossed the Grand Lagoon bridge, and about five hundred yards from his friend's home, he slammed head on into a speeding semi. His friend was thrown out of the car and died instantly. Imp died at the wheel. Neither was wearing a seat belt. The driver of the truck was seriously injured and had to be air lifted to San Fernando General Hospital.

News of the terrible accident spread quickly the next day. It was reported on radio and television. All of the major news papers published articles about it. One tabloid even ran a commentary about the incidence of drunk driving in a nation where the number of motor vehicles were fast approaching the number of people, and apart from the major highways, the streets were narrow and sometimes winding and undulating.

That Tuesday morning Peter Aranguez' reaction to the death of his friend, Imp, was mixed. He was sad to hear of Imp's untimely demise but he did not think of it as a great loss. He felt confident that with the large chunk of the Karch family fortune he had buried in the Trinity Hills Nature Preserve in Guayaguayare, he could take his time in looking for, and selecting another person he can trust to follow his instructions as they pertained to his illegal activities.

Christopher and Ebita arrived at Crown Point International Airport in Tobago early that morning and returned the rented car. They then walked over to the terminal and checked in. They did not have to wait long for a flight to Trinidad. About twenty minutes after their arrival, they boarded a small jet and were airborne. A mere fifteen minutes later they touched down at Piarco International Airport in Trinidad.

"How are we getting to Mayaro?" Ebita asked as they disembarked.

"We can do one of two things."

"Just what may those be?"

"Well, we can rent a car, or we can hire a taxi."

"Which is feasible?"

"Both are," said Christopher. "It would have cost less for us to rent a car if I didn't have a vehicle of my own in Mayaro. Right now, however, it makes more sense for us to hire a taxi."

"Okay."

THIRTY-ONE

AMANDA ARRIVED AT KHLEO'S PLACE at 9:00 a.m. Both Khleo and Eli were already dressed and ready to embark on their assigned routes to investigate the crime perpetrated against the Karch family, including Khleo, and inadvertently, Amanda. They wasted no time in getting started. Amanda drove them over to the auto rental place on Gill Street. On arrival, she handed her car keys to Eli and said, "Use my car. I am going to rent something for myself."

"Wouldn't it be better for me to drive the rental and you drive your own car?" Eli asked.

"Why?"

"I am not sure," said Eli. "I thought you might be more comfortable driving your own set of wheels. Most people are."

"Your point is well taken but I will drive the rental. Thank you," said Amanda. "My piece of junk is still fully insured if that is what you are worried about."

Although Eli never said that he was worried, he clearly was concerned about his lack of experience with right hand driven vehicles, and driving on the left side of the road. Amanda quickly picked up on it. She realized that his real concern was that he might have an accident and be asked to pay for the costly repairs. He was recently deported from the USA, was unemployed and had no savings. She understood his concern and tried to reassure him that he would do just fine. When all the paper work was completed and they received the keys for the two vehicles, they drove off the lot and headed out on their assigned routes. Amanda went to continue her quest along the Manzanilla/Mayaro Road. Khleo headed out along the Mayaro/Guayaguayare Road, and Eli continued along the Naparima/Mayaro Road.

Christopher and Ebita had arrived in Mayaro by then and went directly to Christopher's place. From there he immediately dialed his parents' phone number.

"Hey! Christopher," answered his mother. "Where are you, son?"

"I am at home, Mom."

"Is Etiba with you?"

"Ebita," he corrected her. Then he said, "Yes, she is here."

"Why didn't you bring her directly here?"

Christopher did not answer that question specifically but said, "We are coming over right now, Mom"

"Great! I am looking forward to meeting Etiba."

"Her name is Ebita, Mom."

"Okay. I am certain I will get it right by the time she arrives with you."

"See you soon, Mom."

Christopher hung up the telephone and without further hesitation, he and Ebita left Plaisance and headed out on the relatively short ride to his parents' place in Ste. Marguerite. The journey was familiar to Christopher but Ebita was uneasy. It wasn't because she had no confidence in Christopher's driving skills. She was confident about his ability but the speed at which other vehicles were traveling on the narrow roadway made her uncomfortable. Every time a commercial vehicle whizzed by them, she winced, sat up in her seat, and stepped on an imaginary brake. Often Christopher looked over at her and tried to allay her fears with some comforting words. In response, she always pleaded with him to keep his eyes on the road ahead.

Breaking news on the radio about the horrific accident on the same road the previous night, or rather, earlier that very morning, did not help Christopher's efforts to calm Ebita of her fears. Fortunately, they had arrived at Ste. Marguerite's Road by then, and Christopher quickly turned right, and drove up the hill to his parents newly built posh dwelling overlooking the ocean. It was an unusual piece of modern architecture that was known only to those who had the privilege of entering the building. On the outside it seemed as just a respectable habitat, a decent but ordinary house. However, upon entry the grandeur of the layout was revealed and Ebita was truly impressed. There was a glistening winding staircase that took them to the second floor. Alternatively, the physically challenged could ride a shiny, spotlessly clean elevator to the second floor. That was where the living room, dining room, kitchen, media room, library, or reading room, as the Boyz family called it, were located. At the front, outside of the living room, was a veranda overlooking the roadway below and the Atlantic Ocean a short distance away. The veranda was enclosed in glass and self-contained. It served more like a sitting room. There were coffee tables, a couch, two end tables, a couple of armchairs, a television, a stereo system, and a well-stocked bar on the veranda. Amazingly, all four bedrooms in the house were located on the first floor. The four bathrooms were evenly distributed on both floors. One, however, the largest was located in the master bedroom and unavailable to guest.

Christopher showed Ebita the entire house. She was in awe but tried her best not to show it. During their university years, she always admired Christopher's humility in spite of his successes. She had no idea that his parents were so well off or that Mayaro, a place that Christopher truly loved, was so beautiful. After the grand tour, he escorted Ebita to the veranda. He sat with her for a few minutes, then excused himself to join his mother in the kitchen.

"Christopher, she is gorgeous, and so well mannered," said Mrs. Boyz. "I am willing to bet that she is also very smart."

"She is, Mom. Ebita is all of that."

"Ebita, Ebita, Ebita," Mrs. Boyz repeated softly to herself to help her remember the name for conversations later on. For a brief moment she thought of Khleo, made a mental comparison of the two young women but never mentioned the Karch woman's name.

"Help me with this Christopher," she said as she pointed to a tray she had prepared to serve coffee and tea. He took up the tray. Then he said, "Ebita might prefer something cold, Mom"

"Why don't you ask her. If she does, we have sorrel, mauby, ginger beer, and freshly prepared sour sop (guanabana) drink."

"I will ask her, Mom."

Christopher left the kitchen with the tray and headed to the veranda. His mother followed him. They entered the veranda smiling. Ebita was smiling back at them. That made Christopher very pleased. Ebita was well received by his mother, and they were at ease and comfortable in each other's presence. That was a clear indication that his father would have no reason to object to his choice. His mother was always the fastidious one.

Christopher inquired of Ebita whether she would have preferred to drink something cold and she indicated that she preferred the hot drink because the air conditioning in the enclosed veranda was so very efficient.

"The enclosure is retractable," said Christopher. "Would you like to have it open?"

"Not really. I am okay with it."

As Christopher and his mother sat with Ebita to partake of their coffee and tea, the door bell rang. Neither Christopher nor his mother, Mrs Boyz responded right away, so the visitor rang the bell again.

"Who could that be?" Mrs. Boyz wondered aloud as she excused herself and got up to investigate.

Ebita looked at Christopher as if to ask, *Can one just ring other people's door bell without first making telephone contact?*

"This is Mayaro, my dear," said Christopher. "As I understand it, this town has a long history of open door policy......." At that point his mother returned to the veranda and said, "It looks like Khleo."

"What does she want?" Christopher asked, not really expecting his mother to answer but she did.

"I wouldn't know that, Christopher," she said. Then she asked, "Don't you think that you should go down and asked her?"

"No, Mom," Christopher said.

"You probably should, Christopher," said Ebita. He looked at her puzzled and she said, "It might be important."

Reluctantly, he got up and walked down to the front door. His mother looked at Ebita and said, "Thank you, Ebita." That was her first real opportunity to practice calling the name, and she got it right.

"You are welcome, Mrs. Boyz."

Khleo Karch knew that Christopher was there because his SUV was in the driveway. For a brief moment she thought of bypassing the Boyz family home but she was well aware that if Amanda ever heard of it, she would receive a lecture on determination, strength, and purpose, which she did not need. As Christopher opened the front door, Khleo smiled broadly. He, however, was not smiling but politely asked, "Why are you here alone?"

"It is quite a long story," said Khleo. "You perhaps heard or read of the difficulties Amanda and I have been having."

"Actually, I haven't," said Christopher. "I just returned from Tobago where I spent the weekend."

"Well, what happened is terrible. As a result, Amanda and I am trying to speak with residents with the hope that someone may know something, anything at all that might give us and the police a lead to the perpetrator or perpetrators." Khleo was careful not to mention Eli's name.

"Dad is at work, and right now Mom has company."

"Then, can I speak with you for a few minutes?"

"As I said before, I just returned from Tobago. I would know nothing about what ails you or Amanda. Perhaps you can speak with my parents later."

"Perhaps I would, Christopher. Thank you."

"You are most welcome. Oh, give them a call before you come out again."

"I will. Thanks again. Bye."

"Bye." Christopher closed the door and returned upstairs. Khleo moved on to the home of the next-door neighbor. It was as if they were strangers or at best, mere acquaintances. Christopher was void of emotion toward her and Khleo quickly realized it.

Eli was not having anymore success than Khleo. On the contrary, he was only having fun. With so many people expressing how glad they were to see him after a ten-year absence from Mayaro, and willing to shower him with gifts, food, and drinks, he was becoming a little complacent. Perhaps he was too self-satisfied for his own good. Amanda on the other hand, was working as hard as she could. The leads she thought she was getting, however, led nowhere. Too many people were reporting nothing of consequence that she could have taken to the police. On her particular route, the most frequently suggested scenario was that the kidnappers may have used the forested areas of Cocal to hold their victim. That was because too many people knew so little about the case, while most of the others forgot that the kidnapping was *staged*, and that no one was physically held for ransom. Amanda and Khleo were psychologically victimized and that is what motivated them to launch the search for the culprit or culprits. Eli lacked the same level of motivation and chose instead to use the time and resources made available to him to become reacquainted with the village folks.

News of the quasi investigation circulated throughout the town by way of conversations. It engaged people. Most people were sympathetic toward the young women but there were some skeptics who weren't so sure that they were innocent of the crime for which they were suspected. The inaction of the police neither confirmed that nor laid it to rest.

After Imp's untimely death, Peter Aranguez waged his own campaign to cast doubt on any thought of innocence on the part of Khleo Karch and Amanda Flagg. By doing so, he hoped to deflect any glimmer of suspicion that may be cast on him or his brother. He was very concerned that sooner or later the rogues in town would be scrutinized. Although the Aranguez brothers were never convicted of a crime, they were well known to be unorthodox and unpredictable in their quest for money. They lived ostentatiously, although, neither held a job in the last seven years since Paul was dismissed from the Police service. Other vagabonds in town were considered to be more dangerous and solitary, and the Aranguez brothers often engaged them to perform the dirty leg work in their criminal adventures.

Peter knew that drunkards at the bars and beer parlors he visited spoke indiscreetly about everything and often without knowledge or understanding of the subject of discussion. He, therefore, seized on every occasion that the *staged kidnapping* was discussed to interject his supposed belief that the young elementary school teachers were the culprits. More often that not, the drunkards would believe him, and soon the rumor spread. Although the believers were few, Peter's strategy shifted the focus of attention if there were any, away from the vagabonds that might have been suspected, and they included Peter Aranguez himself and his brother, Paul.

THIRTY-TWO

AMANDA AND ELI REJOINED KHLEO at her place in Pierreville to compare notes, discuss their successes and /or failures, and decide on a new strategy if necessary, for future forays into the realm of criminal investigation. Eli had little to contribute other than he had spoken to a lumberjack named Zachary who informed him that at the time Khleo Karch was rumored to have been kidnapped, he observed several individuals in two vehicles acting suspiciously as they entered a wooded area off Chrysostom Road. Eli did not get descriptions of the vehicles. He did not get the license plate numbers, or descriptions of the individuals occupying or operating the vehicles. Amanda ruled that the effort was good although the information gained was not credible. Eli simply smiled. He couldn't care less. All that mattered to him was the good time he enjoyed getting reacquainted with people he had not seen, heard from, or heard about in ten years.

Apart from what she considered to be an unpleasant encounter with her former sweetheart, Christopher Boyz, Khleo's experience was similar to Eli's. Several individuals described what they considered suspicious behavior on the part of others. Amanda didn't think that any of those warranted a follow up.

Nevertheless, she commended Khleo for her effort and promised that she would deal with Christopher herself when the time was right.

The information Amanda received on her route was similar to what Khleo and Eli gathered. Many people she spoke to informed her either of unusual activity along the Ortoire River in Inner Mafeking, or in wooded areas off Cocal Road. She told her companions, Khleo and Eli, "It was an uneventful day but that is no reason for us to give up. We will go out tomorrow with even more enthusiasm. As for Christopher, I am going to call him as soon as I get home."

"Please don't let him know what I told you," Khleo pleaded.

"Why not? What do you have to lose at this point?"

"I just ...." Khleo started to say something but Amanda interrupted and said, "You dumped him. Did you forget? What do you have to lose now?"

Amanda had a habit of saying whatever came to her mind, irrespective of how other people were affected by it. That Tuesday evening was no different. What she said made Eli cringe, and tears welled up in Khleo's eyes. In the midst of all that Eli exclaimed, "I am hungry!"

"We are trying to solve a serious problem that threatens our livelihood, our future, and our good names, and all you can think of is food?" Eli did not respond, so Amanda continued. "You are a grown man, if you are hungry, get up and get something to eat. No one here is your babysitter, housekeeper, or cook." Still there was no response from Eli. The remark about his hunger was an attempt to change the topic of conversation from a discussion about Christopher Boyz. Obviously, it was the wrong choice of words.

"I will call up for some food," Khleo said.

"You are pathetic, girl," said Amanda. "I am out of here. I will see you tomorrow."

Amanda was still having a difficult time with Khleo's choice of Eli over Christopher. Apart from being a friend and colleague of

Christopher, she saw him as an intelligent, ambitious, upwardly mobile individual with a bright future. On the contrary, she saw Eli as lazy, selfish, and exploiting her friend, Khleo.

Mrs. Elizabeth Boyz told her son, Christopher, "Let me take Ebita away from you for a few minutes."

Christopher raised no objection and the two women walked down the winding stairway to the master bedroom on the first floor. There, Mrs. Boyz took out three family albums from a chest-of -drawers and handed them to Ebita. "These are family treasures," she said .

Ebita smile and started turning the pages that held the black and white wedding pictures of Elizabeth and Stanford Boyz. Most intriguing to her though, was the album with pictures of the couples only child, Christopher, from his infancy to his graduation from the University of the West Indies.

While Ebita and Mrs. Boyz chatted in the master bedroom, Christopher's mobile phone rang. He checked the caller ID and saw that it was Amanda calling, so he answered, "Hello!"

"Christopher, this is Amanda."

"What's up, girl?"

"A lot has happened in the last few days," said Amanda. "We need to sit down and talk."

"That would be nice. How does 10:00 a.m. on Thursday sound?"

"Not good. What I want to talk about is urgent."

"What could be so urgent, Amanda?"

"That whole thing about Khleo's kidnapping," said Amanda. "You perhaps heard that it was _staged_ by some individual or individuals who extorted two hundred and fifty thousand dollars from the Karch family."

"My God! I didn't hear that. I was of the opinion that she was kidnapped and released after her parents paid the ransom."

"That's not how it happened," said Amanda. "In one way it is good that she was not physically captured and possibly harmed. However, at some point we both were mentioned as suspects in the *staged kidnapping* , and that I believe could do irreparable harm to our reputation and careers."

"Oh my! I am so sorry to hear that," said Christopher. Then he asked, "Is there anything I can do to help?"

"Yes. That is exactly why I would like to sit with you and talk."

"That can present some difficulty for me right now."

"How? Or rather, why? Didn't you ask if there is anything you can do to help?"

"Well, I did ask that but right now we have company whom I cannot just abandon. Secondly, I do not want to sit with Khleo and Snake, or whatever his name is."

"You wouldn't have to," said Amanda. "You and I can meet at *The Junction,* at my place, or at yours."

"Let me think about it and get back to you."

"Today, I hope."

"It is already 6:00 p.m. Can I call you early tomorrow morning?"

"You can, Christopher, but please try and call me back this evening," said Amanda. "If you want I can come over now."

"That may not be a good thing. I am at my parent's right now, and as I said before, we have company."

"Then call me back this evening, please."

"I will do that."

"Thanks, Christopher."

"You are welcome."

Amanda said goodbye and hung up the telephone. Christopher felt pressured but he realized the desperation in Amanda's voice and could not ignore her plea.

Elizabeth Boyz and Ebita had viewed all of the pictures when Mrs. Boyz suggested that they return to the veranda. They took the elevator up to the second floor because Mrs. Boyz' arthritic knees were achy. She was in excruciating pain but tried her very best not to show it. She was determined to make Ebita feel welcome and comfortable during her stay.

Christopher had not discussed his disagreement with Khleo Karch and his mother did not question him about it. She knew that something was wrong but just what that something was escaped her. Just as she had always done in other situations, she placed complete trust in her son's judgment and determination.

Khleo Karch was in her kitchen preparing a salad when the delivery man arrived with the Chinese food she had ordered. She answered the door, received the shopping bag, tipped the delivery man, and returned to the kitchen. Eli sat in the living room with the television on in front of him for the duration. He did nothing to help her, and she did not complain about it. He thought, *had Amanda been here, she certainly would have raised some sort of objection, although it was none of her business.* Just then Khleo asked, "What would you like to drink?"

"I will have a beer."

"What type?"

"The local brew."

Khleo took a cold beer out of the refrigerator, opened it, and was attempting to pour it into a glass for Eli when he said, "I prefer my beer in the bottle."

"What difference does it make?"

"The difference is in the taste."

"Okay. Have it your way."

"Thanks."

Just as they sat down to have their dinner, a vehicle was heard in the driveway. Eli became anxious even though Amanda had assured him that her 1998 sedan was still fully insured. He was fully aware of the prevalence of auto theft in T&T and dreaded the responsibility of having to pay for the replacement or repair of a vehicle that was not his. The other car, the one that Khleo drove was a rental. She, therefore, was not at all concerned. Eli's fears were put to rest when the operator of the vehicle sounded the horn several times. Khleo looked out and informed Eli that it was his newly found friend, Peter Aranguez. Eli was not swayed and simply sat down at the dining table.

Khleo opened her front door and Peter stepped out of his SUV. He stood with the door open and stared at her without saying a word. Eventually, she asked, "What can I do for you, Mr. Aranguez?"

"Hmm! Hmm," was all Peter exuded.

"I have no time to waste," said Khleo. "If you do not state your purpose for being here, I am calling the police."

Peter laughed and said sarcastically, "Please don't do that, Ms. Karch." He knew that neither Khleo nor Eli had access to a telephone. He was the person who arranged the theft of her cellular phone and he was personally responsible for putting her land line out of commission. He knew all along that the telephone company would take an eternity to repair the damage he had done. As Khleo turned to close the door behind her, he asked, "Is Snake in, Ms. Karch?"

"He is, but he is having dinner right now."

"That's okay. I will come back later."

"Later?" Khleo asked as she looked at her watch. "It is already 9:30 p.m."

"You are right. It is already very late for couples."

"What is that supposed to mean?"

"Nothing, nothing really. Just tell Eli that I will see him in the morning."

"He will be busy tomorrow morning."

"What! Did he find a job?"

"Good night Mr. Aranguez." Khleo said as she closed the door. She did not answer Peter's last question. Her only concern was that they had to continue their investigation the next day, and she did not want anyone or anything to distract Eli."

As Khleo re-entered the dining room, Eli asked, "Who was that?" As soon as he did, he regretted it. He remembered that Khleo considered those sorts of questions to be intrusive. He was pleasantly surprised when she answered without a fuss.

"That was your so-called friend, Peter."

"What did he want?"

"He wanted to speak with you but I told him that you were having dinner." It never crossed Khleo's mind that Eli might have found that to be controlling and intrusive. If she did wonder about it, Eli's answer would have cleared any doubt.

"You did good because I want to steer clear of him and his brother."

THIRTY-THREE

WEDNESDAY MORNING CHRISTOPHER WAS AWAKEN early by the ringing of his cell phone. Ebita had spent Tuesday night at his parents' home so that only his sleep was interrupted so early that morning. He answered the phone and was not surprised at who the caller was when he heard the voice.

"Christopher! This is Amanda. I hope I didn't wake you up."

"You did, but that's okay."

"We are going out early today to speak with residents again. Would you care to join us?"

"Amanda, I promised I will do what I can to help on Thursday. That's tomorrow I believe."

"I know you said that you would make yourself available to help on Thursday but you are here now and we are desperate for help."

"That is just too bad, Amanda."

"Is that it? You really don't care, do you?"

"It is not that I do not care about you, Amanda. It is that I had prior commitments for today."

"You are trying to avoid Khleo, aren't you?"

"No. Why would I want to do that? She made her choice. That was her decision. I have adjusted well."

"You are sounding bitter."

"If I do, that should not come as a surprise. I was hurt and responded as any normal human male would."

"I understand, Christopher. Nevertheless, think about it and give me a call later. I will leave here at 10:00 a.m.

"Okay."

They hung up the telephone simultaneously without saying goodbye. That brief conversation with Amanda weighed heavily on Christopher's mind. He decided there and then that perhaps he can accomplish two things at the same time. That is, he could accede to Amanda's request, take Ebita along the route or routes designated to him, and by so doing, investigate the *staged kidnapping* and show Ebita around Mayaro at the same time.

He called Ebita at his parents' home and informed her that he would pick her up at 9:00 a.m. that morning. She agreed. He immediately called back Amanda and told her that he would make himself available immediately. She was elated and asked, "Would you like to work the Guayaguayare/Mayaro Road with Khleo?" Amanda hoped she might have been able to reunite her two friends. She really did not like Eli.

"I will not."

"Well, Eli is covering the Naparima/Mayaro Road. I know that you wouldn't want that route."

"Absolutely not."

"Then that leaves my designated route."

"What route is that?"

"The Manzanilla/Mayaro Road from Pierreville to Cocal."

"It sounds like a political campaign route."

"That is somewhat the approach we are taking."

"I see."

"You can work the beach area parallel to the Manzanilla/ Mayaro Road up to *Beau Sejour,* or you can work the main road with me. We can alternate households."

"I will take the beach route," Christopher said. He was thinking of Ebita. The beach area, he thought, would be scenic and pleasant for her.

"Okay. I will meet you on the beach at the *Rest House* in about three to four hours from now."

"See you then."

"Thanks, Christopher. You are such a wonderful, caring individual."

"You are welcome," said Christopher. "Oh! I almost forgot to mention that I will have a friend with me."

"That's okay. I suppose it is the only way you can be available today."

"You are so right."

"See you as planned. Bye."

Christopher got dressed and drove to his parents' place in Ste. Marguerite. His father had already left for the day but his mother and Ebita had breakfast prepared and were waiting for him to join them. As they sat down to breakfast, he explained the role he had been asked to fill in solving the bogus kidnapping of his former girlfriend, Khleo Karch. Both women listened attentively and with great concern. Foremost in their minds was his safety. The safety of the other participants did not go unnoticed as Mrs. Boyz remarked, "Whoever did that is a ruthless vagabond who would stop at nothing less than the elimination of those who may try to uncover the truth."

Ebita was visibly upset by what she heard. Although, she made no attempt to dissuade Christopher from what he was about to pursue. While they were in Tobago, she previously expressed her concern for his safety in that regard. She was determined not to badger him relentlessly with the same rhetoric. That turned out to be the right decision. It became apparent when Christopher remarked, "It is the ruthless nature of the individual or individuals who committed this crime that makes it necessary for us to stop them."

"That should be the undertaking of the police," Mrs. Boyz said.

"To depend entirely on the police here is an exercise in futility. You know that, Mom"

"I do not personally know that. I have heard other people say it before."

"Even so, Mom, that is reason enough to necessitate their capture."

"If that is the only reason you are so willing to pursue the matter, then it is the right reason. However, my concern is that your real motive is quite different from that."

"Mom?"

The quizzing manner by which Christopher addressed his mother made Ebita glance at both of them as if to ask, *what was that all about?* Neither volunteered any information, and Christopher suggested that they get an early start. Mrs. Boyz wasn't too happy about that. She was enjoying Ebita's company. It was a welcomed change from being at home alone every day when Mr. Boyz left for work on Point Galeota. Nevertheless, she did not disclose her disappointment to either her son or to Ebita. She simply said, "Try and be home in time for dinner."

"We will, Mom" said Christopher. He then turned to Ebita and said, "If you are ready, we can go."

"I am ready."

"Then let's go."

"Okay," Ebita said. She then hugged Mrs. Boyz and said, "I hope you have a good, pain free day."

"Thank you , dear," Mrs. Boyz said.

"I will see you later, Mom," said Christopher. "Is there anything you want from Pierreville while we are out there?"

"No, son."

Christopher kissed his mother on her forehead. Then he and Ebita headed out to Plaisance. On arrival there, they parked on Gill Street and walked out to the beach. Ebita was in awe of the expanse of beach. There was an ebb tide, so it looked even more magnificent. She had never before seen anything like it. As she stood in wonder, Christopher pointed to the horizon and told her to look South East. She did and saw the massive oil drilling platforms in the distance.

"They are beautiful at nights when the flares are visible," Christopher said.

"What flares?"

"Flares from the burning off of excess natural gas." That was the best explanation Christopher could offer.

"Could we come back tonight to see the flares?"

"We could. Actually, we can see them from anywhere on the beach." Christopher hesitated to tell Ebita that the beach was not as safe at nights as it used to be, especially for young couples. He wanted her to enjoy the beauty of Mayaro without fear or reservations.

After a few minutes, they held hands, turned, and started walking North when Christopher said, "We will not meet anyone on the beach whom we can interview."

"Who are all these people here?"

"Most are tourists."

"Then there must be some local residents you can talk to."

"I doubt that. These people are either local or foreign tourists."

Ebita looked back and said, "There are lots of people back there."

"So it seems. That area, however, is assigned to someone else."

"Whom?"

"Khleo Karch."

There was a moment of silence before Christopher suggested that they move off the beach and start knocking on doors. They started to climb the embankment, intending to approach the homes that were interspersed beneath the palm trees, just beyond the row of guest houses that lined the Atlantic shore. That is when Christopher noticed a familiar object in the sand. He bent down and picked it up. It was a cellular telephone that had been washed ashore. The purple and silver phone looked very similar to one he had given to Khleo the previous Christmas. He turned it over and saw that the initials KK were etched into the plastic.

"Oh my God!" Christopher exclaimed.

"What is it?" Ebita asked.

"We are on to something."

"What?"

"I am not sure yet but this is Khleo Karch's cell phone. Or, it used to be at least."

Ebita didn't particularly want to hear Khleo Karch's name but she realized that the very nature of what they were undertaking made it necessary for the name to come up from time to time so she asked, "How can you tell?"

"I just know it."

"I am sure the manufacturer made thousands of those."

"These are her initials," Christopher said, as he pointed to the letters KK that were written on the back of the phone.

"Hmm!" Ebita murmured.

"It is probably inoperable but it could not have been in the water very long."

"How can you tell?"

"The color has not faded very much," said Christopher. "Usually, the salt water, sun and sand can damage any object, sometimes beyond recognition."

"When did she lose the phone?"

"I don't know. I did not try to call her since last Thursday when I left here."

"How exactly does all this help her case?"

"I really don't know yet. The phone is washed free of fingerprints."

"That is exactly why cases like this should be left to the experts."

"I couldn't agree with you more. However, law enforcement

seemed disinterested, and I didn't want to appear callous and heartless."

"People who know you could never think of you that way."

"Well, thank you."

"You are welcome."

Christopher placed the sea-washed cell phone in his pocket as they proceeded to knock on doors of the dwellings in the area. While Ebita was new to Mayaro, Christopher himself had never before been in that area. He was surprised at the many sub-standard housing he was seeing. Some of his students lived there, and that made him feel somewhat guilty to have grown up as privileged as he did. Nevertheless, he continued meeting and speaking with people.

After they visited a dozen households and had spoken to as many people between Plaisance Road and Lewis and Sucre Roads, They decided that they should stroll up the beach to the Rest House. They arrived there at 12:10 p.m. Amanda was already there. Christopher introduced her to Ebita. Amanda stretched out her hand to Ebita as a gesture of goodwill and an attempt at making acquaintance. They shook hands. "It is so nice to finally meet you," said Ebita. "I have heard so much about you."

"Good things I hope."

"Of course. Christopher is extremely proud of you."

"Thank you. It is always nice to hear something like that. After all, we have been friends for a long time."

Amanda seemed to be in a state of shock. *My God! She is beautiful. Even so, he never gave Khleo a chance to redeem herself. Then again, Eli was still attaching himself to Khleo like a tick on a cow*, she thought but asked, "Have you had any interesting conversations with people along the way?"

"Interesting conversations, yes. However, there were no leads as to who might have committed the crime."

"You did find that cell phone," Ebita reminded him.

"Oh yes! I found Khleo's cell phone washed up on the beach."

Christopher took the phone from the pocket of his jeans and handed it to Amanda. She recognized it right away as being Khleo's. *Who could have stolen it?* she wondered, but asked Christopher, "Why would someone steal an expensive cell phone and discard it in the ocean?"

"Shouldn't you be asking also, who would do it?" Ebita asked.

"Yes. We should," Amanda said.

"Several possibilities come to mind," Christopher said."

"What are they?"

"It is possible that the youngster who snatched her purse, stole her cell phone but lost it while working in the seine."

"You can rule that out."

"Why?"

"Any teen who works in the seine and has the audacity to snatch a woman's purse, would steal her money, in addition to her cell phone, and anything else of value."

"That point is well taken."

"Well, can you think of another scenario?"

"Yes."

"Let's hear it."

"Perhaps that tough, agile, hood-wearing thug was paid by someone else to mug Khleo and deprive her of her cell phone."

"Still, the question is, why?"

"For the same reason her land line was disabled," said Christopher. "To limit or eliminate her means of communication."

"That sounds plausible, except…….."

"Except what?"

"Except, she could have used my mobile phone while we were on the North Coast."

"Did she know that her phone was missing? Did she feel the need to call somebody? Or is it that she just wanted to be secluded? She certainly didn't try to call me."

That series of questions from Christopher made Ebita uneasy.

She looked at Amanda and said, "Please excuse me. I will be right back."

Where is she going? Does she even know where she is right now? Amanda wondered but nodded her head as if to say okay. She then said to Christopher, "Our purpose is to help Khleo, not castigate her."

"That might be your purpose," said Christopher. "The only reason I am here is to assist you if I can."

"Thanks for reminding me," Amanda said sarcastically.

Ebita meanwhile had walked down to the shore line and sat on a fallen coconut tree. She was looking out on the ocean and crying. She wasn't certain why but she thought that Christopher's reaction to the misfortune of someone he once loved had something to do with it. Although she loved Christopher dearly, on that occasion, her sympathy was with Khleo, someone she never met.

Amanda looked at Christopher and without saying a word, they both walked to the shore line to join Ebita. By then she had dried her eyes and was her smiling, ebullient self again.

"It is way past lunch time. We should break for lunch," Amanda said.

"Where around here can we eat?" Christopher asked.

"There is not a decent place here for us to sit down to lunch. We will have to go back to Pierreville or Plaisance."

"It would be wise for us to go to Plaisance."

"Why Christopher?" Amanda asked. She was thinking of taking them to Elaine's, her favorite restaurant located up on the Old Road.

"My car is parked in Plaisance," Christopher said.

"I can drop you off to where your vehicle is parked. Then you can meet me at Elaine's."

Christopher hesitated at first. He didn't think that he wanted to dine with Ebita where Snake and Khleo ate frequently. Eventually, after careful consideration, he conceded and said, "Okay."

"Then we have a plan," said Amanda. "Let's go."

THIRTY-FOUR

PAUL ARANGUEZ' HEALTH HAD IMPROVED considerably and he
resumed his idle, furtive ways. He and his older brother, Peter,
were always looked upon as unproductive citizens. Yet, they were
able to amass considerable wealth. That Wednesday afternoon,
while Christopher and Ebita joined Amanda at Elaine's for lunch,
Paul met his brother at *The Junction*, arguably, the best watering
hole in the nation. Before Paul's mishap with the viper, they met
there regularly. It was a place where local oral historians gathered.
Budding politicians assembled there. Those who thought they
knew it all gathered there, and so did those who knew nothing
at all.

It wasn't long before everyone present at the bar was offering
an opinion about the *staged kidnapping* of Khleo Karch. The
laconic Paul Aranguez contributed very little. That was not
because he had nothing of value to contribute. He was always a
quiet, reserved, and unassuming individual. During his training
as a police office he learnt that by keeping his mouth shut he can
always prevent self-incrimination. His loquacious brother, Peter,
though cautious, was more inclined to slip up at times and say
what he shouldn't.

When Christopher and his friends were seated at Elaine's, Ebita looked around and said, "This is a lovely little place."

"Yeah. Isn't it amazing how well we are doing all the way out here?" Amanda asked.

"It sure is. If you keep it up, this could be the fastest growing town in Trinidad and Tobago."

"It already is," said Christopher. "In 1970 the population was eight thousand. Today, it is forty thousand."

Neither Amanda nor Ebita questioned Christopher's statistical presentation. Ebita could not challenge the figures because she wasn't aware of the facts. She was visiting Mayaro for the first time. It is doubtful, however, whether she would have challenge Christopher in Amanda's presence even if the figures were familiar to her. Amanda knew the facts and realized that the statistics, as stated by Christopher, were not false. He simply quoted the figures for the entire county, instead of the stats that applied only to Mayaro proper. That is, the town of Pierreville and the surrounding villages.

After they placed their orders and the waitress left, Christopher inquired whether they would like to stop at *The Junction* after lunch.

"What's at *The Junction*? Ebita asked.

"*The Junction* is a bar and lounge," Amanda informed her.

"The best little bar and lounge in town," said Christopher smiling. "Perhaps it is the nation's best."

Ebita looked at Amanda puzzled, as if to ask, *is he for real?* Amanda smiled and shook her head in the affirmative.

"Would you come with us?" Ebita asked. She was smiling too. The question, and the manner in which it was asked, clearly placed Amanda in a quandary. She found Ebita to be very personable, and she and Christopher had been friends for a long time. However, Khleo Karch, who used to be Christopher's girlfriend was her best friend. It was a dilemma she would have preferred not to be faced with. Nevertheless, that was the situation and she had to make a choice. It would have been undesirable, no matter how she chose. She decided, therefore, to choose what she thought was the lesser of two evils and said, "Yes. I certainly would."

Christopher was stunned but Ebita was smiling happily. Her visit to Mayaro was turning out just fine. By then the waitress returned with a well chilled bottle of 1998 Bocce Pino Grigio. She looked at Amanda and said, "For our most valued patron and her friends.

"Oh! That's so sweet. Thank you."

"You are welcome."

The waitress left and Christopher said to Ebita, "She is special."

"Who? Amanda or the Server?" Ebita asked.

"Amanda , of course."

"I thought so since we met at Beau Sejour earlier this afternoon."

"Please stop guys. You are going to cause me to cry."

"That's not like you," said Christopher. "You have always been a strong, confident woman."

"Sensuous and emotional too it seems." Ebita said.

"Thanks for the compliment. Thank you Ebita for realizing that beneath the strength and confidence is a gentle, emotional woman. Now would you taste that wine, Christopher?"

"Oh, sure." said Christopher. He poured a little of the Pino Grigio into his glass, tasted it, nodded his head and said, "It's okay."

"Just okay?"

"It is complimentary, for Christ sake. Do you really expect it to be superb?"

"Okay is good enough."

The waitress returned with the orders and asked whether there was anything else that Amanda and her friends needed. There was nothing they needed or wanted. Amanda smiled and said, "We are fine. Thank you very much."

"You are welcome."

The trio enjoyed their meal while Amanda and Christopher discussed the progress they made in talking to people in the neighborhoods, and their strategy for questioning people they would continue to encounter along their assigned routes. Ebita listened attentively but refrained from making any comments or suggestions. She was happy in the company of Christopher and Amanda and was enjoying her visit to beautiful Mayaro. At that moment, nothing else mattered to her.

After lunch, over objections from Amanda, Christopher assumed responsibility for the check and gratuity. He tendered his credit card for payment, thanked the waitress, and the group left. They drove a short distance, about five minutes away, parked, and went directly to *The Junction*. There were not too many patrons there at 2:30 p.m. so they sat together on a large couch at a low, round table. There was a single armchair opposite to them at the same table.

Amanda and Christopher's chief reason for going to *The Junction*, was to observe, and when possible, speak with other customers. What they didn't know, was that they were being observed themselves. After a few minutes of viewing the sparse crowd, they left their seats to help themselves to some snacks and finger foods that were served buffet style under an ultraviolet light at one corner of the lounge. Upon their return, Peter Aranguez was sitting in the single armchair. He had a drink in one hand and a cigarette in the other. Christopher thought nothing of it but Amanda saw it as being intrusive, unmannerly, and rude. She said, "Excuse me, sir. That seat is occupied."

"Of course. I am sitting in it." said Peter. All the while his eyes were fixed on the stranger, Ebita. She was smiling but it was only because of her embarrassment and perhaps her effort to diffuse what she perceived could escalate into an ugly scene. Amanda, meanwhile, looked around for another vacant seating arrangement to which the group could have moved. However, she quickly and quietly decided against it, realizing that it might be construed as a snub at Mr. Aranguez.

Christopher was more accommodating when he said to Peter, "It is awfully quiet here today."

"Yeah. That is because it is Wednesday and the middle of the day too," said Peter. Then with his eyes still fixed on Ebita he asked Christopher, "Is this lovely lady your sister, Teach?"

"Oh no. This is Ebita, my ...." Without waiting for Christopher to say what he intended, Peter stretched out his hand to Ebita and said, "It is a pleasure to meet you. My name is Peter Aranguez. I know, I do not look Spanish. Ours is one of those original Mayaro surnames."

"That's nice," Ebita said.

"Nice accent! I can tell that you are not from these parts."

"I am not," Ebita said. At the same time she rested her head on Christopher's shoulder and looked at Amanda, as if to ask, *Doesn't he see that I am here with a gentleman?*

Amanda smiled for the first time since they returned to their seats and found Peter sitting there. She then said, "He cannot see Christopher. He is blinded by your stunning beauty. You should let him know though, that you are a prosecuting attorney. Maybe he can use your services."

Ebita was puzzled. Christopher was laughing, but Peter was not amused. He left immediately without saying another word. Christopher composed himself just enough to ask Amanda, "Girl! Why did you embarrass the dude?"

"I did not embarrass the man. He did it to himself with his bad manners. He and his dumb ass brother seem to think that they are God's gift to women. They have to be stopped."

"You stopped him in his tracks, for now at least."

"You also may have missed an opportunity to gather some valuable information about the *staged kidnapping,*" said Ebita. She could not have known it but she made a key statement. After all, no one knew more about the *staged kidnapping* than Peter Aranguez.

Amanda was not aware that Peter had plotted with Imp, the recently deceased vagabond, to do her harm. Suddenly though, she felt that he was just the type who would have tried something like that to gain a large sum of money quickly, easily, illegally, and without much sacrifice, to satisfy his greed and desire for the finer things of life that others acquired legitimately through hard work, education, business investments, or a combination of all of those. Suddenly she was feeling badly for having dismissed him with the veiled threat in her reference to Ebita being a prosecuting attorney. *How can I redeem myself?* She wondered. The opportunity presented itself almost immediately when the person sitting with Peter, or just sitting next to him at the bar, left.

"Excuse me," she said to Christopher and Ebita. Then without any explanation to her friends, she walked over to where Peter was sitting alone and said to him, "Do you mind if I sit down?"

"It's a free country. You can sit wherever you want."

"You are mad at me, aren't you?" Peter did not answer so Amanda said, "I am sorry. I just wanted you to know that the young lady was here with Christopher."

"I knew that."

"Then why were you trying to hit on her?"

"Is he married to her?"

"No."

"Is she married to someone else?"

"Not that I know of."

"Then she is free, single, and disengaged. The game is fair."

"No Peter. It is not a game. It is true that she is single but she is here as a guest of Christopher. It was rude of you to intrude on a private gathering."

"What private gathering? This is a public place. You were there. Weren't you?"

"I was there but clearly you weren't interested in me."

"Look Teach, I do not need a lecture from you."

Amanda realized that all school teachers in Mayaro were referred to as *Teach* in private or casual conversations. It occurred to her immediately that Peter was beginning to calm down. The anger he felt toward her a few moments earlier was subsiding. She saw an opportunity to engage him in conversation, with the possibility of deducing important information about the kidnapping. She believed, rightly or mistakenly, that people of disrepute are more likely than not to know about the terrible things that happened in the community. She was about to apply the art of skilful questioning she learnt in Teachers Training College to a wayward adult. She knew that she had to proceed with caution and exert extreme care not to give any hint of suspicion of anyone in particular. She glanced at Peter's glass. It was empty by then. Without asking him, she said to the server, "Can we have two more of the same?"

"Two scotch on the rocks?" the server asked.

"No! Sorry. One scotch on the rocks and one sauvignon blanc."

"You've got it."

"Are you buying me a drink?"

"Sure. Can't a lady buy a gentleman a drink?"

"Yeah! Yeah! Why not?" Peter was elated and patted Amanda on her back. She tried not to cringe although she thought that he was becoming too familiar too fast.

THIRTY-FIVE

KHLEO TRIED TO REACH AMANDA but couldn't. She then called Eli to ask how his interviews were going. It wasn't that she wanted to monitor Eli's progress. She was bored. Khleo Karch was a privileged young woman who had become accustomed to a small circle of friends. Meeting and greeting ordinary people, and being invited into their modest little homes to have coffee, tea, or a cold beverage was an education in itself for this young school teacher. She was graceful but not enjoying it. Eli Ebbs on the contrary, was basking in the hospitality. Khleo could hear the laughter and chatter in the background when Eli answered his cell phone, "Hello! Eli speaking."

"Eli. This is Khleo."

"Hey, girl! What's up?"

"Nothing spectacular," said Khleo. "I am down here in Lagon Doux where I met a young man who said that he observed some unusual activity where he had been hunting this morning."

"Just where was that?"

"Some place down here," said Khleo. "He pointed across the street away from the ocean and offered to take me there."

"Is he with you right now?"

"He is here but not with me," said Khleo. "He is speaking with someone. They are a few yards from where I am standing."

"Okay! Don't go anywhere with him until I get there."

"Where are you right now?"

"I think the area is called Chrysostom," said Eli. "Isn't that right Diamond?" Eli could be heard asking someone.

"How long will it take you to get here?" Khleo asked.

"I don't know but I am going to leave right away."

"Then I will see you soon."

It was early evening and *The Junction* was crowded with patrons. Peter Aranguez was his talkative self in his conversation with Amanda Flagg. The alcohol he consumed was taking its toll. He was talking a lot but in a very controlled manner so that he would not reveal what he knew about the *staged kidnapping*. Just as he had done previously in conversations with other drunk patrons, Peter placed the blame squarely on Khleo Karch. He absolved Amanda, probably because he was in her company and was becoming comfortable with her. She on the other hand, was not about to be so easy on him. That became evident when she asked, "What proof do you have Peter, that Khleo staged her own kidnapping?"

"Proof?" Peter could not think of, or fabricate any evidence.

"Yes! What have you witnessed that can prove her guilt."

"Nothing."

Then you shouldn't go around accusing people wrongfully," said Amanda. "How would you feel if you are being accused of this *staged kidnapping?*"

"I...I...I...cannot be held responsible for that." Peter was not known to have a speech impediment but he was stuttering. That caused Amanda to say, "You see! The mere suggestion of the possibility of someone accusing you, makes you very nervous."

"I am not nervous."

"So why is your hand shaking? Why the stammering?"

Before Peter could answer Amanda's last question, his cell phone rang. "Excuse me," he said and took the call. After saying goodbye to the caller, He said to Amanda, "Sorry. This is urgent. I have to go but we will continue this discussion another time."

"When?" Amanda asked with some urgency in her voice.

"I will call and let you know."

"How will you do that? You do not have my number."

"You will be surprised.........." Peter hurried out before saying what might surprise Amanda. She, however, conjectured that he might find a way to get her phone number, or perhaps he already had it. Was he being clever or was he cornered? The latter seemed to have been the case. The phone call he received was from his brother who was on his way to *The Junction*. It gave him the perfect excuse to leave. As it turned out, the timing of the call was just right. It saved Peter, for the time being at least, from self-incrimination in the *staged kidnapping.*

Eli arrived at Lagon Doux relatively quickly. Khleo was sitting in her rented car but stepped out when she looked in the rear-view mirror and saw that Amanda's car was approaching slowly. Eli was driving. The car stopped right behind hers and he came out.

"Did I keep you waiting long?" he asked.

"No. I occupied myself with a couple of magazines I brought with me."

"Good. Where is the young man?"

"He had to leave but he promised to be back soon."

As Khleo and Eli stood between the cars in conversation, the young man approached. He was in his early twenties, very tall, unshaven, and scruffy looking. That made him appear much older. When he reached where Khleo and Eli were standing, he introduced himself to Eli and asked, "Are you going with us?"

"Yes," said Eli. He wondered, however, *What could we be looking for in the forest. The kidnapping was staged, Khleo is safe. We are not looking for a victim. We are trying to find the perpetrator or perpetrators. We certainly would not find them in the forest of Lagon Doux.*

Eli was suspicious. Nevertheless, he and Khleo left their

vehicles parked and followed the young man up a narrow path that took them over an incline, and through a depressed coconut plantation. The land was undulating and rugged. Khleo was struggling, and so was Eli. The young man escorting them, however, made the journey effortlessly. After walking about half a mile, they ascended the third major hill, looked down beyond the valley below and saw a forested area.

"It's down there," the young man said as he pointed to the forest in the distance.

"That could be another mile's walk," Eli said.

"No," said the young man. "It is much less than that."

Khleo said nothing. She was too out of breath to speak. She was truly out of her comfort zone. Never before did she experience anything like it. She was aware that her father worked in the forest at one time or another, but she had no concept of what type of work was involved until they came upon several logs in the valley below.

"What are these for?" she asked.

"Those are timber, logs that are to be carted out to the sawmill and made into lumber."

"How many trees did they have to cut down to get this many logs?"

"A lot," said the young man. "One tree would yield two logs at most."

"My God! Do they ever replant the trees?"

"No conscious or organized effort is ever made to replant the trees. Everyone involved, consciously or unconsciously, depend on the natural dispersal of seeds to do that."

"What a shame," Khleo remarked.

Eli had no comment. He couldn't care less about the environment, trees, or other natural resources, renewable or non-renewable. He just wanted to see whatever they were going to see so he could have something to report to Amanda. Neither he nor Khleo was aware that Christopher and his new girlfriend were working with Amanda along her route.

They arrived at the area the young man wanted Khleo to see. It was a small clearing in the underbrush of the tropical rain forest that appeared as if something had been buried there.

"This is it," said the young man as they approached the spot. "It looks as if a treasure or a body could be buried there."

"Why would you think so?" Eli asked.

"My dog, Rex was sniffing and digging at it."

"Why didn't you dig it up?" Eli asked.

"There were a few reasons why I didn't."

"What could those have been?" Khleo asked.

"One, I only had a cutlass (machete) with me. Secondly, I was afraid that it might be a body."

"Why? No one has been reported missing in Mayaro," Eli commented.

"While that might be true, you must bear in mind that criminals take their kidnapped victims anywhere in this country and dispose of their bodies."

"You are afraid of the dead I presume."

"I am more afraid of being falsely accused."

Those statements from the young hunter and from Eli really frightened Khleo but they somehow invigorated Eli. "Let me borrow your cutlass. If this is a grave, it has to be a shallow one," he said.

"Suppose it's a buried treasure?" asked the young man.

"It probably will be buried at the same depth," Eli said.

The young hunter handed Eli the machete. He took it and immediately started digging up the suspicious area. It wasn't very long or very deep before the cutlass struck something hard. At first they all thought it might have been a rock. However, as Eli continued digging around the hard object, it wasn't long before human remains were revealed. Eli stopped digging and stood up. Khleo screamed and held onto him. The young man who took them to the scene was frozen with fear. Several seconds elapsed before anyone said a word. When someone eventually spoke, it was the young hunter who asked, "What do we do now?"

"Call the police," Eli said.

"*Mayaro* police?" Khleo asked.

"That's the only choice we have," Eli said.

"He is right," the young man said.

Khleo understood that there was no other recourse. She was skeptical nevertheless. Her own experience with the Mayaro police when her purse was stolen was terribly disappointing. Nevertheless, she said to Eli, "Let me use your phone." He handed her his cell phone and she dialed the local police station. Officer Sookram answered, "Hello. This is the Mayaro Police Station. Officer Sookram speaking."

"Good evening, sir. I am calling to report the discovery of human remains in a shallow grave."

"Who made that discovery?" Officer Sookram asked.

"We did," Khleo said.

"Who exactly are you referring to as we?"

"Two friends and I," Khleo said.

"What is your name, miss?"

"Khleo Karch, sir."

"The Khleo Karch! Formerly kidnapped victim. Or rather, victim of a kidnapping hoax?"

"Yes, sir."

For what seemed a very strange reason, Khleo was somewhat relieved by the questions Officer Sookram asked. One question in particular gave her the impression that she, at least, was now being considered as the victim of a kidnapping hoax by law enforcement. Before she had a chance to bask in the thought that she, and possibly Amanda no longer had to fear being hauled in by police, Officer Sookram asked, "Where are you right now?"

"We are in Lagon Doux." She looked at the others as if to ask, *is that correct?* The young man shook his head to indicate that she was right.

"Where exactly in Lagon Doux are you?"

"I couldn't say exactly where. However, our cars are parked together on the Guayaguayare Road." She described the vehicles and gave the officer the plate numbers. Then she said, "We walked from where the cars are parked straight up the hill until we entered the forest beyond the coconut plantation."

"Stay where you are. Two officers are coming out there right now."

"Do you want us to stay with the remains?"

"Yes." Before Khleo could think of anything else to ask Officer Sookram, he hung up the telephone.

THIRTY-SIX

AFTER PETER ARANGUEZ LEFT *THE Junction*, Amanda rejoined Christopher and Ebita on the couch. She felt somewhat dejected and was inclined to blame herself for being too aggressive in her approach to getting information from Peter that may have been pertinent to the *staged kidnapping*. "I think I might have pressed him too hard," she lamented.

"Whom do you think you pressed too hard?" Christopher asked.

"Peter Aranguez," she said.

"Were you conversing with that creep?"

"Yes. Why shouldn't I? Isn't that the reason we are out here?"

"It is true that we are here to meet and speak with people, but certainly not his type."

"I have to disagree with you Christopher. He is exactly the type we need to engage in conversation."

"People like him are less likely to reveal what they know."

"Why do you think so?" Amanda asked.

"There is an unwritten rule amongst rogues that information

that can aid in a criminal investigation should never be revealed to anyone other than those already involved."

"I have not heard that before. Although, there is a possibility you might be right."

Ebita felt that she had nothing to contribute to the discussions but listened intently. She found the arguments for and against speaking with everyone to be very interesting. She thought, however, that if she had to choose, she would have sided with Amanda. *The people you refuse to speak with may just be the ones with the information you need most*, she thought. Whether or how one got them to reveal that information would have been dependent upon the individual's approach. Christopher was firm, direct, and to the point. He asked exactly what he wanted to know. Amanda on the contrary, was deliberate but charming. She smiled, pampered and cajoled the men she spoke with. Somehow that did not work quite so well with Peter Aranguez. When speaking with women, Amanda took a different approach. She was relaxed, friendly, talkative, but flexible. She strayed from the topic whenever she found it convenient.

While Amanda was having those exchanges with Christopher, her cell phone rang. She answered. It was Khleo calling to explain the situation they were in while waiting for the police to arrive. Amanda couldn't understand why Khleo and Eli had that predicament in the first place. Nevertheless, she listened attentively to what Khleo had to say. Ultimately, she agreed, as did Khleo, that the choice was clear. They had to stay with the human remains in Lagon Doux until the police arrived.

Amanda suggested that at the end of the day the group would gather at Khleo's place to compare notes and propose any future plans. What she didn't say, was that Christopher and his new girlfriend were with her. She also neglected to inform Christopher that they all will gather at Khleo's by day's end.

Khleo was still on the telephone with Amanda when the Mayaro police arrived in the area of Lagon Doux where she, Eli, and the young hunter were with the human remains. Surprisingly enough, there were four officers with two trained dogs instead of the two law men Officer Sookram had suggested would arrive.

The officers unearthed the remains completely and contacted the Medical Examiner's Office. That office immediately dispatched a crew to retrieve the remains for identification, including DNA testing. In the interim, before the Medical Examiner's crew arrived, the police officers questioned Khleo, Eli, and the young hunter.

The senior officer who originally questioned Eli in connection with Khleo's supposed disappearance, looked at him and said, "You look very familiar. Aren't you Mr. Ebbs?"

"Yes, sir. Eli Ebbs is my name."

"What are you mixed up in now?"

The question bothered Eli. He was dreadfully afraid of getting into trouble with the law again, so he answered cautiously, "We stumbled on this corpse while investigating the staged kidnapping of Miss Khleo Karch."

"I thought it was decided that there was no culpability on her part."

"No one informed us of that, sir."

"So you have taken it upon yourself to investigate? Since when are you with law enforcement anyway?" the senior officer asked.

"I am not with law enforcement, and neither are my friends. We are acting on our own as private citizens."

"That's fine as long as you act within the realm of the laws of the land. What we are looking at here appears to be a serious criminal act. I do hope that none of you is involved, and perhaps revisiting the scene of the crime."

Once again a statement from a police officer frightened Khleo. She huddled close to Eli as her arms and legs shook nervously. That prompted the officer to ask, "Who are you?"

"Khleo Karch, sir."

"Is it that controversy simply follows you? Or are you a magnet for trouble?"

Khleo was afraid. She did not answer but her fear did not go unnoticed by the officers as they continued their work. They secured the site as a crime scene after the Medical Examiner's crew had taken pictures and removed the remains. Khleo, Eli, and the youngster who made the discovery, were advised to leave the scene, but not before the officers got their names, proper identification, and personal contacts.

As they made their way back to the Mayaro/Guayaguayare Road, Eli's cell phone rang. He answered, "Hello!"

"Eli! This is Amanda," the caller said.

"Hey, Amanda! What are you up to?"

"I want to suggest that we meet at Khleo's this evening at six o'clock."

"Does she know that?"

"Not yet. As you know, I have no way of contacting her directly."

"She is right here."

"Where?"

"With me in Lagon Doux."

"Why are you still there? That is her assigned route."

"It is a long story. One you will find to be very interesting once you hear it this evening."

"Okay. Then let me speak with Khleo."

"Sure." Eli handed the telephone to Khleo and said, "It's Amanda."

The two women spoke briefly and agreed that they would meet that evening at six o'clock. Amanda did not tell Khleo that she was with Christopher and his friend, Ebita. She felt certain that Christopher would not have cared much about joining them at Khleo's place. She did not know though, how Khleo felt about the possibility of having Christopher and Ebita visit her.

That evening Peter Aranguez made a desperate attempt to prevent his brother , Paul, from visiting the local establishment known as *The Junction*. His concern was that Amanda Flag, the school teacher investigating false accusations against Khleo Karch and herself might attempt to question his brother. Paul, however, was having none of it. He was feeling much better after being bitten by a venomous snake, and he had no intention of staying at home alone. *The Junction* was the logical choice of a place to go for entertainment and companionship. Peter's concern was that for some individuals in town, alcohol acted as a truth serum. His brother was one of those; a normally quiet, and reserved man who became extremely talkative and brutally honest when drunk.

After his failed attempts to get his brother to stay at home, Peter Aranguez agreed to return to *The Junction* with him. He didn't know that Amanda, Christopher, and Ebita had already left the Place. His concern was that Amanda's aggressive questioning technique might be too much for Paul to endure in the physical and emotional state he was in. What Peter did not realize was that Paul had improved considerably since he was bitten by the fer-de-lance.

It wasn't long after they arrived at the bar and lounge that the *staged kidnapping* was mentioned. To the press and other news media that subject was no longer news worthy. It had been abandoned in favor of current breaking news stories. The bar patrons, however, did not let the story rest. It was the biggest news coming out of Mayaro in years.

Peter Aranguez was sober and controlled. He was determined to stay that way. He had a few drinks earlier that evening and decided that, regardless of how long he and his brother stayed at the bar, one drink had to suffice. With that in mind, he ordered a round of drinks for his brother, two friends, and himself. They sat at the bar, drank their liquor, and took turns ordering drinks. After the third drink, one of the patrons whom the locals knew only as Melwish, noticed that Peter wasn't drinking and asked, "What is the matter, Peter?"

"Nothing man, nothing at all."

"It seems as if something is bothering you."

"Me? No. Why do you think so?"

"I know you, man. You are not yourself today." Peter did not respond to that. He was fixated on his brother's behavior and what he might say. Anytime Paul spoke, Peter interrupted. It became obvious that he didn't want Paul to speak. At one point Melwish asked, "Why wouldn't you allow the man to speak for himself?" Once again, Peter ignored the question, so Melwish continued, "It looks to me as if you are afraid he would say something you do not want us to hear."

"I had enough of your shit. We are out of here, Paul," Peter said and got up to leave. He expected Paul to follow him as has always been the case; whatever Peter did, Paul imitated. That day, to Peter's disappointed, was different. "You can leave. I am not going anywhere," Paul said. Peter sat down again.

THIRTY-SEVEN

AMANDA, CHRISTOPHER, AND EBITA LEFT The Junction long before Peter Aranguez returned there with his brother. They had gone to Amanda's place earlier but six o'clock was fast approaching and Amanda was preparing to meet with Khleo and Eli at Khleo's home. She invited Christopher and Ebita to join her but wasn't disappointed when Christopher politely declined. He and Ebita returned to his parents' home for dinner while Amanda proceeded to Khleo's. She arrived there at the same time that Khleo and Eli returned from Lagon Doux. They exchanged greetings as Khleo unlocked her door and invited them in.

As soon as they were seated, Amanda remarked, "You had a very exciting day, I would imagine."

"You do have a vivid imagination. Although, I am not sure that exciting is the word that best describes our day," said Khleo. "Dramatic is more like it."

"Dramatic is right," Eli said.

"Yeah! For a while I thought that we were going to be interrogated by the police."

"Why?" asked Amanda.

"One officer suggested that either controversy follows me, or I was a magnet for trouble."

"He did not suggest that, Khleo. He simply asked."

"Whatever! I was intimidated to say the least."

"Everything frightens you, Khleo," Eli said.

"So I am a coward. What else is new?"

"Okay! You had a dramatic sort of day but did you uncover any new evidence pertinent to our case?" Amanda asked.

"We did not. Did you?" Eli asked.

"In fact, we did find something that may shed some light on the case."

"Good! We have been in the dark too long," said Khleo. She then asked, "What is it?"

"Your cell phone." Amanda took the water-damaged cell phone from her pocket and handed it to Khleo.

"Oh my God! Where did you find this?"

"Christopher did."

"Where?"

"On the beach in Beau Sejour."

Khleo fidgeted with the phone for a while, then she tried to dial someone's number. Nothing happened. She tried again, using a different phone number but got the same result; nothing.

"Do you really expect that damn thing to work?" Amanda asked.

"I was hoping that it would."

"Girl! You are pathetic."

"Stop! Please!" Eli shouted. "I have been thinking," he said.

"That's all you ever do, think," Amanda said.

"Well, let him express his thoughts. His ideas might be good but you'll never know otherwise," Khleo said.

"Thank you," Eli said.

Amanda hissed her teeth in disgust. *He never has anything to offer,* she thought but sat back to listen. Khleo too was eager to hear what Eli had to say.

"I do recall Peter Aranguez asking me if Khleo had a cell

phone," Eli said in response to Khleo's statement. Nevertheless, he looked directly at Amanda as he spoke. She quickly sat up to listen. Then she asked, "When was this?"

"Just before you went away for the weekend. In fact, it was the day before Khleo's purse was snatched from her."

"That creep! No wonder he became so nervous when I questioned him at *The Junction*"

"Why was he interested in my cell phone?"

"Right now we do not know. We will soon find out though," said Amanda.

"How?" Khleo asked.

"I would be speaking with Peter again," said Amanda. "In the mean time, tell us, what else he ask you Eli."

"He wanted to know how much she paid for the phone, and where she generally kept it."

"Huh," murmured Amanda. "The first may be irrelevant. The second question; *where she generally keeps it?* definitely has some bearing on the mugging incident."

"You are so right," said Eli. "I do remember telling him that I thought Khleo kept her phone in her purse."

"Yeah! Unfortunately, you had no way of knowing what he was up to."

"Are you suggesting that Peter stole my cell phone?" Khleo asked.

"We all know that the physical act of snatching your purse and removing the phone was perpetrated by someone younger. That young man, however, was paid to commit what initially appeared to be a petty crime."

"Now it seems that we have been speaking with the wrong people," Khleo said.

"You do have a valid point," said Eli. "We should have been engaging a much younger crowd from the beginning."

"You may be right. We will soon find out," Amanda said.

"Do you think Peter paid the young man to do that?" Khleo asked.

"Directly or indirectly, Peter Aranguez was involved," said Amanda. "How? That is what we must find out."

"You speak as if you are quite certain."

"I am not absolutely sure but I intend to prove without a doubt that he was responsible."

While Amanda was speaking, her cell phone rang. It was Christopher calling. She answered, "Hey, Christopher!" Before Amanda could say another word, Khleo walked away. She went to her bedroom and closed the door behind her. Eli rolled his eyes as if to ask, *what's up with her?* Amanda ignored them both and continued speaking with Christopher.

"Have you made any progress?" he asked.

"Amazingly, that telephone you found on the beach this afternoon might present the break we were hoping for."

"That is great news," said Christopher. "It is now up to us to act on it."

"I am going to see to it that we do."

"I know you will, Amanda. I know you will."

"We will, Christopher. This is a cooperative effort."

Amanda was contemplating how she could get Peter Aranguez to sit down face to face with her in conversation. She turned to Eli and asked, "What does he like to talk about?"

"Who is he?" Eli asked.

"Peter, of course."

"I don't know him well enough to say unequivocally."

"Come on now, Eli. I am not asking you to tell me without any doubt. You have spent more time in his company than any of us. You had to have made some observations."

"Do you set out to observe people's demeanor, choice of conversational topics and other preference whenever you speak with them?"

"I never set out to do that but when I am in the company of most individuals, I do. You have associated with Peter, even if briefly, you had to have observed something about him."

"Well, I did notice that he belittles his brother, even though he does it in jest."

"There you go. That's something," said Amanda. "What else did you observe?"

"Huh, He likes to talk about women and money."

"Does he speak about all women?"

"No," said Eli. "Actually, he looks at beautiful women and makes nasty comments."

"Do you think he hates women?"

"No."

Amanda did not question Eli any further. She heard as much as she needed to hear and decided to act on that information immediately. She turned to Khleo and said, "Get your tape recorder and come with me. I have a plan."

"What now?" Khleo asked.

Before Amanda could answer Khleo's question, Eli said, "You are not planning to go missing for another three or four days. Are you?"

"No. Nothing like that," said Amanda. "Come on Khleo. Let's go."

Khleo grabbed the tape recorder from where it was on the dining room table and on the way out said to Eli, "I will see you later." She did not know where Amanda was taking her or what they were about to do, so she could not tell Eli when she would be back. She suspected that whatever they were about to undertake had something to do with Amanda's obsession with solving the *staged kidnapping* case, a case law enforcement had obviously abandoned.

As soon as they entered Amanda's rented car and buckled themselves in, she started the vehicle and sped off. Within minutes they arrived at her place. She parked and rushed in. Khleo followed and asked in an astonished sort of way, "What's up now, Amanda?"

"This is when we get a chance to put our investigative skills to work."

"What investigative skills?"

"It's called charm, Khleo. Have you forgotten."

"I hope you are not trying anything that would get us both killed."

"No. We are going to entertain Mr. Peter Aranguez in a way he has never been entertained before."

"What?"

"You heard me. Brew some coffee. Then put that bottle of scotch and the bottle of sherry on the coffee table," said Amanda. She pointed to a mini bar in her living room. Then she said, "Also, put two glasses on a tray while you are at it."

"Am I your damn maid and butler?"

"No, girl. You are only helping out while I take a quick shower," Amanda said as she left the room.

Khleo did what she was asked and sat back. She checked the voice activated tape recorder to be sure it was in good working condition. It was. So she turned on the television, crossed her legs, and surfed the channels to see whether there was anything worthy of looking at. There wasn't in her opinion. She turned off the TV. By then Amanda came out looking radiant and ravaging in a low cut baby blue satin dress. The hem was just above her knees and she was not wearing hoses or stockings.

"Where are you going dressed so salaciously?" Khleo asked.

"What is wrong with you, girl?" asked Amanda. "I wore this to Kelna's wedding and everybody loved it."

"I know. I was there. That was a wedding and all of the other women were similarly dressed."

"So?"

"So right now you are at home. What is the point."

"It is all part of the charm, girl," said Amanda. "Just look and learn."

"I am supposed to sit here in t-shirt and jeans and look at you dressed to kill while you and Peter converse."

"No. That is not the plan."

"Just what is the plan?"

"As of now, Peter and I will be lounging here in the living room. You will be in the bedroom with the tape recorder placed just behind the door. You would have to be quiet though. No TV channel surfing until he leaves."

"Did I hear you say lounging in the living room?"

"Yes."

"How quiet can I be? Suppose I want to sneeze?"

"You cannot."

"What?"

"You heard me. Stifle it if you feel the urge."

"That sounds as if I am going to be incarcerated"

"It will only be for a short while."

"Suppose he doesn't want to leave? What then?"

"Don't be so pessimistic, Khleo. Everything is going to be just fine."

"What time will he be here?"

"I don't know yet. I have to call him."

Khleo started laughing at Amanda's last statement. Then she said, "You are funny, truly funny, girl."

"There is nothing funny about this, Khleo."

"Suppose when you make the call, he tells you that he has other plans. Then what will you do?"

"Change my clothes I guess," said Amanda. "What would I lose?"

"Nothing, I guess."

"There you have it." Amanda said. Just then her cell phone rang. She answered, "Hello!"

"Amanda, dear. This is Peter."

"Oh! How are you Peter?" asked Amanda, but before Peter Aranguez could answer. She said, "I see you did manage to get my number." Khleo started to snicker, so Amanda placed her right index finger across both of her lips to indicate to Khleo that she should remain silent.

"I told you I would," he said

"That's great. You are really good"

Peter was smiling and feeling proud of himself. Amanda suspected that and thought it was just the right moment to invite him over, so she asked, "What are you doing this evening, honey?"

Peter smiled, pumped his right fist in the air and said joyfully, "Nothing really."

"How would you like to share a drink?"

"With you....? Anytime baby," he said stammering. Then he asked, "Where are you?"

"I am at home."

"Would you like to meet at *The Junction*?"

Amanda paused, pretending to think about Peter's suggestion for a while. Then she said, "You can meet me at home if you like."

"At what time?"

"I just got home. You can come now if you wish."

"I'll be right over."

"See you then. Bye." They both hung up.

THIRTY-EIGHT

WHEN EBITA AND CHRISTOPHER RETURNED to his parents' home in Ste Marguerite that evening after leaving Amanda's, Ebita met Mr. Standford Boyz, Christopher's father, for the first time. He had been busy with his responsibilities at work, trying to complete assignments and meet deadlines. As a result, he left home very early and returned late. Ebita was as happy to meet Mr. Boyz as he was ecstatic about meeting her, and he made no secret of it.

"I was looking forward to this day as soon as I heard that you were expected to visit Mayaro. I am truly happy to meet you," he said.

"I am very pleased to meet you, sir," said Ebita. "Christopher told me so much about you."

"I am surprised. Generally, he speaks mostly about his mother."

"Oh, he is so very proud of you too."

He is a good boy." said Mr. Boyz. Although Ebita had heard the reference to a grown man as boy in Trinidad before, she was no less taken aback by it. However, she did not comment and Mr. Boyz continued, "Why couldn't he have met you years ago?"

He did, she thought but didn't express it. Instead, she said, "We have had time to get to know each other very well."

"Better late than never," Mr. Boyz said.

Christopher smiled at his father's comment. That prompted the old man to ask, "Do you think that's funny?"

"No, Dad. I just...."

"You just what? Don't you think it is time for you to associate with someone whose parents will not object to that association?" There was no response from Christopher and that statement from his father took Ebita by surprise. Christopher had never told her that Khleo's parents had objected to their relationship. She thought of telling Mr. Boyz, *that could not happen in our case, sir. My parents are dead.* She refrained because Mr. Boyz was speaking directly to his son and not to her. Christopher did not follow up on the discussion. So his father said, "This family welcomes you, child."

"Thank you, sir."

Stanford Boyz had a bold and direct manner of speaking that was very unlike that of his wife or his son. That no doubt, intimidated Ebita. She was reluctant to speak in his presence until he said, "We as a family would always cherish you my dear."

"Thank you, sir," said Ebita. "My parents would never have objected to a fine young man like Christopher."

"Would never have....?" Mr. Boyz questioned.

"Yes, sir. My parents are deceased." Ebita told Mr. Boyz what Christopher already knew. He was surprised and genuinely concerned about what he heard and said, "I am so sorry. You seem so young to have lost both your parents. How are your brothers and sisters handling this?"

"I am an only child, sir."

"Oh my!" exclaimed Mr. Boyz. "Christopher is our only child too."

Ebita was discovering that in spite of his gruff, bold, direct and deliberate manner of speaking, Mr. Stanford Boyz was indeed a concerned and caring individual, much like his son,

Christopher. Uncertain as to what else he should ask, Mr. Boyz said, "Obviously you were on your way out and here I am holding you up. Go, enjoy yourselves. There will be plenty of time for us to talk."

"We weren't going anywhere special," said Christopher. "Ebita wanted to see the flares that are off shore."

"Christopher! You know that we have always discouraged you from going to the beach at nights. Now you are attempting to go there with a beautiful young woman at your side."

Christopher smiled and said, "We will be okay, Dad."

"Okay is not good enough. Where do you plan to enter the beach?"

"At Eccles Road in Grand Lagoon."

"Alright! Go ahead. I will get Liz and come out there to make sure you are safe."

"Thanks, Dad," said Christopher as he and Ebita got into his SUV for the drive over to Grand Lagoon Beach.

Christopher knew that his father's concern was for Ebita. His offer to get Mrs. Elizabeth Boyz and go down to the beach just to be sure that they were safe, was his way of showing that he cared, and not just saying it. Christopher had no objection, and neither did Ebita. They drove out of the driveway and headed to Grand Lagoon. When they arrived at the beach, the flares were visible from where they parked. At any other time, Christopher would have left the vehicle and walked with Ebita on the beach. That night, however, his father's words, *Christopher! You know that we always discouraged........"* kept ringing in his ears. For the first time he felt afraid and decided to sit in the truck. A few minutes later, he looked in the rearview mirror and saw the headlights of another vehicle approaching behind them. He became very anxious. His heart was racing but he was determined to stay calm and not cause Ebita any anxiety. Soon the car stopped directly behind his. Only then did he realize that it was his parents' car. As promised, his father had driven his mother there. "Is everything okay?" Mr. Boyz asked the couple when he stepped out of his car and approached their's.

"Yes, Dad."

"We will stick around for a few minutes. Please call us when you leave here."

"Sure thing. Thank you, Dad."

Mr. Boyz returned to his car. Backed up the vehicle about twenty feet, parked it, and turned the lights off. "Are you comfortable, Liz?" he asked his wife.

"I would prefer to be in my bed."

"Okay! We are leaving in a few minutes. Are you upset?"

"No. Why?"

"The manner in which you spoke caused me to ask."

"I was only wondering, how long do you think you can continue to protect him? He is grown. You have to let go."

"That is something I would have to learn to do. After all, he is our only child."

Ebita, meanwhile, turned to Christopher and said, "You Dad is very protective of you."

Christopher chuckled and said, "I think this time he is being protective of you."

She realized that Christopher did not deny that his father was very protective of him. She understood the behavior very well and said, "My father was just like that toward me. Everyone said I was sheltered. I, however, felt imprisoned. I was very surprised and relieved when I was accepted to the university and he allowed me to attend."

"Parents do shelter their daughters. At least, the more proactive ones do."

"I realized that early in life and always wondered whether the same was true when the only child was male. Now I know."

"Do not rush to publish that theory. It may not be true of all parents."

Ebita started laughing. Before her laughter stopped,

Christopher looked in his rearview mirror and saw that his parents were gone.

"We are alone," he said. He expected Ebita to be happy about that. To her though, it was not particularly significant. Perhaps because she had grown accustomed to being alone with Christopher during the week prior. She turned to him and said, "These lights are pretty but without a camera, I think I have had just about enough of them."

"Would you like to stroll the beach," asked Christopher. "You may get a better view of the flares."

"Didn't your father caution you about walking on the beach with a beautiful young woman at night?"

"Yes! I know. He really swelled your head." said Christopher. Then he looked at his watch and said, "It is only six forty-five. Technically, it is still evening"

"Evening or not, it is dark. I do not want to walk out there."

"It isn't completely dark out there. The flares do provide some light."

"Please, Christopher. Let's just go home."

"Okay."

"We should stop at your parents' and let them know."

"Somehow I thought you were referring to my parents' place as home."

"How could you?" asked Ebita. "In the first place, you do not live there. Secondly, Everything I brought with me is at your place."

"Oh. I am sorry, darling. I forgot. Let's go."

Christopher and Ebita left the Grand Lagoon Beach area. On their way to the Mayaro/Guayaguayare Road, Christopher called his parents' home and his mother answered.

"Hey, Mom! It's Christopher," he said.

"What are you up to now, son?"

"Ebita and I will return to Pierreville. She needs to get a change of clothing."

"Does that mean that you will not be here for dinner?"

Christopher paused and mumbled the word *dinner* to Ebita who shrugged her shoulders and asked, "What can we say? Yes!"

"We will be there , Mom," Christopher said.

"At what time?"

"Seven-thirty."

"Okay. Seven-thirty is fine."

"See you then, Mom," said Christopher. He turned to Ebita and said, "We should get dressed and still take a change of clothing with us."

"You are right. We can save a great deal of time if something new comes up in the morning."

"Okay!"

Just then Christopher's telephone started ringing. Ebita was sitting next to it, so Christopher asked, "Will you please answer that?"

"Sorry! No, sir." said Ebita. She immediately remembered what happened in Tobago when she answered his phone while they were on their way from Charlotte Ville to Plymouth. Christopher was left with one choice. He leaned over, picked up the phone and said, "Hello!"

"Christopher! This is Khleo," the caller said. She was barely audible, and at first Christopher did not recognize her voice. Eventually he did and asked, "Why are you whispering?"

"It's a long story. I cannot speak freely now. I will call you back." She hung up abruptly. Christopher removed the telephone from his left ear, looked at it and said, "What the hell!" He was looking at Ebita as if expecting a comment from her. She was silent. So, they moved on with their plan and started putting together the clothing they intended to take with them to his parents' place that evening. Christopher, however, was uneasy. His mood and demeanor changed after he received that phone call and Ebita sensed it. He did not say who the caller was or what the call was about but he seemed concerned and that bothered her. As she thought of the water damaged cell phone belonging to Khleo Karch that they found on the beach, and their encounter with Peter Aranguez at *The Junction*, she suddenly realized that she too had become involved in the investigative process she had cautioned Christopher about. She viewed the situation as dangerous. That frightened her but she resisted the temptation to ask Christopher; *who called?* or whether it was a threatening phone call. *If it is something I should know, I trust that he would tell me,* she thought.

THIRTY-NINE

PETER ARANGUEZ HAD ARRIVED AT Amanda's home in Plaisance sooner than she expected. He was very uncomfortable at first, so she tried to allay his anxieties by attempting to appear at ease and relaxed in his presence. She ushered him to a seat on the couch in the living room and he sat down at the right end opposite the door. He was obviously nervous as he fidgeted with a gold ring on the pinkie of his right hand. Amanda suggested that he relax and have a drink. He did not respond. However, she recalled that he drank scotch on the rocks while at *The Junction*.

"Can I pour you a scotch on ice?" she asked. He nodded in agreement, so Amanda poured the drink for him and poured a glass of sherry for herself. She handed Peter his drink and lifted her glass to his in a celebratory manner and said, "Cheers!" Peter smiled for the first time since he arrived there, and he responded, "Cheers!"

Khleo was beginning to feel sleepy from lying down with nothing to do. She was becoming bored. She sat up and wondered, *Why wouldn't those two converse?* Suddenly laughter emanated from the living room and the voice activated tape recorder behind the door clicked softly. She smiled and laid back. She could hear Amanda's chatter but Peter was subdued and she became concerned that Amanda's plan might just be an exercise in futility. *I could have spent my time doing something worthwhile,* she thought. Suddenly, more laughter came from the living room. Both Amanda and Peter were laughing loudly. The TV was on softly, so Khleo had no way of knowing whether they were laughing at something that was being aired ,or whether they had simply bonded and found that they had more in common than either previously thought. Then she heard Amanda ask, "Did you really think so?"

"Yes! In fact, at first I thought you might have authored the script to execute such a caper," Peter said.

"That was not a lighthearted adventure. You know that. Don't you?" asked Amanda. "How much money was extorted from Mr. Karch? I forgot now."

"I heard it was five hundred thousand TT dollars."

"You thought that Khleo and I could have pulled that off?"

"I certainly did."

Peter did not count his ill gotten gain before burying it in the Trinity Hill Nature Preserve. There just wasn't enough time to do that and get his brother the urgent medical care he needed after he was bitten by a venomous snake. Five hundred thousand dollars was his original demand. He assumed, therefore, that 500,000.00 was the amount delivered.

"Let me pour you another drink," said Amanda. She did not wait for Peter's response before placing more ice in his glass and pouring more scotch. Then she poured a little more wine in her glass. She had only sipped the sherry. Therefore, very little more could have been poured into the glass. She then asked, "How could you have assumed that Khleo and I were capable of ripping off her father when the *staged kidnapper's* voice was that of a man?"

"Was it? I... I didn't know that." Peter stammered to deliver that lie.

"How could you not know, when the crime was reported in every newspaper and on television?"

"I don't pay attention to the news."

"Oh, I am sorry. I forgot that you are a busy man."

"Are you trying to be funny now?" Peter asked. That was when she decided to take a gentler but more direct approach, depending on how one looks at it. "No, sweetie. Why would I want to be funny with you?" asked Amanda. "I thought we were here to enjoy the evening together?"

"I thought so too."

"Now, you don't think that it's going well. Do you, sweetie?"

There was no response from Peter, so Amanda moved closer to him on the couch and asked, "Is that any better?"

Once again, there was no verbal response from him. He simply smiled and placed his left hand on her right thigh on an area just above her knee from where her mini-skirted silk dress had risen. Amanda smiled too but it wasn't genuine. *Am I taking this too far?* she wondered, but made no effort to remove Peter's warm hand from where it rested. Instead she asked, "Would you like to have some cake?"

"That might be nice."

"What's your preference?"

"What do you have?"

"I have black cake *(a type of fruit cake)* and I have sponge *(pound)* cake."

"I would prefer the black cake."

"Will you excuse me for a moment?"

Peter said nothing in response, but he lifted his hand from her thigh. She got up, went to the kitchen, and returned with a dessert-type plate containing several slices of black cake.

Peter was still playing with the ring on his pinkie when Amanda served him the cake. She noticed his uneasiness and asked, "What's the matter, Peter? Are you unable to relax here?" He did not answer the question but he did say that the cake was good. She informed him that she baked it herself, and that making pastries was her favorite pastime. Then she asked, "What do you like to do in your spare time?"

"Spare time?" he asked.

I forgot that all you have is spare time. You do not have a job. Amanda thought, but she said, "Yes. Seriously, what do you do for fun?"

"I like to hunt and go deep sea fishing."

"Do you have dogs?"

Peter's eyes sparkled. Amanda was delighted. She had found something to talk about that was of interest to him. However, she constantly reminded herself why she invited him over to her home in the first place. Her strategy then, was to steer the conversation toward the things Peter liked to do and talk about, and frequently veer to what he does for a livelihood.

"I have a guard dog and a couple of hunting dogs." Peter said in answer to Amanda's question.

"What's the difference?"

"We never take the guard dog into the forest."

"That's it? Aren't there certain characteristics that make hunting dogs more suitable for what they do?" The question puzzled Peter. He had no knowledge of DNA or genes and was unable to offer a scientific explanation for the abilities of the canines he owned. *Where is she going with that?* He wondered but reluctantly said, "Yes."

"So what are some of those characteristics?"

"For one thing, the guard dog is vicious. The hunters just hunt."

"Did you have the dogs with you when Paul was bitten by the Fer-de-lance?"

"No."

"Why not?"

"We were not hunting."

"Then what were you doing in that snake infested forest reserve?"

"We were hiking. Is that against the law?"

"No, but it is common knowledge that the forested Trinity Hills are teeming with poisonous snakes."

"We didn't know that."

"Every child in Guayaguayare knows that."

"We are not from Guayaguayare and we are not children."

I know. A couple of dumb asses are what you are, Amanda thought but said, "You needed Petrotrin's permission to be there though."

"We had permission," Peter said. He didn't say it was Petrotrin's permission but that was what Amanda assumed.

"I think those dogs would have alerted you of the snake."

"Maybe."

"You may never want to hike in that forest again," she suggested.

"I would not say never."

"Do you mean that you are willing to take such risks again?"

"I may have to."

"Why?"

"Who knows?"

You are either incredibly stupid, or you have some vested interest in there, like Mr. Karch's money, Amanda thought but asked, "Will you take me with you if you ever decided to go hiking there again?"

"Are you out of your mind?"

"Why? Don't you think girls can do what boys can do?"

Khleo who was in the bedroom listening to the exchanges between Amanda and Peter was snickering softly. She was not suspicious of him but Amanda was. Although Peter was careful enough not to reveal anything to Amanda that could be self-incriminating, she was satisfied that if the tape recorder worked properly they would have captured Peter's voice which, hopefully, Mr. and Mrs. Karch would have been able to identify as the caller who demanded the ransom payment for the *stage kidnapping* of their daughter.

To Amanda's delight, Peter helped himself to another drink,

his third. He also had some more of her black cake. *He might be hungry. If we had an opportunity to dine together, he just might talk a lot more,* she thought. She pinned her hopes on an old adage in Mayaro, *a parrot talks most when it is well fed.* With that in mind, she asked Peter if he had dinner. Her hope was that he would say no. That would have given her the opportunity to suggest that he stayed a while and she would have ordered dinner. What she didn't know was that Peter was becoming wary of her line of questioning. He looked at his watch and said, "It is wonderful being here with you but it's getting late."

"Late for what or for whom? You live alone and I live alone," she said.

"What the hell is wrong with her?" asked Khleo of herself softly. "What would she do if he decides to stay?"

Fortunately though, Peter said, "While it is not that late for two single people, I have some important things to take care of."

Yeah! Right! Count Mr. Karch's money perhaps, she thought. Then she said to Khleo's relief, "Oh, Peter! It was so nice to have you. I hope we can do this again soon."

"I hope so too. Tomorrow maybe?" he asked with a broad smile on his face.

"We'll see how the day goes."

"Okay!"

Peter got up to leave and Amanda stood up with him. They walked toward the door, they hugged, but when Peter attempted to kiss her, she turned and offered him her cheek. He kissed her there. Then he said, "I am a tad disappointed."

"Don't be, hon," said Amanda. "This is only our first date. We have all the time in the world for more."

"Good night."

"Have a good night, Peter."

He walked down the step, turned around, smiled, and blew her a kiss. She reciprocated and closed the door when he drove off. "Wow!" She exhaled with great relief.

Khleo rushed out of the bedroom exuberantly, "Girl! Do you think you pulled it off?" she asked.

"What was I supposed to accomplish again?"

Khleo laughed and said, "Don't tell me that you are falling for that creep."

"No, girl."

"Oh, I was beginning to wonder how far you were prepared to take that needs thing you spoke about last weekend."

"I may take it very far but not with him. Trust me on that."

"I am willing to bet that he is not thinking like that."

"He may not right now, but very soon he will." there was a brief period of silence when both women said nothing. Then Amanda said, "Let's hear the tape." Khleo pressed the play button and they listened. When the recording ended, Amanda asked, "Do you think we have something here?"

"Besides having your conversation on tape, I don't know," Khleo said.

"Okay! We will listen to it again tomorrow."

FORTY

AFTER LISTENING TO THE TAPE recording of Peter Aranguez' voice the next morning, Khleo and Amanda agreed that they should listen to it again together with Khleo's parents, Eli, and possibly Christopher and Ebita. For some reason which Khleo herself could not explain, she was eager to meet Ebita. Amanda seemed unable to stop talking about how pretty and smart she was, and that perhaps heightened Khleo's interest.

Right after they had breakfast, Khleo called her parents to ask whether it was okay for her, Amanda, and a few others to visit later that day. Amanda called Christopher and invited him and Ebita to join them. He politely declined. He said that they had plans to visit the under water volcano off shore in Ortoire. Amanda tried unsuccessfully to convince him that the meeting time could be arranged to their convenience. He, however, was having none of it. He had absolutely no desire to be in the company of Eli, Khleo, or her parents, especially her father. He also did not want to place Ebita in a situation that would have caused any uneasiness or embarrassment.

Mr. and Mrs. Karch were glad that their daughter was planning to visit. She had been estranged from them for a while, and although she called them occasionally, she had not visited in more than two years. Mrs. Karch did not know how many people intended to visit. Khleo did not say. Nevertheless, Mrs. Karch hurried to prepare whatever she could.

The trio; Khleo, Amanda, and Eli arrived at the Karch family home at 11:00 a.m. that Friday morning. In spite of the *staged kidnapping* of Khleo, an egregious crime that was perpetrated against them, the door of the Karch's home was wide open and the group walked in. Khleo called out, "Hello! Mom, Dad. Are you there?"

At the sound of her daughter's voice, Mrs. Karch hobbled out in spite of a painful knee, and her husband followed. When they reached the living room, Khleo and the other two were standing there. "Oh my baby! My baby! Mrs. Karch shouted as she hugged her daughter. Mr. Karch was more subdued. He simply hugged Khleo and said, "It is so nice to have you back. Thank God."

Khleo's parents greeted Amanda and Eli whom they were very glad to see. The reunion with Khleo to some extent overshadowed Eli's return.

"Please sit down. Make yourselves comfortable," Mrs. Karch said. Khleo and her friends complied while Mrs. Karch returned to the kitchen to fetch the goodies she had prepared.

Amanda took the tape recorder out of her handbag and placed it on the coffee table. She said nothing about it, and no one asked. Khleo of course, was privy to what they were there to reveal on the tape. Eli, however, had no knowledge of it.

Mr. Karch found that his wife was taking exceptionally long to return from the kitchen. He asked his daughter and her guests to excuse him and he walked back to check on her. Khleo followed him. A few minutes later all three returned with a tray of delicacies Mrs. Karch had prepared. Khleo cleared an area on the large coffee table, and her father placed the tray on it.

"Oh! Everything looks so good." Amanda said.

"Please help yourselves," said Mrs. Mancelia Karch. "I was

so happy when Khleo said she was coming and that Eli was with her, I might have been a little bit excessive."

"Thank you," said Amanda. "Before we partake of this gastronomic delight, however, I want you to listen to something." Everyone nodded their agreement and Amanda pressed the play button on the tape recorder. There was utter silence as Eli, and Mr. and Mrs. Karch paid rapt attention to the conversation on the tape. At the end Amanda asked, "Do you recognize the voices?"

"The female sounds like you." Mrs. Karch said.

"The male voice sounded very much like that of Peter Aranguez." Eli said.

"Please listen to it again." Amanda said as she rewind the tape and pressed the play button again. The group listened, though less enthusiastically. At the end she asked the same question as she did previously.

"The voice of the female does sound like yours," said Mr. Karch.

"Definitely!" Mrs. Karch said.

"The male voice is certainly that of Peter Aranguez." Eli said.

Amanda wanted positive identification of the recorded voices and she got that. The next step she thought, was for Mr. and Mrs. Karch to positively identify the male voice as that of the caller who demanded the ransom payment for the *staged kidnapping* of their daughter, so Amanda said, "Now that we have reached a consensus as to whose voices are on this tape, do you, sir, recognize any of them as the voice of the caller who, a week ago, demanded $500,000.00 from you supposedly for Khleo's safe release?"

Mr. Karch shook his head to indicate, no. He was choked up for a minute and was unable to speak. His eyes welled up with tears which he somehow managed to keep from flowing down his cheeks.

"What about you Mrs. Karch? Do you recognize any of the voices as someone you spoke to about Khleo's staged capture?"

"No," she said while shaking her head, either to emphasize her answer or reinforce it.

"Huh!" Amanda murmured. She was not about to give up her pursuit of the criminal. At that moment though, her facial expression showed her disappointment. Mr. Karch recognize it and said, "Come on. Let's eat."

"First we must give thanks for having Khleo home safely." No one objected, so Mrs. Karch said a short prayer. Everyone then helped themselves to some of what she had prepared.

While members of the party ate and spoke on a variety of topics except the *staged kidnapping*, Amanda stayed focus. She spoke very little, something that did not escape either Khleo or Eli, both of whom knew her to be talkative, especially when in a social setting like that, with several people.

Amanda's thoughts were racing but one thing in particular kept recurring, *he must have disguised his voice. It really didn't sound like him.* She was perplexed. Eli recognized that and said, "Cheer up, Amanda. If this thing is bothering you so much, then let's speak with Paul Aranguez. The brothers do everything together."

"You are so right, Eli." said Amanda. "When can we do that?"

"The sooner the better."

"Well, it is already late. Early tomorrow morning might be a good time to pay him a visit."

"Tomorrow is Saturday. Some people sleep late. Others move very early. How do we know what Paul Aranguez will do?" Khleo asked.

"We really have no way of knowing that," said Amanda. "What we do know is that neither he nor his brother has a job. The likelihood is that he may not leave his home very early."

"10:30 a.m. might be a good time," Eli suggested.

Amanda laughed and said, "I see that you too do not want to leave your bed early."

The others in the room laughed as Eli agreed with Amanda's

assessment. She in turn conceded, and they reached a consensus. Ten thirty was decided upon.

Mrs. Karch asked Khleo to stay the night and she agreed. She got up and hugged her mother . Then she hugged her father. The last time she slept at her parents' place had been three years earlier.

"Oh! That is so sweet," Amanda said.

Mr. Karch looked at Eli and said, "Thank goodness you decided to return home. Welcome!"

How did he come to that conclusion? Amanda wondered. Then she said to herself, *If it makes him happy, what the hell!*

Eli, meanwhile, nodded to acknowledge what he viewed as a compliment from Mr. Karch. He offered no clarification and none was asked of him or expected. Since Khleo agreed to stay the night at her parents' home, Amanda and Eli felt it was the appropriate time for them to leave. They wished the Karch family well, said goodnight and were on their way. Eli headed to Khleo's apartment which became his abode since he was deported from the USA. Amanda went to her place in Plaisance, and for the first time she double locked the front and back doors. Although both doors were equipped with two sets of locks the very day she took up residence there, she had never before used both locks at the same time. She wasn't even sure what prompted her to adopt the new security measure. It was apparently just a hunch.

She slept soundly and was interrupted only by the sound of her telephone ringing the next morning. She woke up, stretched, yawned, and reached for the telephone. Before she could answer, a male voice said, "Amanda! It's Christopher. I am sorry that I wake you up."

"You already did, so speak to me."

"I wanted to know if you had any success with your plan to speak with Peter Aranguez."

"He did show up here yesterday evening but he was a tougher nut than I anticipated."

"Are you saying that you got nothing?"

"Nothing at all, Christopher."

Amanda went on to explain that neither Mr. nor Mrs. Karch was able to identify Peter's voice as that of the person who demanded the ransom."

"Damn!"

"Don't be like that, Christopher. He might very well be innocent."

"Then what's your next move?"

"Our next move is more like the first."

"Okay! Then what is it."

"I am not really sure. We are planning to pay his brother a visit today. Do you want to come with us?

"Thank you for asking but I do have to decline."

"I understand. You can't stand to see Eli with her, can you?"

"Sorry, Amanda. I am not going there with you."

"Fine! I understand, Christopher."

"All the best when you speak with Paul today."

"Thanks."

"You are welcome . Bye now. I will speak with you later."

"Okay! Bye." They hung up the phones together and Amanda laid back in the bed. *He could have been a real asset to this investigation if only he had been a bit more liberal*, she thought for a while. Then she fell asleep again.

It was 8:30 a.m. before Amanda woke up again. She called Khleo. Then she called Eli to remind them of the plan to visit Paul Aranguez at ten o'clock that morning. Both were dressed and ready to go. Suddenly, Amanda realized that she was the one running late. "Where shall we meet?" she asked Eli.

"I can call Khleo and ask her to meet us at your place."

"That's okay. I can call her. Both of you can meet me here at, say 9:45."

"Good! I will see you then."

Amanda called Khleo. They agreed to meet at her place and use one car to take them to Paul Aranguez' home in Beau Sejour. As soon as she hung up the telephone to end her conversation with Khleo, she got dressed in a hurry. Eli arrived there precisely at 9:45 a.m. and Khleo arrived about one minute later. They got into Amanda's rental and drove the short distance to Paul's home. Amanda took a note pad and pencil from her handbag and approached Paul's driveway. Khleo and Eli followed with their tape recorders. When they reached the front door, Amanda rang the door bell and waited. No one answered. After two minutes of waiting, she rang the bell again. That time a male figure approached the door. He was pulling a t-shirt over his head. "Good morning, sir," she said. At first Paul looked puzzled. No one in Mayaro had ever called him *sir*. When he composed himself he said, "Good morning," Khleo and Eli echoed the same greeting.

"I guess you are wondering why we are here so early on a Saturday morning," Amanda said.

"No," replied Paul. "Whatever it is that you are selling, forget it. I am not interested."

"We are not selling anything, Mr. Aranguez," Amanda said.

Paul looked at the note pad in Amanda's hand and said, "I do not need any religious literature."

"We are not from the......." Before Amanda could complete her trend of thought, Paul Aranguez said, "I know where the *explicit* you are from and what you want. I am telling you once more, I am not interested. So get to hell off my property."

Amanda, Khleo and Eli stood there as if they were frozen in time when Paul shouted, "Now!" He walked away and closed the door behind him.

The three friends turned and walked away. Their most recent attempt at private investigation seemed to be a total failure. They sat in the car trying to decide among themselves what their next move could be when Khleo suddenly screamed. The shrill, blood chilling scream startled both Amanda and Eli who realized that there were two large dogs, Pit bulls perhaps, standing with their front paws on the front passenger window where Khleo sat.

Amanda and Eli quickly rolled up their windows and Amanda drove off. "What do we do now?" Eli asked.

"We go to the police with what we have," Amanda said.

"Huh!" Eli murmured.

"It might be a good time for us to speak with Christopher," said Amanda. "He usually has some good ideas."

"For us to speak with Christopher....." Eli mimicked Amanda. Khleo said nothing. Amanda realized Eli's displeasure and repeated her earlier statement, "We go to the police with what we have."

"What do we have?" Eli asked. He sounded impatient and agitated.

"We have the water-damaged cell phone. We have evidence of where we were that weekend. We have the tape recording of Peter's voice, and hopefully, you caught Paul's obnoxious language on tape today." To Khleo and Eli the evidence seemed sufficient to present to law enforcement. Amanda, however, felt she needed to consult with Christopher but did not mention that to either Khleo or Eli again.

Lunch time was approaching fast. Amanda knew Eli will be thinking about food and it would be Khleo as usual, who would be strapped with the bill. The mere thought of that made her irritable. She decided, therefore, to return to her place, and made that known to her friends. They parted amicably at noon and agreed to get in touch for a Saturday evening junket at either *The Junction* or at Elaine's. Amanda promised to pick up the tab. She would have liked to have Christopher and Ebita there but realized that was not possible.

She arrived home and quickly called Christopher. When he answered she asked, "Where are you, Chris?" It was rear that anyone called him Chris although he never objected to the name.

"I am at home," he said.

"Your home or your parents'?"

"What's wrong with you, girl? Home refers to where I live."

"Is Ebita with you?"

"Yes," Christopher answered but he wondered, *why all the questions?* Almost immediately he got the answer when Amanda said, "I would like you to join me for lunch."

"When?"

"Why would you ask when? Today of course."

"At what time?"

"In about an hour from now."

"Hold on a second," said Christopher. He spoke with Ebita about it. She had no objection, so he looked at his watch and told Amanda, "Okay. That will be 12:30. We will see you then."

"Thanks."

Amanda quickly ordered food and arranged to have it delivered just before Christopher and Ebita were to arrived. The restaurant was efficient and prompt with the delivery. She then set an elegant table for three. Christopher and Ebita showed up precisely at 12:30 p.m. They brought with them a bouquet of freshly cut flowers and a bottle of local tropical fruit wine. They hugged Amanda and presented their gifts which she appreciated. She cleared a spot at the center of the table and placed the flowers there. When they sat down to dine she asked Christopher to open the wine. He did, and poured some in her glass. She sipped it and nodded her approval. Christopher continued to serve the wine. When all of their glasses had enough of the cashew wine, Amanda bowed her head in a short, silent prayer. Then they ate. As they did, they conversed. As expected, the main subject of their conversation was, of course, the evidence they had to present to law enforcement.

Amanda wanted to know whether the information they gathered was worthwhile to present to the police, and she asked for Christopher's input.

"Quite frankly, Amanda, I do not think that there is much of anything," he said.

"To us it may seem as if there is very little. A trained

investigative mind, however, may detect something that we overlooked," Ebita said.

"Then we take what we have to the police," Christopher suggested.

"Can we do that after lunch?" Amanda asked.

"Sure," said Christopher.

"Good. I would let Khleo and Eli know what we plan to do but I wouldn't ask them to come along."

"Okay."

"Great."

"That was easy," Ebita said.

It was 2:00p.m. when Amanda, Christopher, and Ebita arrived at the police station. Before they left the vehicle, Christopher glanced inside the station and said, "Officer Sookram is at the desk. Amanda looked at her watch. "This is not his shift. He might be filling in for someone else," she said.

"That could be to our advantage. He tends to be emotional but he is the most thorough and perhaps the most knowledgeable officer in this town," said Christopher. "I would prefer to deal with him on any given day."

They entered the station and greeted the officer. He returned the greeting in a unique sort of way by saying, "Oh! Look who are here. My favorite teachers. What a pleasant surprise." He then looked at Ebita and asked, "Who is the beautiful stranger?"

"This is Ebita, a friend of ours. She is Christopher's fiancée really." Amanda said. She lied.

"I thought............" Officer Sookram started to say something but Amanda interrupted.

"I know what you thought, Officer Sookram. You were wrong," she said.

"I can tell that this is not a courtesy call," Officer Sookram said with a smile.

"It is always nice to speak with you but the reason we are here today is that we believe we have some evidence that can tie someone to the *staged kidnapping* of Ms. Khleo Karch," Christopher said.

"Oh, yes! Your ex-fiancée," said Officer Sookram." Then he asked, "Who can be implicated in that case?"

"The Aranguez brothers, Peter and Paul," Christopher said.

Officer Sookram sat up straight. He stopped smiling and became very focused. *We have had so many reports of wrong doing on the part of those two, I hope this one will stick*, he thought but asked, "What do you have?"

"First, we have Ms. Karch's cell phone which was stolen when she was mugged. We also have a tape recording of Peter Aranguez' voice which we believe would match the voice of the supposed kidnapper which you have on record as he demanded the ransom."

Officer Sookram raised his eyebrows and asked, "What else do you have?" He was embarrassed to say outright that the police had no recording of the kidnapper's voice.

"There is nothing else we can add but we know that you in law enforcement have the shoe prints of the culprits and the tire impressions of their vehicle," said Christopher. "Certainly, you can tie all of that together and get them in for questioning."

"Well, let me ask you this. Did you handle the cell phone in a manner that preserved the finger prints?"

"No. We found the phone washed up on the beach."

"So, how do you know it belongs to Ms. Karch?"

"Her name is engraved on the back of the phone."

"Do you have it with you?"

Christopher looked at Amanda as if to ask, *Do you still have the cell phone?* She, somehow anticipated the question and pulled the water damaged phone out of her bag and handed it to Officer Sookram.

"This is just too bad," said the officer after he examined the phone. "Now, let me hear the tape recording."

Amanda took the small voice activated tape recorder out of her handbag, rested it on the officer's desk, and pressed the play button. Officer Sookram leaned back in his chair and listened. Christopher and Ebita also listened attentively. At the end, Officer Sookram said, "Guys, that was merely a social conversation. Nothing was said that could be incriminating."

"True! What you want is a voice match to that of the person who demanded the ransom from Mr. and Mrs. Karch," Christopher said.

"Unfortunately, we do not have such a recording," said Officer Sookram. "By the time we were able to get an officer out to the Karch family home, the family had already paid the ransom."

Christopher hissed his teeth in disgust. Then he asked, "What about the tire prints? Did they match Peter's SUV's?

"No. They were distorted because of the rainfall earlier, before the pictures were taken. The photography was also of poor quality because of the lighting, or lack thereof," said Officer Sookram. "In spite of all that, we were able to determine that the tire prints we got were from a much smaller vehicle."

"Shit! Another crime goes unsolved," Christopher said.

"The only thing we can hope for now is that one of the brothers does something stupid and illegal, so that in the course of investigating that infraction, we can question him about the *staged kidnapping* of Ms. Khleo Karch," Officer Sookram said.